DIRTY LI ECRETS

ELISE NOBLE

Published by Undercover Publishing Limited

v4

ISBN: 978-1-912888-44-3

This book is a work of fiction. Names, characters, organisations, places, events, and incidents are either the product of the author's imagination or are used fictitiously.

Edited by Nikki Mentges, NAM Editorial

Cover design by Abigail Sins

www.undercover-publishing.com

www.elise-noble.com

secret

(noun)

something you tell everybody to tell nobody

1

BROOKE

Some people called Baldwin's Shore the end of the world.

Until I turned eighteen, I'd just called it home, but now at the age of twenty-six, having made my escape and ended up right back where I started, I had to agree with that sentiment.

Another twig cracked, and this time, I knew I hadn't imagined it. There *was* something behind me. Or someone. My fingers tightened around Vega's leash, and I began to walk faster. Did I have a phone signal? Not even one bar. Dammit.

The forest that surrounded the town changed with the seasons. In winter, when the sun shone through skeletal branches and frost glistened on textured bark, when the snow crunched underfoot on an otherwise silent trail, the place was magical. In spring, when the trees burst into life and in fall, when leaves drifted in riots of colour, I jogged or hiked every chance I got so I didn't miss nature's magic. And in summer, the dappled shade provided a welcome respite from the heat.

Today? Today, on this gloomy Monday in early April, it felt like hunting season, and I was the prey.

I never used to get jumpy like this. A year ago, I'd have written off the rustles as a deer in the bushes, or maybe a squirrel, but today? Today, my mind cycled through wolf, cougar, and bear, then settled on *man*. The worst predator of all. Think I was overreacting? Perhaps...perhaps I was.

After all, I wasn't totally sure I'd been assaulted in my own bed just over a year ago. Not a hundred percent, but definitely ninety-five. I couldn't remember a thing between feeling hot and a little headachy and waking up naked at eight o'clock the next morning with an ache between my legs and bruises on my arms that hadn't been there the day before. The smell of stale sex still hung in the air, but I had no idea who I might have brought home with me. And I might even have wondered if I'd dreamed the whole thing, if not for the note. One line on a piece of paper torn from the pad I kept on my bedside table.

YOU WERE EVERYTHING I IMAGINED.

There was no signature, only a heart with an arrow through the middle. *Cupid.* I'd read the words. Read them again because my brain had barely taken them in the first time. Read them a third time, and then staggered to the bathroom and vomited everything left in my stomach.

My recollections of that morning were fuzzy, but I remembered sitting by the toilet with my arms wrapped around my legs, rocking back and forth as I tried to work out what had happened the night before. *Had* I met a guy? Every time I reached for a memory, it skittered out of range. What had I done? I'd been drinking, but not that much. At least, I didn't think so.

Turn over, Brooke.

It came as a whisper, but where from? Was it a memory or just my mind trying to fill in the blanks? I struggled to my feet, nearly fell because of the pins and needles in my legs, and stumbled into the bedroom. The sun had risen higher in the sky, light streaming in through the window and illuminating the marks on my pillow. Two ovals of spidery black streaks and a pair of smudged red lips, all surrounded by a pale peach halo. At some point the previous night, I'd had my face smushed into the cream cotton, hard enough to rub off my make-up. I wouldn't have slept like that. Would I? The sheets were clean, but that musky scent... It still lingered.

A chill ran through me, partly because I hadn't turned the heating on but mostly because...because I thought I might have been raped, but I had no way of proving it. I didn't need to get a degree in criminal justice to work that one out. All I had in the form of evidence was a few unexplained marks, a note that could have been sweet or creepy depending on the interpretation, and a *feeling*.

And now, one year and sixteen days later, I had a dog I'd adopted in the hope that he might help me to feel safe again, a "Happy Anniversary" card from my bogeyman, something behind me in the trees, and a heart threatening to hammer its way through my ribcage.

I ran.

Vega didn't really understand what was going on, but he lolloped along beside me anyway. The shelter had guessed he was a year old, but he still had big puppy paws he'd never quite grown into and a tongue that hung out of one side of his mouth whenever he got hot. I'd picked him out because he looked scary, but having gotten to know him over the past two weeks, I worried he might just drool on a would-be attacker instead of defending me.

Was that a branch snapping back?

Maybe, but I didn't want to wait around to find out. I darted sideways into the trees, pulling Vega with me because if I took a shortcut through the undergrowth, I'd reach the lower trail faster, and from there it was only three hundred yards to the trailhead.

We so, so nearly made it. The other trail was in sight when Vega stopped, yanking the leash out of my hand. When he tried to run again, all he managed was a yelp and a hop, and then I saw the rabbit hole his leg must have gone down and realised he was hurt. Badly hurt. He wouldn't even put his back foot on the ground. Fear prickled at my spine like cryogenic cockroaches with icy little legs. I couldn't stop, I couldn't, but leaving Vega wasn't an option either. I might have adopted him less than a month ago, but the big goof had already wormed his way into my heart.

"Shh, shh."

I paused to listen, but all I could hear was my own thumping heart. Was there anyone else around to hear me scream if…if…? I didn't even want to think about it. A muscle twanged in my back as I hefted Vega into my arms, and for a moment I thought my knees would buckle. Fear had made them weak, and Vega had to weigh half as much as I did.

Adrenaline helped me to stagger to the start of the trail, and I almost wept with relief when I spotted a couple on mountain bikes headed toward me. Tourists? I didn't recognise either of them, and Baldwin's Shore was…well, I couldn't call it a two-horse town because Bobbie Jo who bred Quarter Horses at the Little Creek Ranch would take offence, but when the new resort by the ocean was full, the population practically doubled.

Before the paper mill closed fifteen years ago, the town had been much bigger, but without jobs, people had moved away.

"Hey, are you okay?" the woman asked.

She was around my age, but she looked much perkier than I felt. Life had worn me down over the past few years. The assault had just been one more kick in the teeth, albeit a particularly vicious one. I lowered Vega to the ground, and he stood on three legs.

"My dog's injured, and I think there might be something out there in the forest."

"Something?" The woman glanced toward her boyfriend. Or fiancé, judging by the huge diamond ring that glinted in the sunlight. "Like a mountain lion? Or Sasquatch?"

"I didn't actually see it."

The guy rolled his eyes. "Probably a deer."

"I don't want to go that way if there's a mountain lion."

"Cougars don't usually approach people," I told her. "They mostly keep out of the way."

"There you go, Kelly. You're out of excuses. She'd rather stay at home and use her Peloton," the guy explained. "I have to drag her into the great outdoors kicking and screaming." He put his hands on his hips and drew in a deep breath. "Smell that fresh air."

"What happened to your dog?"

"He wrenched his leg in a rabbit hole."

"Do you need help?"

"I don't suppose you have a car nearby?"

"I wish. We've ridden, like, fifty miles already."

"Five miles, Kelly. We've ridden five miles. Can we call someone for you?"

I checked my own phone. Two bars of signal, thank

goodness. “I can call my brother. He lives in town, but would you mind waiting with me until he arrives?”

“Sure, sure, we can wait.” Kelly crouched to pet Vega, and even injured, he immediately backed away and hid behind my legs. So much for his guarding instincts. “Your dog is *so* cute. He should totally have his own Instagram page. He’s not badly hurt, is he?”

“I hope not. I’m planning to take him straight to the veterinarian.”

Even though my brother’s office was at the other end of town, it wouldn’t take him more than fifteen minutes to drive to the trailhead. Aaron still tended to act annoyingly overprotective, but today, I had to be grateful for that.

“Aaron?”

“Brooke? What’s up?”

“Vega had an accident near the start of the Eagle’s Nest Trail.”

“You had an accident? What happened? Are you hurt?”

“No, Vega had the accident.”

“Sorry, the line’s bad. Is *he* hurt?”

“He needs to go to the veterinarian. Can you pick us up?”

Aaron cursed under his breath. “I’m over in Coquille. Lonnie Jackson got himself arrested again.”

“Again? Isn’t that twice this month?”

And as if Lonnie’s habit of taking his clothes off in public wasn’t bad enough, Coquille was three-quarters of an hour away. More with my brother driving—he’d always preferred the brakes to the gas pedal.

Maybe my boss would pick me up? I hated to ask Darla for a favour because she’d done so much for me already, but Paulo wouldn’t mind watching the store for half an hour. Darla was more of a cat person, but Vega would charm her the way he charmed everyone. Perhaps I should take Kelly's advice and set up an Instagram page? My friend Adeline always told me I should make more of an effort to be sociable.

I could have discussed the matter with Darla, who knew far more about social media than I did, but unfortunately, my brother had another plan.

"Yeah, Lonnie's been picked up twice, and this time he managed to wave his frank 'n' beans at Judge Hamble's wife, so making bail's gonna be a challenge. But don't worry; I'll send Luca."

"Luca?"

"Don't tell me you've forgotten him? He practically lived at our house when we were kids."

The cryo-cockroaches spontaneously combusted and sent a flash of heat through me. Luca Mendez? My brother was talking about Luca Mendez? His sexy, brooding best friend Luca Mendez? Of course I hadn't forgotten him. I'd *never* forget him.

"B-b-but I thought Luca was in Ethiopia."

"Eritrea, and there was a problem, so he had to come back in a hurry."

"What kind of a problem? Is he okay?"

Luca had been in the army, but he'd switched to private security work around the same time as I moved back to Baldwin's Shore. I'd rather he quit the military life altogether—the news was full of horror stories every night —but Aaron said private work was safer and I sure hoped he was right about that.

"Yeah, he's fine—just the usual government bureaucracy. He can borrow Deck's truck and pick you up."

Decker was the carpenter helping to remodel my brother's half-finished house. Actually, half-finished was being generous, and it wasn't even a house. It was a former indoor car dealership he'd acquired after it had sat empty for a decade, and it still looked decidedly industrial. But eventually, it would become his home, and my home too. He'd offered me the second floor, plus he was going to convert the biggest of the two outbuildings into an office for the law firm he wanted to run someday. At the moment, Aaron lived in a single-wide trailer in the backyard-slash-parking lot and worked with Asa Phillips from an office off Main Street. Asa was getting on in years, and they planned for Aaron to take over the firm when he had more experience. And I rented a garage apartment from Adeline's parents. Her grandma used to live there before she moved into a retirement home, and on a warm day, it still smelled of mothballs.

"Couldn't Deck come? Or Brady?" Brady was the electrician, a friend of Adeline's who'd agreed to take on the mammoth task of rewiring the cavernous interior of the building formerly known as Deals on Wheels.

"No, because I pay Deck and Brady by the hour, and Luca's helping out in exchange for room and board."

"Room and board? What do you mean, room and board? Where?"

"One of the bedrooms at Deals on Wheels is almost finished, and he said he's slept in worse places. Hell, he's probably sleeping now. He looked like shit when he arrived this morning."

Luca was living in my future home? This got worse and worse.

"Maybe I should try calling Colt?"

Colton Haines—another of my brother's friends—was also a sheriff's deputy. It was literally his job to rescue people. And now I was kicking myself for not calling him in the first place.

"Colt's here at the courthouse. He had to drive Lonnie over for his bail hearing."

"Why don't I just call a cab?"

"Brooke, why don't you want Luca to pick you up?"

Because eight years ago, I blurted out my feelings for him and he rejected me. The pity. I'd never forget the pity on his face when he turned me down. As if he felt sorry for my stupidity.

"What do you mean? Why wouldn't I want him to pick me up? I'd hate for him to go to any trouble, that's all. I mean, if he's just flown back from Eritrea, won't he be tired?"

"Tired?" Aaron snorted. "Luca's a machine. Wait in the parking lot, and he'll be there in fifteen minutes."

2

LUCA

"Buddy, I need a favour."

One advantage of spending seven years in the US Army, most of them as a Ranger, was that I could go from fast asleep to wide awake in half a second. Who needed more than an hour's shut-eye anyway?

"Sure. Did you run out of beer again?"

Whatever Aaron wanted, I'd do it. He'd saved my ass more times than I wanted to count, including the night before last when I'd found myself on a plane out of Asmara with thirty minutes' notice.

"Run out of beer? Are you kidding? No, Brooke's dog hurt its leg. Can you borrow Deck's truck and drive them to the veterinarian?"

"Brooke?"

"My sister? The brat who borrowed your Seahawks hoodie to use as a superhero cape and fell off the roof? Don't tell me you've forgotten her?"

If only. I'd sure as hell tried. For years, I'd tried, and it was the only thing I'd failed at since I left Baldwin's Shore. Brooke Bartlett was the forbidden fruit I'd dreamed about every damn night, the girl whose photo I'd secretly carried with me from Afghanistan to Algeria and everywhere in between. My lucky charm. If Aaron ever found out, he'd kill me. No matter how much training I might have had, I'd be a dead man.

"Sure, I remember her. She lives in Coos Bay, right?" Which would give me thirty minutes to get my game face on. "She has a dog now?"

"Yeah, she adopted the mutt from the shelter two weeks ago. And she's in Baldwin's Shore."

"Visiting?"

"No, she moved back. Decided the city wasn't for her and rented the Crowes' garage apartment."

Ah, fuck. Why the hell hadn't Aaron told me that? Actually, I could answer my own question: because every time he mentioned his baby sister, I changed the subject.

"I thought Brooke had a car?"

"She does, but she went out hiking on the Eagle's Nest Trail."

Brooke was on the trail? Alone? There were cougars up there. And bears, and rattlesnakes. I had one leg in my pants before I finished the thought.

"How far did she get?"

And where was my gun?

"She's waiting at the trailhead. Do you remember where the veterinarian's office is?"

"Behind the feed store?"

"Yeah, that's right."

"I'll be there in fifteen minutes."

"Thanks, buddy."

I threw on a T-shirt, tossed a handful of mints into my mouth, and debated shaving. Nah, didn't have time. And besides, women found the stubble sexy, or so they said. One night in a bar, an army buddy had asked a group of Rangerettes to rate my attributes, and the stubble had come in third, right behind my muscles and my smile. For some reason, chicks dug the dimples. Which kind of made up for being nicknamed "crater face" in junior high, but—

Hold that thought right there.

I didn't need to look sexy around Brooke. There was only one thing worse than wanting my best friend's little sister and not being able to have her, and that was knowing she wanted me too. And once upon a time, she *had* wanted me. Two weeks before I left for boot camp, she'd broken down in my room and told me she didn't want to lose me. That she liked me. That she'd wait for me. And I'd done the honourable thing and lied. I'd lied and told her I didn't feel the same, and then I'd sent her away.

Fuck.

Okay, no smile, no muscles, no stubble.

I spotted a plaid shirt someone had left on a workbench, pulled it on over my T-shirt, and grabbed a razor from my washbag. I could shave at the stop lights. When I got to the trailhead, I'd act like an asshole and everything would be fine. In a week, maybe two, I'd get offered another security contract and ship out to some godforsaken sandpit, and everything would be fine.

Everything would be fine.

I made it to the trailhead in thirteen minutes and screwed up almost immediately. Brooke was exactly where Aaron said she'd be, and she looked fucking radiant. Stunning. She'd turned from a pretty teenager into a beautiful woman, curvier than I remembered but with the same sparkling eyes. Her thick chocolate-brown hair was braided into a pair of pigtails just made for tugging on, still long, and my mind went from zero to filthy in nought point five seconds. So much for not smiling. I grinned like an idiot before I caught myself.

Had she noticed? Probably not—it was a sunny day, and the glare on the windshield covered my mistake.

The dog lying in the dirt beside Brooke had the head of a German shepherd and the stocky body of a pit bull. He might have been intimidating if it hadn't been for the tongue lolling out of his mouth and the fact that the tip of his tail started wagging as soon as I got out of the truck. A couple I hadn't seen before was standing with them. Friends? The man was staring at her tits, and as I got closer, I could hear the blonde woman chattering about a Japanese tea garden and Turtle Rock. Probably tourists. I had no idea where the Japanese garden was, but Turtle Rock was the town's biggest claim to fame, although that wasn't much to brag about. It was a rock. Shaped like a turtle. Rumour said a ghostly siren had made it her home, but that was just bullshit, probably invented by some hotel owner in the dim and distant past. Tourists wanted their photos taken in front of it, and idiots swam out to sea to try and climb it. Lucky there was a coastguard station nearby.

"Ready to go?"

"Luca?"

She seriously had to ask that question?

"We'll have to put the dog in the back seat."

"I-I don't think I can lift him. I hurt my back carrying him the first time."

"You should have waited."

Brooke's mouth set into a thin little line. "I didn't want to stay in the forest."

The blonde's head was swinging back and forth as she followed the conversation, and judging by her scowl, she didn't think much of me either.

"Uh, do you want us to come with you?" she asked Brooke.

Translation: that guy seems like an asshole.

"No, I'll be fine. He's friends with my brother."

"Okaaaaay. If you're sure."

"I really am, and thanks so much for helping me."

"Maybe we'll see you at the craft store?"

"I'd love that. And I promise you won't regret a visit to the tea garden. It's lovely all year round."

Time to get going. "Will the dog bite me if I pick it up?"

"Vega. His name is Vega. And I don't think he'll bite, but I only just adopted him and sometimes he gets scared."

I knelt down and petted the mutt, and he licked my hand. I'd never had a dog of my own, or any other sort of pet, mainly because my father would have beaten it the way he beat me. But when I was stationed in Afghanistan, a pack of stray dogs hung around at the base and I used to buy food for them. We'd gotten along okay.

"Hey, boy, you wanna go visit the veterinarian?"

When he didn't seem averse to the idea, I wrapped my arms around his belly and heaved him into the cab. He must've weighed sixty pounds at least. No wonder Brooke had struggled—how far had she carried him?

"Should we tie him to the seat belt or something?"

"He has a harness for the car, but I didn't bring it today, only his leash."

"Well, unless you want to jog home and pick it up..."

"I don't think he'll move. As long as you drive carefully, that is."

"Have I ever not driven carefully?"

"Well, there was that time when you parked your dad's truck in the ditch..."

It had been icy that morning, and Dad had beaten me

black and blue over the dented fender. Brooke didn't know that, of course. I'd kept the bruises hidden the same way as I always did because I didn't want her to realise just how bad things had gotten at home. And in some ways, the accident had been a blessing. At sixteen, I'd stood over six feet tall, but I'd always been kind of skinny. Then Aaron got a weight bench, only a cheap thing he'd bought second-hand from an internet auction, but we used to pump iron every weekend in Nonna's garage and we thought we were the shit. By the time I turned seventeen, I'd begun to fill out. I started watching old boxing videos on YouTube, Muhammad Ali and Joe Frazier, "Sugar" Ray Leonard and Thomas Hearns, and when I couldn't sleep, I'd shadow-box in front of the spotted old mirror in my bedroom. Night after night after night. It gave my anger an outlet.

So when my father finished with his fists and took off his belt, I decided enough was enough, and I broke his fucking nose. He came at me with a whisky bottle, and I broke that too.

It was the last day he'd ever laid a hand on me.

Why didn't I simply leave, you ask? Why didn't I join the army at seventeen? Fair question—I mean, my dad would've given his consent just to get rid of me. But I had a sister Brooke's age. Romi was smart and beautiful but vulnerable too, and I didn't trust our father not to hurt her. To break her. When he drank, he just...lashed out. So, I stuck around for another three years until she could graduate and get the hell out of town too. We'd spent a lot of time with the Bartletts in those days. Hell, Mrs. Bartlett had insisted I call her "Nonna" the same as Brooke and Aaron did. In the eight years before today, I'd returned to Baldwin's Shore twice, once to attend Hannah Haines's funeral and most recently to attend Nonna's. On that cold, clear January afternoon, I'd stood there silent and full of regrets as the casket was lowered into the ground in the little cemetery by the ocean. *I should have visited more often. I should have done more than send money. I should have said a proper goodbye.* That Brooke and Aaron's grandma had passed away while my father was still—presumably—breathing showed how little justice there was in the world.

"Yeah, well, I learned my lesson. I'm not gonna crash, okay?"

Brooke climbed into the passenger seat, and I dragged my gaze away from her legs. Shit, coming here had been a bad, bad idea. I should've taken a vacation instead, sat on a beach somewhere with hot women and ice-cold beer. Instead, I was stuck in a truck with a farting dog and a woman I could never have. She folded her arms when I started the engine, leaving me under no illusion as to where I stood in her affections. She thought I was a jerk.

I should have been relieved.

Why, then, did I feel so damn hollow inside?

3

BROOKE

What was Luca Mendez doing in Baldwin's Shore?

Why had he come back?

Was his father sick? One could hope.

And why did Luca have to look so horribly good?

The last time I'd seen him, he'd been standing solemnly at Nonna's funeral in his dress uniform, although he'd looked kind of blurry through my tears. The asshole. First, he'd treated me like a virtual stranger that day—he'd hugged my brother, then shaken my freaking hand—and afterward, he'd left town without saying goodbye. I understood that he'd felt awkward after I offered myself to him on a plate—okay, his bed—but I'd been a month past my eighteenth birthday and stupid. Couldn't he cut me a little slack?

"Vega's torn his cruciate ligament, Ms. Bartlett," the veterinarian said, dragging me back to the present. Vega tried to slurp at his face, and he ducked out of the way with practised ease. The dog seemed to lick people as a defence mechanism, I'd noticed. Almost an apology. *Please don't hurt me.* "See the way his tibia slides forward when I move his leg? It's not meant to do that."

"Please call me Brooke," I said out of habit.

"And I'm Isaac."

Isaac Ward had bought the veterinary practice after Dr. Stockton retired to Florida to be near his daughter. I'd never visited before, but Darla had brought her cat for shots a few months ago, and when she got back to the store, she'd giggled and said he was a definite improvement. And now I knew why. His bedside manner, obviously—nothing to do with his tousled brown hair or the way those blue eyes twinkled when he looked up at me.

Isaac's charms didn't have the same effect on Luca, though. He leaned against the wall by the door wearing the faintest scowl, which I ignored. It wasn't as if I'd asked him to come inside, anyway. He could have waited in the car.

Or gone back to Deals on Wheels.

Or flown to a whole other country.

Isaac cleared his throat. Ah, right, Vega's leg.

"Will it be okay? I mean, will it heal?"

"In a smaller dog, an injury like this can improve with rest, but for an animal of Vega's size, surgery's the best option."

"S-s-surgery?"

When I adopted Vega from the shelter, I'd been looking for a guard dog, but I also wanted to give him a happier life. He'd looked so sad sitting at the back of his kennel, head hanging down, and the volunteer who showed me around the dogs said most people walked right on past because he never came over to greet visitors. But I saw him. And I saw that he'd lost his spirit the way I'd lost mine.

So far, he'd kept to himself at home, or as "to himself" as he could keep in a one-bedroom apartment. In the evenings, he curled up in his bed in the corner of the living room, but he liked his dinner and he happily trotted along beside me on walks. Last night, he'd crept along on his belly as I watched TV, getting closer and closer to the couch. He'd stopped halfway, but it was definite progress.

And now he was hurt. Because I couldn't keep my fear under control, he was hurt, and I'd only had him for two weeks. *Well done, Brooke. You score a D-minus as a pet owner.*

"It's a fairly straightforward operation, and there's an excellent orthopaedic surgeon in Coos Bay. If Vega doesn't have the surgery, his limp might improve slightly, but without stabilisation, the bones will rub together, and that's going to lead to arthritis later in life."

"How soon can we get an appointment?"

"I'll send over a referral right away."

"Do you know how much it might cost?"

"With today's appointment, the surgery, medication, and follow-ups, I'd estimate around fifteen hundred dollars."

I swallowed hard, but what choice did I have? Vega deserved the best treatment. I had money set aside to buy bathroom fittings for my new apartment at Deals on Wheels, but who needed faucets anyway? The Crowes' garage apartment came with the basics, and I could stay there for as long as I wanted. Renting for a few more months wouldn't kill me. Adeline's grandma had been good friends with Nonna, and the Crowes charged me way less than they should have.

"Right. Okay."

Isaac must have felt sorry for me. There was no mistaking his look of sympathy. Had he heard about my sudden move back to Baldwin's Shore? Or the fact that I was always first in line at yard sales? That was the problem in a small town—gossip travelled faster than a hat in a hurricane.

"The surgeon might be willing to work out a payment plan. Do you want me to call the practice and see what they can do?"

"Thank you," I said around the lump in my throat. "I'd be grateful."

Vega expressed his thanks by farting—again—and Isaac wrinkled his nose.

"Maybe I'll just open a window first."

That's what I did at home, but only the bathroom window and the small one above the kitchen sink because an intruder couldn't fit through those. The rest of the time, I lived with the smell. And got angry. Angry that a man's selfish actions had left me jumping at my own shadow. Angry that he'd come back to torment me. Wasn't scaring me out of Coos Bay enough for him?

Speaking of Coos Bay, the specialist veterinarian had one appointment left that afternoon, and if I skipped lunch, I could make it in time. I owed that much to Vega.

"I'd better check that Deck doesn't need his truck this afternoon."

What was Luca talking about? "Why does that matter?"

"Because it'll take us a half hour to get to Coos Bay and a half hour to get back."

"I'm sorry—us?"

"You were planning to drive yourself? How are you gonna lift Vega out of your car at the other end?"

"I'll manage."

"You already hurt your back, Brooke."

I'd rather take Tylenol than spend another minute in the truck with Luca Mendez. It would be less painful, both to my heart and to my head. I already had red-hot needles stabbing behind my eyeballs. And could he stop scowling, just for a minute? Yes, I understood that he'd rather be somewhere else, a fact that made his offer to come to Coos Bay all the more mystifying.

"So? I might as well get used to carrying him—I live in a walk-up apartment."

He pinched the bridge of his nose the way he always used to when he got stressed. "Fuck."

"Luca, what are you doing here?"

"Driving you and your dog to the veterinarian," he said, using his "isn't it obvious?" voice.

"No, I mean why did you come back to Baldwin's Shore? Why now?"

"It's my home."

"But you always hated the place. You couldn't wait to leave."

"No, I hated living with my father. There's a difference."

"I thought that maybe you'd come back to see him. He broke his arm falling out of the Cave not so long ago, and…"

Now Luca turned to look at me, and that gaze had only grown more intense over the years. I was close enough to see the gold that flecked his rich brown irises, to wonder whether the network of fine lines around his eyes had been born out of laughter or out of stress. I knew from my brother that he'd transferred into special forces soon after he joined the army, and every time I heard a news story about soldiers being injured or killed in a high-tech operation, or a daring raid, or a rescue mission, I'd prayed Luca's name wouldn't be mentioned. But I'd never thought about the toll the job would take on him. Probably because I'd tried to avoid thinking about him at all.

"I didn't even know for sure that my father was still alive, and I don't give a shit that he broke his arm. I always figured he'd drink his way into an early grave." Luca sighed. "Why did I come back? Habit, I guess. I always used to crash with Aaron in New York when I came to the US on leave. But don't worry; I'll be leaving soon."

"Worried? Why would I be worried?"

"I'm not a fuckin' idiot, Brooke. I feel the daggers you shoot at me every time my back's turned."

Had I been doing that?

"That's a bit of an exaggeration."

They were more like...craft knives. And the blades retracted and bounced right off him anyway. Luca was one big wall of muscle.

Luca's shrug said that he either didn't care about my thoughts or didn't believe my words. "While I'm here, I promised I'd help your brother out, and that means carrying your dog into the veterinarian's office. He'd be pissed if I let you hurt yourself. And one of us will carry him into your apartment too. He said you were staying at the Crowes' place?"

I might be able to convince Luca to leave me the hell alone, but when it came to Aaron, I had no hope. Ever since our parents died in a car crash, he'd played the protective older brother. The *over*protective older brother. Even when he was living in New York, he'd called or texted every day and come home to visit whenever he could. He'd drop everything if I was in trouble. During his first year at college, I'd slipped and fallen during a late snowfall and fractured my wrist, and he'd flown back to Oregon the very next day to help me out. And then struggled with his first set of exams because of all the lectures he'd missed.

Which was why I hadn't told him about what happened in my apartment that night last year. He'd been preparing to sit his finals at law school, and if my stupidity at letting my guard down on a night out had led to him failing, I'd never have forgiven myself. And by the time the exams were over and he'd passed, it was too late for me to spill my secret. He'd only have been hurt that I'd kept it from him in the first place, and I'd never dreamed that it would come back to haunt me a year later.

"Yes, I'm staying at the Crowes' place." My turn to sigh. "Thanks for helping."

4

LUCA

What was I doing here? A good question. I could have driven Brooke back to her apartment, moved Vega from Deck's truck to her car, and crawled back to bed. The veterinarian in Coos Bay would've helped to get the dog out when Brooke arrived. He probably had staff for that. But I'd seen the way the new veterinarian in Baldwin's Shore had looked at her, and I didn't like it. So no, I didn't want to take a chance that his colleague in Coos Bay might feel the same way, and yes, I was an asshole.

What had happened to Dr. Stockton, anyway? He'd taken care of the animals in Baldwin's Shore for as long as I could remember. Had he retired? Or died? I'd have to ask Aaron because Brooke was giving me the cold shoulder again.

My own fault, but I still hated it.

Not for the first time, I wished we could turn back the clock. Wished I'd travelled to Fort Benning two weeks earlier. I'd considered it. My sister had already left to backpack around Europe, my father was being more of a prick than usual, and a cheap motel in Georgia had never been so appealing. But I'd stayed. Because of her.

I'd bunked at the Bartletts' home, spent too much time with Brooke, got too close, and ended up hurting her. Now I had to live with the consequences.

"Want to pick up food on the way?" I asked.

"Do we have time?"

"If you're hungry, we have time. Is the Steak and Shake still open?"

"Viola May's gonna run that place till the day she dies."

"At least someone's stuck around. What happened to Beer Me Up?"

That place had been a Baldwin's Shore institution. Skip, the owner-slash-barman, had rolled into town when I was seven years old, along with his conspiracy theories and a crow named Barbara that sat on his shoulder like a pirate's parrot and squawked at anyone who came near. When she died, he'd had her stuffed, and she took up residence in a glass cabinet behind the bar, glaring out from her spot between a leprechaun perched on a rainbow and a chunk of metal Skip swore came from a spaceship. But when I'd driven past on the way to rescue Brooke, the bar's name had been changed to Applejack's. *Applejack's.* Sounded like a place that served fancy cocktails and designer peanuts.

"Well, Skip got busted for serving alcohol to a minor..."

"Busted by who?"

"Uh, Colt."

"*Colt* busted Skip? But Colt started drinking Pilsner at Beer Me Up the day he turned sixteen."

Which, by Skip's twisted logic, was just fine because sixteen was the legal drinking age in Germany. When drinking German beer, do as the Germans do—that was his philosophy.

"A couple staying over at the new resort kicked up a fuss. Their son got so drunk he couldn't even walk, and the boy was only fifteen. Tall for his age, but Skip didn't ask for ID."

"So maybe the parents should have kept a closer eye on the kid?"

"That's what Sheriff Newman said, but they kept complaining and complaining, so he figured the easiest thing to do would be to have Colt pick up Skip on a misdemeanour and then dismiss it once the idiots had gone back to LA."

"LA? Figures. But that still doesn't explain how Beer Me Up became Applejack's."

"Because when Colt fingerprinted Skip, he realised that he wasn't Skip at all. He was a fugitive who'd been on the run for two decades."

"A fugitive? What'd he do, rob a liquor store?"

"No, an armoured car."

What the fuck? Skip had acted like everyone's crazy uncle. Sure, he kept a baseball bat behind the bar, but robbery? Shit, my mom had worked for him as a barmaid, and she used to take me there to pet the crow.

"Are you serious?"

"Yup. He worked for the armoured car company, and when his partner stopped for an emergency bathroom break, he hit him over the head and drove off with the truck and four million dollars' worth of gold."

"What happened to the loot? He sure didn't spend it on the bar."

"Nobody knows. He wouldn't say. And after he went to prison, a girl from Seattle bought the joint and turned it into Applejack's. It's nice. Classier, and a hundred times better than the Cave."

I wasn't sure Applejack's was my kinda place, but you

know what *was* nice? That Brooke was talking to me in whole sentences. And she was right about the Cave—or the Cavan Arms, as it was more formally known—which was the other bar in Baldwin's Shore. The place had been run by the O'Donnells for three generations. Sean O'Donnell, the youngest of the clan, was my age, and he was the jerk who'd come up with "crater face." So that meant if I wanted to go out for a drink, I was stuck with Applejack's whether I liked it or not.

The Steak and Shake came into view on the left, and apart from the picnic tables that had appeared on a square of patchy grass at the edge of the parking lot, the place looked exactly as I remembered—a low brick building with a blinking neon sign on a pole outside. Through the big glass windows, I could see the turquoise vinyl booths where I used to sit for hours with Brooke, Aaron, and Addy, making a single milkshake last all evening because it was the best way to avoid going home and I was too poor to buy another.

The lady behind the register hadn't changed either. Viola blinked a couple of times, then ran around the counter and crushed me in a hug.

"Luca Mendez! Nobody told me you were in town."

"Only got back yesterday."

"Well, it was about time you came back to take care of that father of yours. Family's important. And is that young Brooke in the car with you?"

I ignored the first comment. "Yes."

"Aw, I always said you'd make a lovely couple."

"I'm only driving her to Coos Bay as a favour. Her dog's sick."

Viola's face fell. "That's a disappointment, and the dog

too, but I'm sure you'll see sense. Girls like that don't come along every day. What can I get for ya?"

I'd almost forgotten how persistent Viola could be. Sweet, but persistent. Even if she had the wrong end of the stick, she'd use that stick to push you around to her way of thinking. But since I didn't plan on staying in town for long, the smartest thing to do was nod, smile, and order our food.

"Three cheeseburgers and fries, plus two chocolate milkshakes and a bottle of water."

Viola winked at me. "I'll slip some cookies in too. Good to see you again, Luca."

Back in the car, Brooke's earlier chill soon evaporated.

"Three cheeseburgers? Didn't they feed you on your top-secret mission?"

"One of them's for Vega, and it wasn't top secret. I was running security at a new Eritrean gold mine."

And then the mine's owner had fallen out with the government, the project got put on hold, and all the foreign employees were kicked out of the country with twelve hours' notice. I'd barely had time to pack my bags before I got escorted to the airport. Hence ending up on a mattress in Aaron's half-built home. I hadn't had time to make an alternative plan, and then I'd promised to lend a hand with the construction work...

"Vega's not meant to eat cheeseburgers. The lady at the shelter said to feed him on kibble."

"Do you have any kibble with you?"

"No, but—"

"Look at those eyes. You want a cheeseburger, don't you, boy?"

"Luca..."

"How can you say no to that face?"

Brooke folded her arms. "Fine. He can have a small piece of cheeseburger."

"How about fries?"

She just glared at me, and my testicles shrivelled.

"It's a no on the fries?"

At least the dog liked me.

And so did the orthopaedic veterinarian, it turned out. Carly was a pretty redhead in her mid-thirties who'd moved to Coos Bay after her divorce. And the more she smiled at me, the more Brooke scowled.

Interesting.

And also awkward.

"It should be straightforward to fix," she told Brooke. "It's good that you brought Vega in so quickly. He can stay overnight, and I'll operate in the morning."

"And you've done operations like this before?"

"Many, many times. Cranial cruciate ligament injuries are one of the most common orthopaedic problems we see in dogs."

"How long will it take him to recover?"

"Five to six months, and it's imperative that his movement be restricted at first in order for the repair to heal. He'll need to be confined to one room, or crated if you leave him unattended. Can you remove the furniture in case he gets tempted to jump?"

"Uh, not really. My apartment's really tiny. He'll have to stay in the living room, but I only have a couch."

"You could put cardboard boxes on the seats to discourage him."

"I will, I'll do that." Brooke nodded. "How long until he can climb stairs again?"

"As long as everything's healing as it should, around four months."

Brooke chewed her lip, and I'd seen that look in the past, right before she ran out of my bedroom crying. Hell, I'd never forget those tears.

"I'll come over and carry him into your apartment whenever you need me to," I told her.

"For how long? Aren't you leaving town again?"

"You two don't live together?" Carly asked. "I just assumed…"

"Luca's a friend of my brother's," Brooke told her. "We barely even know each other."

Ouch. That hurt. That really fucking hurt.

"Okay, I understand. If you keep Vega confined and perform mobility exercises every day—I'll give you notes on those—that can help to speed up the recovery. Do you have access to a swimming pool? Hydrotherapy can be beneficial."

Brooke shook her head "no," and she looked so miserable that I wanted to grab a spade and dig a damn pool myself.

"Where can I get a crate?" she asked softly.

"The pet store might have one, or you could try Isaac back in Baldwin's Shore. He keeps one or two to lend to patients. I'd offer myself, but all of mine are being used right now. And I understand from Isaac that you'd like to work out a payment plan?"

"Is that possible?"

"I'll accept half up front, a quarter at the end of next month, and a quarter the month after?"

I'd have paid the whole amount right then, but Brooke was both proud and stubborn and I knew she'd turn the money down. I also knew that I'd be calling the office to pay the outstanding balance before the next installment was due. As she'd said, I didn't plan on sticking around, and if I wasn't there, she couldn't argue with me, could she? On the way to the truck, I wadded up the phone number Carly had slipped into my hand and dropped it into a trash can. Maybe in a different time, in a different city, I'd have been tempted, but not here... Not with the sweet scent of Brooke's vanilla shampoo still lingering in the air.

The trip back was quieter without Vega panting in the back seat. Brooke spoke to Isaac, and he promised to have a crate available for her tomorrow morning. I offered to borrow the truck again to pick it up, and she shrugged, which I took to mean "yes."

The sky was darkening by the time we got back, but my suggestion that we stop at Mary's Coffee House—a family enterprise that morphed into Papa's Pizza in the evenings—on the way was met with a frown.

"I just want to go home."

"You need me to move your couch? Make space for that crate?"

"I can do it."

"I don't doubt that for a moment, but do you want a hand?"

"No."

Great. We'd graduated to one-word answers. Were we destined to dance awkwardly around each other for the rest of our lives?

"So I guess I'll see you tomorrow. Call me when you're ready to go?"

"I don't even have your number."

"Give me your phone."

"Just give me the number. I can type it in."

Out of stubbornness? Or because there were things on

her phone she didn't want me to see? I hoped for the former. Stubbornness, I could handle, but we'd trusted each other once, and the thought of that trust being gone for good left me with an ache worse than a bullet wound—I knew that from experience.

Still, I recited the number and then waited as Brooke climbed the steps to her shoebox of an apartment. The home Aaron planned to build for her was ten times the size, and I'd do my part for as long as I was in town. Muscle in exchange for a roof over my head—that seemed like a fair deal to me.

Brooke paused at the top of the stairs that went up the side of the garage, then bent to pick something up. What was it? A package? No, more like a vase of flowers. The headlights lit up the white blooms. Fuck. Who was sending her flowers? The overly attentive vet? A secret admirer? Or a boyfriend I wasn't aware of? All three options sucked, and worse, there wasn't a damn thing I could do about it.

5

BROOKE

"You okay, hun?" Darla asked two minutes after she arrived at work.

My boss was entirely too perceptive at times. Kind, but too observant for comfort. Was it the black circles under my eyes? The tear streaks? My pale skin? Because I'd tried to cover those up with make-up. Or was it the fact that my hands wouldn't stop shaking?

Since Adeline, who'd been my bestie since elementary school, was still living in Coos Bay, Darla was the closest thing I had to a girlfriend in Baldwin's Shore. We'd first met a little over four years ago when Darla started work as a live-in nurse for the oldest Mr. Baldwin—yes, one of *those* Baldwins—and I was still caring for Nonna. We used to bump into each other when I took Nonna for walks by the beach. Well, pushes, because after two strokes she had to use a wheelchair. But she still loved to watch the sea. To listen to the waves. To feel the salt spray on her face. Mr. Baldwin insisted on walking along the coastal path every morning, even toward the end when he could barely manage to shuffle fifty yards with help, and Darla used to hold his arm so he didn't trip. Mr. Baldwin was a kind old soul, not like most of his grandchildren. I'd gone to school with all five of them, and the only one I cared to spend longer than thirty seconds with was Sara. Maybe because underneath the Baldwin veneer, the two of us had something in common—we'd both lost our parents at a young age. Both from automobile accidents too, although rumour said her parents had been forced off the road deliberately.

And while I'd been blessed to live with Nonna, she'd been taken in by her uncle, Easton Baldwin Jr—EJ—plus his second wife and his poisonous offspring. I guess Parker was okay—he was the older of the two boys and not out-and-out obnoxious like Easton the Third—but their two sisters took after EJ's viper of a first wife and reminded me of Cinderella's siblings.

After Mr. Baldwin died, Darla had stuck around in town and opened up a craft store on Main Street, and when I moved back to Baldwin's Shore in a hurry and the only job advertised was a waitressing position at the Cave, she'd offered me a job as a retail assistant, even though she couldn't really afford it at the time. I'd almost cried with relief. After my nightmare in Coos Bay, the thought of waiting on the men who frequented the Cave—and it *was* mostly men—left me nauseated.

Truth be told, I'd figured that I'd only be at the Craft Cabin short-term. A stopgap to tide me over until I'd licked my wounds and found something better. But those wounds refused to close, and a year later, I was still there. Right now, I wasn't sure whether that was a good thing or a bad thing. Years ago, I'd set myself a goal to be happy, and with that goal had come dreams of a college education, a high-powered job, a swanky apartment, and vacations in the Caribbean.

Crawling back to Baldwin's Shore had left me feeling like a failure.

As if I'd lost at the game of life.

The people close to me? They'd all won.

My brother was a lawyer, Luca had travelled the world, and Addy's social life would make an A-lister envious. Romi had battled her demons and made her fortune by walking runways from New York to Milan. Colt had gotten a job in law enforcement. They all adulted properly. Knew what they wanted and moved mountains to get it.

I taught five-year-olds how to make monsters out of modelling clay.

But at least through working for Darla, I'd rediscovered an old love of painting, and just as it had helped me to heal as a child, it was helping me again now. By turning my feelings into brushstrokes, by pouring the darkness inside onto canvas, I found I could breathe again. Of course, I never showed those paintings to anyone. Instead I destroyed them. Crumpled them up, shredded them, sometimes even burned them. It was my own personal therapy.

And it had been working until Cupid raised his bow again.

Now I'd been pushed back to square one, and all I could do was paste on a smile and paint landscapes in public.

Three of us worked at the Craft Cabin now—Darla, me, and Paulo. Three-quarters of our sales came from online, and when we weren't packaging up goods or making tutorial videos for the store's website and YouTube channel, we ran classes for locals plus the occasional tourist as well as manning the register. Paulo was the tech guru, Darla was amazing with her hands, and I'd discovered I quite enjoyed teaching.

In short, I liked working there, except when Darla asked questions I didn't know how to answer.

"Vega hurt his leg yesterday, and I had to take him to the veterinarian in Coos Bay for surgery. Is it okay if I go to get him this afternoon? I'll make up the hours."

"Of course it's okay. I'll see if Paulo can come in, but if not, I'll manage. Could you do me a favour and pick up a package of worming tablets for Pickle while you're there?"

Pickle had shown up on the store's doorstep six months ago—no, seven months now—a skinny waif of a cat, hopping with fleas. When nobody claimed her, Darla had decided that we should take her in, which meant getting her spayed and health-checked and feeding her twice a day. Oh, sure, Darla claimed she wasn't a cat person, but now Pickle had three beds, a scratching post in the break area, and a never-ending supply of organic kitty treats. Plus an Instagram page, courtesy of Paulo.

So I'd known it wouldn't be a problem for me to take some personal time to pick up Vega, but I was still grateful that Darla made things so easy. That was the best part of my job at the Craft Cabin—the people. Sometimes we had to work evenings if we had a lot of online orders, but Darla would buy cakes and put on music, and Paulo was a demon with packaging. Yes, I'd sure lucked out with my colleagues.

"Absolutely. The same tablets as last time?"

"Maybe ask the veterinarian what he recommends?"

"She," I said automatically, thinking of the flirty redhead and the way she'd spent half of the appointment gazing at Luca. "Her name's Carly."

Darla raised a pencilled-in eyebrow. "You don't like her?"

Uh-oh, was it that obvious?

"I'm sure she's a nice person, but she spent more time checking out the guy who gave me a ride to Coos Bay than my dog."

Wrong thing to say. Now Darla's other eyebrow zinged up to meet her hairline. "You went with a guy?"

"Nothing to get excited over—Luca's just a friend of my brother's who's in town for a few days. Aaron sent him to rescue me because he had to go to court."

"It's good that you had help."

That was another thing I liked about Darla—she was interested in my life, but not nosy. She cared, but not to the point of pushiness. Unlike Paulo. If he found out I'd been within ten yards of a guy, he'd be planning my wedding, from the dress to the guest list to the party favours. Even Addy had been hinting lately that I should try dating again. She didn't know the whole story of what had happened a year ago, though, just that I'd made a horrible mistake with a guy. I'd only told one person the truth.

Sammi had been the other executive assistant at Harding and Lucas, the accounting firm I'd worked for in Coos Bay. The hours were long, but there'd been a "work hard, play hard" culture that I'd tried so hard to fit into. With hindsight, it had been like squeezing into a pair of jeans half a size too small—it looked good, but it was never quite comfortable. It was Sammi who'd found me crying in the bathroom late on Monday morning, still groggy and hung-over and trying to process what had happened to me. I'd confessed my mistakes—the blackout, the feeling that I'd done something with a man but I wasn't entirely sure what, the way I felt dirty and sick inside.

And her reaction? *Welcome to the club.*

Everybody drank too much at some point in their lives, she said. Everyone made mistakes with guys. It was practically a rite of passage. Sammi was trying to be kind, to comfort me, but her words left me feeling stupid as well as icky. And was that really surprising? I'd heard what people said about other women.

She'd been drinking.

She wore a slutty dress.

She was asking for it.

The part they never mentioned?

The shame.

I couldn't bear the thought of people saying those things about me. Whispering behind my back. That the event had happened was painful enough, without society telling me it was my fault and if I'd just acted differently that night, everything would have been fine.

And when I'd decided not to report the matter, I'd been too embarrassed to tell Addy the details either. Plus she'd been miserable herself. Her latest boyfriend had broken up with her three days before the party, so I just nodded along with her "all men are assholes" rants and kept my mouth shut about my own problems.

At the time, it had seemed like the sensible approach, but now?

Now, I had nobody to tell about the "Happy Anniversary" card the sick beast had sent me, printed with the same skinny block capitals that he'd used to leave his parting note that awful night. Even the thought of the words he'd written inside made me shudder.

DO YOU REMEMBER ME? BECAUSE I REMEMBER YOU.

And when I'd arrived home last night and found his gift —a dozen white lilies ordered from an online florist with a note telling me that he missed me—all I'd been able to do was sit at home alone with the horrible knowledge that he was thinking about me the same as I was thinking about him.

And worse, he had my address.

Cupid wasn't done with me yet.

Did tormenting me from afar turn him on? Give him a sick thrill? The note had been printed in a card with a cupid's heart on the front, which was one of the store's standard options. I'd checked. A banner ad on the website offered customers the choice of typing their message into a box or uploading a scanned version "for that personal touch." The lilies had set the asshole back forty bucks. Why spend that amount of money? Was he jerking off to my fear? And why lilies? Everyone knew they were funeral flowers. Did he want to scare me twofold or simply remind me of my own mortality?

Either way, it worked.

I hadn't slept. I'd sat on the couch all night with the lights on, jumping at every tiny sound outside, my finger poised over my phone's keypad. I'd longed to call Aaron, but I knew how hurt he'd be that I'd kept my secret from him for so long. Even though I'd made the decision for his benefit, he wouldn't understand. My big brother didn't always think rationally.

That was my job.

I couldn't afford not to keep my feelings in check. If I'd let my emotions overwhelm me after our parents died, after Luca's rejection, through all of Nonna's health problems, I'd have cried myself into an early grave. But no, I'd kept my head. Kept my head so Aaron could finish the law degree he'd already spent years working toward. We were a team—that was the pact we'd made when we lost Mom and Dad. Whatever shit got thrown at us, we'd get through it together.

"Luca said he'd give me a ride to the veterinarian again today," I told Darla. "We need to pick up a crate for Vega on the way, and I think it might be heavy."

"He has to go in a crate? The poor thing."

"I'll have to let him out at lunchtimes. Do you think if I come in early, I could take an extra break in the mornings?"

"Does he like cats?"

"I don't know. Why?"

"Because if he won't bark at Pickle, you could put the crate in the break room instead. That way he'd have company for more of the day."

"Really?"

Darla had always said she wasn't a dog person either.

She shrugged. "It just seems easier, that's all."

It would be. It definitely would be, not least because there weren't any stairs into the store. Far easier for Vega to do his business in the parking lot twice a day than for me to schlep him in and out of my apartment. Or worse, have to ask Luca for more help I didn't want.

Darla might just have saved my back as well as my sanity.

CARLY CALLED at half past two, and although she was polite, friendly even, the sound of her voice set off a tension headache. If I could have fit the giant crate into my Honda compact, then I'd have bypassed Luca and driven to Coos Bay myself.

But the gods weren't smiling down, so I sent him a text message.

Me: Vega's surgery went well. I can pick him up now.

Spending a half-day with Luca had let me see how he'd

changed in the eight years he'd been gone, and not just physically. Yes, he was bulkier in the shoulders and leaner in the waist, but he also carried a tension with him that hadn't been there before. A twitchiness. In the old days, he'd never been able to truly relax—how could he with what he'd had to deal with at home?—but now it looked as if he carried a heavier weight on those broad shoulders. Probably he did. When he was working, he was responsible for people's lives and, if his concentration lapsed, their deaths.

And what about his sister? Had she gotten into any more trouble? I'd heard rumours over the years, and one time, Aaron had taken a cab across New York in the middle of the night to rescue her from a party after a panicked call from Luca. She'd gone to rehab after that. Luca probably thought I didn't know about Romi's meltdown, but I'd been staying with my brother that weekend, and I'd ended up watching a Broadway show alone while he dealt with the fallout from her mess.

But was it any wonder she had issues after the way her father had treated her? Luca had suffered too, physically as well as mentally. That was something else I wasn't meant to know, but I hadn't been blind. I'd seen the bruises they'd both tried to hide.

Anyhow, Luca had changed, but in many ways, he was also the same. The bossiness, the assholic tendencies, the cloud of pheromones that seeped from his pores and made women roll out their tongues like tiny red carpets... Those hadn't changed.

Plus he was still punctual. Ten minutes after I messaged him, he pulled up outside my apartment in Deck's pickup. Was it possible for a man to get hotter overnight? He hadn't shaved, but his hair was still wet from the shower. His faded blue T-shirt might have been painted on. When he got out to open my door, I felt the intensity of his gaze, but his eyes stayed hidden behind a pair of mirrored aviators.

"Morning."

"It's the afternoon."

He glanced at his watch, a chunky digital thing with buttons all over the place. "So it is. Where to first?"

"Can we pick up the crate and take it to the Craft Cabin? Vega's gonna come to work with me each day. And I also need to stop at the pharmacy and get Mr. Bertrand's medication."

"He still lives next door to the Crowes?"

"Yes, and his daughter moved away, so I help out with errands when I can."

"Bet you help out half the damn neighbourhood."

More like a quarter. "Do you have a problem with that?"

"No, no problem. And sure, we can drop by the pharmacy."

Luca didn't ask where the Craft Cabin was, so I assumed that somebody had filled him in on at least some of the changes to Baldwin's Shore since he left. When we got there, Darla had moved the chairs around to make space in the break room, and I noticed she gave Luca the once-over as he wrestled the crate into place and set it up. Just a quick appraisal, but her eyes lingered on his ass for a second, and I honestly couldn't blame her for that.

"Does your brother have any more friends?" she whispered.

"Uh, maybe? Luca's—" I'd been about to say that Luca was single, but then I realised I didn't know that. Aaron had never mentioned a girlfriend, and neither had Luca, but what if he was seeing someone? Plus Carly had given him her number—did he think I hadn't noticed that? "Luca's only in town temporarily. He's between jobs at the moment."

"Ah."

"He does contract work. Security stuff."

"Like a mall cop?"

The thought of Luca riding around the mall in Coos Bay on a Segway made me smile for the first time all day, but when I swallowed my giggle, I ended up choking and he looked at me funny.

"I'm okay, I'm okay." I lowered my voice and leaned closer to Darla. "No, overseas security stuff. He was an Army Ranger."

Darla glanced in Luca's direction again, just as he bent over to clip one of the crate's panels into place.

"Figures."

How did it figure? Because of his ass? It really was a very nice ass. Now that time had dulled the sting of his brush-off, I could look at these things objectively. At least, that's what I told myself.

"I should put blankets in the crate. Or a cushion." Except I didn't have a cushion. "I'll bring something from home tomorrow."

"An old quilt? I have an old quilt you can use."

"Really? That'd be great."

Pickle stalked in, peered into the crate, and gave Darla a questioning look. *Please, let her get along with Vega.* I didn't think Vega would chase her because when squirrels came into the yard at home, he'd make one half-hearted attempt to run after them, then sit at the bottom of the steps and bark as they dug up the lawn, much to Mrs. Crowe's disappointment. Rodent patrol just seemed like too much hard work.

Luca paused what he was doing for a second to gift Darla one of his toothpaste-ad smiles, all teeth and dimples.

"Thanks for accommodating the dog. Brooke worries about him."

"My pleasure. You two want a coffee before you go?"

We didn't have time. "No, it's—"

"OMG!" Paulo appeared at the back door, frantically smoothing down his hair. It was thick and lush and, this week, blond with purple tips. Taming it was his biggest challenge. Today, he'd sprayed it with silver glitter that floated to the ground like overachieving snowflakes. "Nobody told me we were having a visitor. What's the cage for? Are we gonna be running YouTube BDSM sessions now? You know, branching out?"

Now he was staring at Luca's ass, and unlike Darla, he didn't try to hide it. And when Luca straightened and turned, Paulo stared at the rest of him too, unashamedly, including his package.

"Where did you come from, hot stuff?"

That was the first time I'd seen Luca look unsure about anything, and my lips twitched into another smile. Paulo *could* be a tiny bit full-on sometimes, but he was adorable. Or adazzleable, as he preferred to call himself.

"Paulo, meet Luca. He's a friend of my brother's. Luca, this is Paulo, my other colleague."

Luca held out a hand, but Paulo crushed him in a hug instead.

"Ooh, I'm *very* happy to meet you." Paulo stood on tiptoes and mouthed at me over Luca's shoulder. "Straight?"

I nodded. Luca might have been straight, but I was struggling to keep my face that way.

Somehow, Darla managed the feat. "I'm not sure BDSM's allowed on YouTube, hun. Can you put Brooke's friend down? We have thirty packages to ship out today, and a delivery of yarn just arrived too."

Paulo backed away, fanning himself, still not taking his eyes off Luca. "Sure, sure, I'll get right on that."

Yes, I loved my colleagues. With them, what you saw was what you got, and their honesty sure beat the double-dealing and back-stabbing I'd come across in the corporate world.

I'd done the right thing by moving back to Baldwin's Shore.

Hadn't I?

6

BROOKE

"What just happened in there?" Luca asked when we climbed back into the truck.

"Do you mean Paulo? Sometimes he can be a little...extra."

"Extra... Right. Do I have glitter on my shirt?"

"Uh, yes?"

And in his hair, and on his face, and on his pants.

"Fuck." He batted at the fabric with his hands, and then Deck's truck was covered in glitter too. "Glad I kept my sunglasses on."

"How did that help with the glitter?"

"It didn't. But being in that room was like staring into the sun."

"Oh, you mean Darla's outfit?"

I'd gotten used to her fashion choices over the years. Her style tended toward voluminous. Think caftans, muumuus, and tent dresses, which until I met Darla, I'd thought were all the same thing. Apparently, they weren't. Muumuus were yokeless dresses that hailed from Hawaii, often in floral patterns. Tent dresses hung from the shoulder to the hips or floor with no waistline whatsoever. And caftans, they were more exotic garments that originated in ancient Mesopotamia, narrower cut with long, flowing sleeves and a deep, open neck. Working at the Craft Cabin was nothing if not educational. I used to roll my eyes at her outfits, but then she'd made me a muumuu for Christmas and it changed my life. It was just so *comfortable*. Although I only wore it around the house, I was considering investing in a tent dress or two for the summer.

Anyhow, back to Darla. Today, she'd teamed her sunshine-yellow muumuu with a matching hair turban and the hot-pink tasselled earrings she'd made last week for one of Paulo's YouTube videos, plus hand-painted boots in forest green. And yes, I had to concede that she'd looked kind of bright.

"Yeah, I mean her outfit," Luca said. "I thought only grandmas wore caftans?"

"It was a muumuu," I said out of habit, and Luca just stared at me. *Mental note: don't let him see me in my own palm-print version.* "Darla's only thirty-four, but she says lounge dresses are very comfortable."

"There sure are some interesting people in Baldwin's Shore now."

"You know how it goes—most people born here want to leave and see the world, and outsiders want to stay for the peace and quiet."

What a stupid thing to say. Yes, it was the truth, but it left the door wide open for Luca's next question.

"Why'd you come back, Brooke? When we were kids, you always wanted to travel. I mean, I know about your grandma, but... When you moved to Coos Bay, you didn't want to stay there?"

I cursed in my head. All the four-letter words I knew

plus a bunch I made up. Then I did what any sensible girl would do when their former crush was one spadeful of dirt away from digging up their darkest, most rotten secret. I deflected.

Poorly.

"I could ask you the same thing."

"You already did, yesterday, and I told you the answer."

Why did my brain always malfunction around Luca Mendez?

"Uh, yes, I remember. Of course I do. I was just… Look, I didn't much like my job, okay? My old boss used to call me at seven a.m. to remind me to pick up his skinny soy latte on my way to work and at seven p.m. to ask me to make his dinner reservations. In between, I'd have to juggle calls from his wife and his mistress, and fix all his typos, and rearrange his meetings, and on Saturdays, I got to pick up his dry cleaning and feed his cat while he unwound on his boat. So I quit."

That wasn't a total lie. My first boss had been that asshole, but my last boss, he'd been okay. Demanding but fair. He'd wanted me to stay. Addy had wanted me to stay too, but I couldn't. I just couldn't.

"Good."

"I got sick of being treated like a doormat, and— Wait, what did you say?"

"Good. Good for you."

"Uh, thanks."

So many other people in town were incredulous that I'd quit a good-paying, well-respected job. I'd tried to stick it out in the city. I really had. For two months, I'd tried to block out the memories of that night, the little snippets that came back to haunt me. But every time I walked past a man I vaguely recognised, I wondered if it had been *him*. Friends, colleagues... I couldn't relax around any of them. I didn't want to go out, and when I stayed home, I began shaking every time I heard footsteps in the hallway outside my apartment. What if it had been one of my neighbours who violated me in the worst possible way? I became suspicious of everyone, and that was no way to live. A fresh start had seemed like the best option, and I'd always felt safe in Baldwin's Shore. Stifled, but safe.

Until now.

Luca shrugged. "Sometimes, you gotta walk your own path. Follow your heart."

And then, because I hadn't embarrassed myself enough in front of Luca in the past two days, I spewed forth some more word vomit. Vomit with the teensiest hint of the bile that had been building for the last eight years. The oral equivalent of partially digested diced carrots.

"I tried that once before, and it didn't work out so well, did it?"

We both knew what I was talking about, and my brain froze before I finished the sentence. But the words kept tumbling from my lips, the Niagara Falls of stupidity. Luca cursed again, this time under his breath, but I barely heard him because I was already halfway out of the truck.

"On second thought, I'll take my own car to Coos Bay."

Perhaps the veterinarian would help me to lift Vega into the back seat if I asked nicely? Or I could hire someone to help? There was a flyer pinned on the noticeboard at the grocery store, and—

Luca shot out his hand and grabbed my wrist. Holy heck, the man had reflexes.

"The hell you will."

"Hey, let go!"

"Get back in the truck, Brooke."

He held me gently, almost a caress, and I gave an involuntary shiver. Why did he still affect me this way after all this time? Even when he was behaving like a jerk?

"I'm sorry," I muttered. "I shouldn't have said that. I misread the signs back then, and... I'm just sorry, okay?"

"Sit down and put your seat belt on," he said, speaking softly now. "We need to go get your dog."

I slumped back into the passenger seat. Spending time with Luca was uncomfortable, but there was no way to bury the past or even to ignore it. That stupid memory would always be between us, the elephant in the room. And I really couldn't afford to turn down his help. Quite literally—Vega's surgery would cost half of my savings, and I still needed to finish my apartment. Aaron was being beyond generous in building me somewhere to live, but his finances wouldn't stretch to all the furnishings, so I had to chip in too. Although I knew why Aaron was doing it—out of guilt. Guilt that he'd stayed in New York to finish his law degree while I'd given up my college dreams to care for Nonna after her first stroke. Oh, he'd offered to come back, but he'd been more than two years into his legal studies and had a full-ride scholarship, whereas I'd only just started my business degree. The gift of an apartment was his way of repaying me.

But somehow, it still felt like a consolation prize.

Hey, Brooke, you'll never achieve your dreams, but at least you have an en-suite bathroom.

Gah, now I sounded like an ungrateful idiot. It wasn't that I didn't appreciate what Aaron was doing—I did, beyond measure—but I'd always hoped to buy a home in a location I loved with money I'd made myself. To feel as if I'd earned it. Not only had I failed, but I was trapped in Baldwin's Shore now, perhaps forever.

I buckled up, and Luca started the engine. He'd put a pile of towels on the back seat for Vega to lie on, and I recognised them as being from Aaron's linen cupboard.

"Does Aaron know you borrowed his towels?"

"I'll wash them afterward."

A no, then. We lapsed into silence as we drove past the diner and out of town. No milkshakes today.

Every so often, I snuck a peek across at Luca, but he never looked at me. With his eyes hidden behind the sunglasses, I had no way to tell what he was thinking. At first glance, he seemed relaxed, one hand on the steering wheel and the other resting on his well-muscled thigh, but then I began to notice the little signs of tension—the tight skin across his knuckles where he gripped the wheel, his tapping foot, the rigid set of his jaw. It mirrored my own. And as we drove, I thought of the past. Of the fun we'd had as teenagers. Of trips to the Steak and Shake, hikes in the forest with Aaron and Addy and Colt and Romi, picnics on the beach, the way he'd give me a piggyback when I got tired and dunk me in the ocean when I threw sand at him. I missed the old Luca. More than anything else, my mistake had cost me a friend. Tears prickled, and I wiped at my eyes with a sleeve. Why did Luca have to come back and stir up all these old feelings?

We were halfway to Coos Bay before he spoke again, so quietly I could barely hear.

"You didn't misread the signs, Brooke."

What? What was he talking about? "Huh?"

"That night. You didn't misread the signs. I just should've been better at hiding them."

A second passed as his words filtered into my brain. I didn't...misread...signs...hiding... *What*? I stiffened so fast I feared my spine might snap. Was he saying what I thought he was saying?

"I… I…"

"What you wanted to happen, what *I* wanted to happen, it just wasn't an option."

"Why? Why wasn't it an option?"

"Because your brother's my best friend, Brooke. And if you've been friends with a guy for longer than, say, twenty-four hours, you don't sleep with his sister. There are rules about that."

"Rules?"

"A code. Plus I was leaving town two weeks later. Anything we might've had would've fallen apart, and we'd both have hurt Aaron in the process."

"So you hurt me instead."

"And I'll always be sorry for that. Always," he added under his breath.

What was I meant to say to that? In part, it was a vindication, a revelation that I hadn't been quite as stupid as I thought all those years ago. He'd liked me. Luca really had liked me. But whether he'd liked me or not, ultimately, we'd still ended up in the same position, except maybe he'd been hurting too. *Had* he been hurting? Or had he forgotten me as soon as he arrived in Fort Benning? His face was impassive now, a blank mask as he stared straight ahead through the windshield.

He'd never called. He'd never written. Until now, he'd never visited, although he'd gone to see Aaron. Did he *still* like me? Or had I merely been a passing infatuation?

"So what now?"

"Now? Now, we go and pick up your dog."

Had he always missed the point so intentionally? "You know exactly what I meant."

"Yeah." Boy, that was a long sigh. "But nothing's changed, has it? I'll be gone in a week, two weeks max. It's easier that way."

Easier for who?

"Do you have another contract lined up?"

"Nothing's confirmed, but there're a couple of possibilities. I hear Sierra Leone's nice this time of year. But in the meantime, I'll help you to carry the dog up and down your steps whenever Aaron isn't around. Unless you have a boyfriend lined up to lend a hand?"

"There's nobody. I decided to give dating a rest for a while."

"Bad break-up?"

"Something like that."

"Sorry you had such a shitty time."

He sounded as if he meant it, but what did that matter? Our lives were separate now. It occurred to me that despite our shared history, I didn't really know him. Perhaps I never had?

Fifteen minutes until we reached Coos Bay. Quite deliberately, I turned to look out the passenger window and folded my arms, protecting what was left of my heart. With Luca Mendez in town, the risk of further damage was all too real.

And with my stalker in Baldwin's Shore as well, a broken heart wasn't the only danger I faced.

7

LUCA

What the fuck had I done?

The threat of tears plus eight years of festering guilt had pried open my mouth, loosened my tongue, and made me confess a secret that should have stayed hidden. When Brooke's bottom lip had quivered, I'd wanted to pull over and gather her in my arms, but that wasn't an option, and now I'd done even more damage.

It had been far easier to deny my feelings when the girl I'd been in love with for over a decade didn't know about them.

I still remembered the moment when I'd finally seen what had been staring me in the face for years. I was seventeen, coasting my way through high school with no plan other than to get the hell away from Baldwin's Shore, and I'd been kicked out of class for fighting. Again. Going home was out of the question—my father worked the night shift at a warehouse in Coos Bay in those days, and if I'd set foot in the house with obvious bruises, getting suspended would've been the least of my worries.

So I went to the Bartlett place. Nonna was out, but I knew where the spare key was, and nobody minded if I let myself in. Nonna said I was honorary family, even if I didn't always feel like I deserved that title. Brooke was there. Lying on the couch with the drapes pulled, a damp cloth over her forehead to try and ease her migraine. There'd been an awkward moment when I almost sat on her. But despite her own pain, she'd insisted on cleaning up my bloody knuckles, and then we'd just sat together in the dark, silent at first, but when her head started to feel better, we'd begun talking. She'd asked me why I fought, and when I tried to put it into words, I realised there was no good reason. Because I hated to lose, I guess. She asked me what my ambitions were. What did I want to get out of my life? I didn't have an answer for that either. Brooke helped me to see that just hightailing it out of town wasn't much of a plan, and if I was going to succeed, to make something of myself, then I needed to have goals.

That day, we'd both made lists, three items each.

Luca's goals

1 - Take care of my sister.

2 - Get a good job.

3 - See the world.

Brooke's goals

1 - Learn the right lessons.

2 - Fall in love.

3 - Be happy.

Of course, I'd laughed at Brooke's list. I was a teenage boy—what did you expect? Lessons were for dorks. And being happy? That was a foreign concept. The idea of falling in love was dumb—why would I want to do that when I got all the pussy I needed for free? Girls lined up to get a Luca-notch on their bedposts. Sleeping with the bad boy was a rite of passage for the girls at Bayshore High, and I took full advantage of that tradition.

But even as I told her that, the words rang hollow.

Brooke had lain there with her head in my lap as I massaged her temples, and she'd told me that my new goals were wise and noble. That I was a good brother. It was she who'd suggested the army as an option—that way, I could combine goals two and three, and we both knew I liked fighting, didn't we?

That afternoon had changed my life. And now, eleven years later, I'd achieved goals two and three. Goal one was still a work in progress. I tried, fuck, I tried, but Romi still had a tendency to go off the rails, although she'd managed to stay on the straight and narrow for the past three years, more or less. A record. She'd earned her fortune as a model, but that world hadn't been kind to her.

I'd also realised that Brooke's list contained a more worthwhile set of goals than mine, taking care of Romi excepted.

And they were far harder to achieve.

So there I was, stuck in my past, on my way to pick up Brooke's dog and avoid a horny veterinarian. Every few minutes, Brooke wiped her face with a sleeve, and regret clogged my veins like treacle. Regret that I'd put her into this position. But I had no choice.

Not only was there a code, but there was also a pact. A pact with Aaron that we wouldn't mess around with each other's sisters. It happened when we were sixteen, and yeah, alcohol had been involved, but that didn't make it any less serious. We'd been at a party. Him, me, and Romi—Brooke had been somewhere else, probably studying or over at Addy's place. Those two had been thick as thieves. Too much beer and knock-off Jack Daniels led to a game of truth or dare, and because Easton Baldwin was an asshole, he'd dared Aaron to kiss Romi, and when Aaron turned down that dare, Easton had dared him to feel her up instead. Romi's relationship with drink hadn't been much better as a teenager than it was as an adult, and she probably wouldn't have objected, but I sure did.

I'd been about to wipe the smile off of Easton's smug face and probably flatten his nose too when Aaron had stopped me.

"I'll take the truth," he whispered. "I'm not gonna kiss your sister. But you've gotta promise not to touch Brooke either."

"Brooke's not even here."

"I mean ever. You don't touch her ever."

Back then, it had been an easy promise to make. Now, I wondered if he'd known something that I didn't.

"Sure, buddy, I won't touch Brooke. She's not my type anyway."

Aaron had confessed to shitting his pants on Halloween when he was ten, earning himself the nickname "skidmark" for junior year. And I'd kept my promise.

For twelve years, I'd kept my promise, but keeping my lips, hands, and everything else off Brooke got more difficult with every day that passed. So I'd have to keep my distance instead.

Returning to Baldwin's Shore had been a mistake, but I couldn't change the past.

"Don't worry if Vega doesn't eat tonight. He's had a long anaesthetic today, and he'll feel sleepy for the rest of the evening. But if he doesn't eat tomorrow either, give me a call."

Carly was acting more businesslike today, thank fuck. Probably because I stayed by the door, arms folded, and ignored her. She seemed like a nice enough woman, but with Brooke around, avoidance was the best tactic.

"Doesn't he need a bandage?" Brooke asked.

"No, it's important that he be able to extend and flex his leg right from the start. That gives his knee a better chance of healing successfully. But don't let him run around. You're happy with the exercise plan?"

Brooke was clutching the twelve-week planner plus a chart of leg exercises in her hand, and she nodded. "I think so."

"I'm here if you have any questions."

"How long should he keep the cone on?"

"Until the sutures dissolve. That'll take a couple of weeks, but book in for a check-up in ten days. He'll need X-rays at six weeks as well."

Again, Brooke nodded. She was quiet, quieter than usual, and I wasn't sure whether it was the seriousness of Vega's injury that had upset her, or our conversation in the truck. Probably both. That seemed like a good bet. While she finished talking with Carly, I slipped out of the consulting room to pay off the balance on Brooke's account. Seven years spent living on various bases plus the added bonus of hostile fire pay every time I got deployed to a combat zone, which was most of the time, plus a stint in the private sector that paid me more than all my years in the army combined had left me sitting on a healthy nest egg. Spending some of it to fix Brooke's dog was the least I could do.

But of course, that pissed her off too. Back in the truck, Vega snored softly on the pile of towels wearing his giant plastic cone, and Brooke glared at me, arms folded. The glint in her gorgeous brown eyes made me wish I'd brought body armour.

"The vet said you paid for everything."

"Yeah. So?"

"Why?"

"Because I have the money, and you have a half-built apartment."

"So now I'm a charity case?"

I wanted to sigh, but I swallowed it down. "Aren't I allowed to help out a friend?"

"A friend?" She barked out a laugh, a final kick to the nuts. "You think we're friends?"

"You think we're not?"

"Luca, you said goodbye with a note, and you've barely spoken to me since you left."

"I wasn't sure you'd want to hear anything I had to say."

"So you didn't even try?"

I realised now that by attempting to avoid the hurt and the awkwardness, by trying to spare Brooke's feelings and my own, I'd made a mistake. A big one. Perhaps even an irreparable one. While I was busy fighting for my country and getting shot at, ultimately, I'd been a coward. I'd cut our contact down to Christmas and birthday cards sent via Aaron, all because I couldn't face the roller coaster of feelings I rode every time I spoke to Brooke. *Feelings*. They'd become the enemy. By shunning them, I'd become an excellent soldier and a shitty human being.

"I'm sorry I didn't try. I should have." When she didn't answer, I carried on blindly. "But I'm trying now."

"Oh, sure. For two weeks, you'll hang around to annoy me, and then you'll disappear for another eight years."

"I—" I couldn't say I wouldn't, because I would. Brooke was probably right on both counts. "I'm sorry for that too."

"How about we stop discussing this? Our past is so messed up, Luca, and I can't… I just can't…"

Another truth, and I had to respect it.

We rode the rest of the way in silence, and the sun had begun to drop by the time I parked beside Brooke's Honda in front of the Crowes' two-car garage. Back when I was a kid, I used to keep my bike in there so my dad didn't smash it up in one of his rages, but now cobwebs hung at the corners of the doors and Addy's mom's compact and her dad's SUV were parked in the driveway out front. The light was on in the kitchen, and I saw them sitting at the table, eating. Some things didn't change. Dinner in the Crowe house was served at seven p.m. prompt and heaven help you if you showed up late.

"You want to unlock, and then I'll carry the dog upstairs?" I asked.

"I'll let Vega sniff in the yard for a few minutes first in case he needs to go to the bathroom."

"Want me to open the door?"

Brooke handed the key over, and I jogged up the stairs. I'd been in the garage apartment plenty of times when

Addy's grandma had been alive—she used to be a reliable source of candy—and I found it hadn't changed much. The front door opened straight into the living room, with a small kitchen at the back and the bedroom and bathroom to the side. The wallpaper was the same, pale pink with thin white stripes, now peeling around the edges. Yellowed gloss paint on the woodwork showed chips and cracks. The kitchen was stuck in a time warp, and I could swear that was Grandma Crowe's overstuffed couch as well, also pink but a darker shade, more Pepto Bismol than cotton candy. Brooke had made several updates—a flat-screen TV on a side table, new pictures on the walls, too many cushions to count, and a potted plant on the coffee table. All things that could be taken with her when she moved. In some ways, it reminded me of the quarters I'd lived in over the years, spaces I'd called home but which, in reality, had been nothing more than a place to sleep.

I stepped closer to study a painting beside the bedroom door. A small figure stood on the beach, staring out at the waves, and I recognised Turtle Rock in the distance. Had Brooke painted it? Yes, that was her signature in the bottom right-hand corner. Was the figure meant to be her? It should have been serene, but there was a melancholy about the scene. A sadness that made me want to call Addy and get her to give Brooke a hug because sure as shit Brooke would turn down a hug from me if I offered.

If Brooke had painted that from the heart, then mine ached for her.

"Is Vega ready to come in yet?" I called.

"I think so."

The dog was still sleepy, and he didn't protest when I lifted him into my arms and carried him up the stairs. But he did walk into the coffee table as soon as I put him down. And the couch. And the sideboard. Guess that cone took some getting used to. Every time the *crack* of plastic on wood sounded, Brooke winced.

"You want to move some of this furniture?" I suggested.

"Move it where?"

"To the side of the room? Downstairs into the garage? Or I could take it to Deals on Wheels temporarily."

"Uh..." *Crack*. "Could you take the coffee table out? There's a tiny bit of space in the garage, and I have a key."

"Sure. Do you need to keep all these magazines?"

Crafts at Home, *Crochet World*, *American Craft*, *Watercolor Weekly*... Guess I knew what Brooke did in her spare time these days.

"The pile on the bottom shelf can go in the trash." She put her head in her hands. "The trash can's full."

"In the kitchen? I'll empty it."

"You don't have to do that."

"Yes, I do."

Brooke held onto Vega while I gathered up the bag of trash from the kitchen and the pile of magazines, took them to the outside trash can, and tossed them in on top of a vase of flowers. Wait. Flowers? Curious, I reached in and lifted them out. These weren't withered stems, they were fresh lilies. The flowers I'd seen her pick up outside the door last night? Why had she thrown them out? There was a card stuffed into the middle of the blooms, and because I was an asshole, I opened it.

I MISS YOU.

That was all it said, but the sender had drawn a crude heart with an arrow through it at the bottom, Cupid-style to match the picture on the front. The ex-boyfriend? The one who'd put Brooke off dating? If he still had feelings for her, then she sure didn't feel the same way. Part of me, the primitive part fuelled by testosterone rather than reason, wanted to stick around for longer than two weeks just to punch him in the face.

My phone rang, and I forced myself to uncurl my fists. Brooke wasn't mine, and she never would be.

"Aaron? How'd it go in court today?"

"Pretty good."

"You won?"

I didn't know the details of the case, something about a divorce dispute, but Aaron hadn't been sure which way it would go and he'd spent most of the night reading through documents. Between the lawyering and the renovation project, he'd been working harder than a Middle Eastern donkey lately.

"Yeah, it was a good settlement. The client was happy, which is why I'm calling."

What did that have to do with me? "Oh?"

"He's offered me the use of his vacation home in Cabo, and I'd like to take Clarissa for a couple of weeks, but Brooke's dog... How long are you planning to hang around in Baldwin's Shore?"

Ah, shit. But Aaron needed the break, and I didn't have a firm contract lined up. It'd be a dick move to make him give up a free vacation.

"What dates are we talking?"

"Leaving the week after next."

"Take the trip. I can stay until you get back."

"Thanks, buddy. Are you with Brooke right now?"

"Just got back from the veterinarian. The dog keeps walking into the furniture."

"Can you tell her I'll bring dinner over tonight? I haven't seen her in a few days."

"Sure, I'll pass on the message."

And Aaron could tell her about Cabo. Better him than me because when Brooke found out I'd be on dog duty for two weeks longer than she thought, she'd be pissed.

8

BROOKE

"Cabo? You're going to freaking Cabo?"

For two freaking weeks?

Aaron looked at his girlfriend and back to me. Yes, I knew I was overreacting, but this week had been one long series of challenges sent to test me.

"It's only for a vacation," Clarissa told me. "Your brother needs a break, wouldn't you agree?"

Yes, and Clarissa wanted a free trip to Mexico. She stared down her nose at me in that snooty way of hers, and I blinked back tears. Why did he have to pick her over me? Not that I particularly wanted to go to Cabo; I just really, really needed his company at the moment. For a brief second, I was tempted to confess all about my stalker, but I stopped myself in time. *Don't be selfish, Brooke.* Aaron *did* need a vacation. He'd been working way too hard lately, doing his best to create a better future for both of us. Clarissa was right, the same way she was always right.

"Yes, I agree he needs a break, but Vega..."

Vega raised his head at the sound of his name. He was a smart dog. He'd already learned how to sit and stay, and he also knew that if he cocked his head to one side and looked up at me with those doleful eyes, I'd give him a doggie treat.

"Luca's agreed to stay until we get back," Aaron said. "He'll help you each day."

Oh, he had, had he? Just when I thought this month couldn't get any worse.

"Vega needs to be carried in and out, like, four times a day, and more at the weekends. That's a lot to ask."

"He can handle it. Plus he can give Deck and Brady a hand with the renovations, so your apartment will get finished sooner."

I managed a weak smile. "That's great. Terrific. I hope you both enjoy Mexico."

Clarissa helped herself to a slice of pizza. At least they'd brought food with them. "We will. The villa's right on the beach, and the nightlife in Cabo is amazing. You should go sometime."

Did she say that just to rub it in? She knew I was ploughing every cent I had into the renovation project, and also that I was single. I blew out a long breath. It wasn't that I hated my brother's girlfriend—hate was a strong word—but I couldn't help wishing she were nicer. Clarissa was pretty and successful and made all the right choices in life, and she also never passed up an opportunity to remind me of that. Beside her, I felt like a bumbling fool.

"I'm too busy with work to take a vacation."

"Oh, right, the crafting. Your brother showed me a video the other day. People really pay you to fold paper?"

"Origami's very popular, actually."

"Right." She sounded as if she didn't believe me, even though my origami videos had thousands of views. "Have you ever thought about going back to college?"

"So I can work in an office like you?"

Aaron jumped in before Clarissa could bite back. "Clarissa got promoted last week. She's regional vice president of marketing now."

Did that mean she got a bigger stick to shove up her ass? Internally, I poked pins into an imaginary voodoo Clarissa doll, but externally, I smiled.

"Congratulations! That's great news."

To my own ears, my words sounded fake, but Clarissa didn't seem to notice. Probably she was used to people speaking that way.

"Thanks! I'm getting a new company car as well. Are you gonna eat that last slice of pepperoni?"

"No, you have it." I'd lost my appetite. Perhaps that was one small silver lining to this month's clouds—I could button my jeans again. "Aaron, how's the reno work going? Did Deck finish making the kitchen cabinets?"

He truly was making them, like from scratch. Aaron said that if he was going to go to the trouble of building his own home, then he'd build it exactly the way he wanted it. If that took longer, then so be it. Better to do it right the first time than cut corners and have to redo the work a year or two later.

Which meant that Aaron had sketched out his ideas for the whole of his home, and Deck was bringing the wooden parts to life. When Deck first came to town a few years ago, he'd worked as a sculptor, but sculpting didn't pay the bills, so he'd turned to carpentry to make ends meet. A shame, really, because he was so talented. We kept some of his smaller pieces at the Craft Cabin on a consignment basis, and every so often one of them sold, but they weren't cheap. Maybe if we could attract more visitors into town from the Peninsula Resort...

Deck's artistic background meant that everything he

made turned out beautiful. The kitchen, the dining area, and the living room were all open plan, a mix of reclaimed materials and quirky modern touches that I absolutely loved. Personally, I thought my brother's talents were wasted as a lawyer. He should have become a designer. Honestly, he'd have made a fortune.

"They're halfway finished. We managed to get a bunch of old science benches from the high school in Coquille, and he's going to incorporate those into the island. Did you decide on your bathroom tiles yet?"

I thought I had—white tiles with a ripple texture, plus metallic silver tiles to form a feature line halfway up the wall—but that was before I got Vega's vet bill. Yes, Luca had paid it, but I had every intention of paying him back. And although it was very generous of him, I couldn't deny being the tiniest bit annoyed that he'd gone ahead and settled the balance without mentioning his plan to me first.

"I think I'll probably go with plain white."

Clarissa wrinkled her nose because anything plain was anathema to her, but I ignored her opinion the same way I always did.

"You think?" Aaron asked. "Is that a definite maybe?"

"Probably."

He just chuckled. "Let me know if you want me to order them. Brady finished wiring the lights today, and the plumber finished the first downstairs bathroom last week. He's gonna start on yours next month."

Thank goodness. Until now, we'd had to use the old staff bathroom from the building's time as a car dealership. To say it had seen better days was an understatement. Think blackened grout and yellowed porcelain, chipped tiles and pipes that clanked and groaned when you turned the faucet on. I'd kept a pair of flip-flops by the door because no matter how many times I scrubbed the floor, it had still remained a stubborn beige colour.

But now we had proper plumbing. Hallelujah.

At least one part of my life was going according to plan, thanks in no small part to my brother. I *couldn't* burden him with the rest of my troubles. It would ruin his first vacation in years, and I'd make an enemy out of Clarissa too. She wouldn't let a little thing like a stalker bother her. No, she'd probably stab him through the eye with a lip liner or knock him out with her giant purse.

I'd survive alone for two weeks. Well, not entirely alone. I had Luca on speed dial, and if it meant my brother getting a break, I'd put up with Luca's presence and deal with the consequences later.

DEALING with Luca turned out to be easier than I thought. After the rocky start and his overreach with the vet bill, he began acting more...professional? Was that the right word? Probably not, but I didn't like the term "distant."

Aaron came over in the mornings to carry Vega down the stairs and load him into the car. Paulo or Darla helped me to get him out at the store, and he snoozed in the break room all day, apart from at lunchtime when he got up to mooch for titbits. He barked at Pickle once, she hissed back, and he reversed until his butt hit the wall. So much for being a guard dog. From that moment on, they ignored each other, which meant one problem was solved.

Luca showed up three times each evening—right after work to carry Vega into the apartment, once before dinner, and again just before I went to bed—and he never complained. Not once. On the third day, I asked if he wanted to stay for pizza, but he said he had to finish painting a wall. Okay, maybe "distant" *was* the most appropriate term. But having a little space between us was a good thing, right? The evening after, he had to take a phone call about a job, so Colt came over with Kinsley, his little girl, and we made paper daisies. Me and Kinsley, not me and Colt. That would've been weird. But Colt did bring pizza, so the arrangement worked out well for all of us, not that I was hungry because I was too busy worrying about where Luca might end up going next. How dangerous would it be? Concerns I'd pushed to the back of my mind for the last eight years were now front and centre. And worse, there was nothing I could do about them—if I confessed my fears to Luca, that would upset the tentative truce we'd settled into. Having salvaged the remnants of a friendship, I didn't want to lose it.

Nor did I want to be alone when my brother went on vacation. My stalker had been blessedly quiet for the last week, but who knew how long the peace would last?

9

BROOKE

On Wednesday, Aaron took the evening shift—thankfully sans Clarissa—because his flight to Cabo left on Thursday morning and we wouldn't see each other for two weeks after that.

"You didn't make *me* a cake on my birthday," he grumbled as I sifted flour into a bowl.

"That's because you were on a health kick. I made you a vegetable lasagne and stuck candles in it, remember?"

Paulo preferred sugar to veggies, so he was getting a three-tier chocolate sponge with buttercream filling. Darla had promised to drop by and help us to eat it, even though it was her day off tomorrow. We each worked five days per week in the store—I covered Tuesdays and Wednesdays with Darla, Thursdays and Fridays with Paulo, and all three of us worked Saturdays.

Saturdays were my favourite days. Not only because I had Sundays and Mondays off, but because I ran a craft group for older children in the mornings. I also taught adults on Wednesday afternoons and younger kids on Tuesdays. The classes were my favourite part of the job—

they were sometimes chaotic and usually messy, but always fun.

And this Saturday, I had Paulo's birthday dinner to look forward to as well, plus another cake, one I didn't have to make this time. All I had to do was get through the rest of the week first.

"The lasagne was good," Aaron admitted, patting his stomach. "And I should have stuck with the diet. Not sure I've got much of a beach body at the moment."

"Clarissa loves you just as you are." Gag. "What time is your flight tomorrow?"

"Nine thirty. You sure you'll be okay while we're not here?"

Not even a little bit. "I managed to survive for nearly seven years while you were in New York."

"Yeah, I know, but I'm allowed to worry about my little sister, aren't I?"

"Hey, less of the 'little.'" I flicked flour at him, then cursed when he ducked. "I'm only three inches shorter than you."

"Sure, if you stand on tiptoe."

Maybe that was true.

"Now you're just being picky. Want me to make you a cake when you get back?"

"I'm never gonna say no to one of your cakes, and you'll be able to make it in your new kitchen soon. Deck's gonna start work on it while I'm away." Aaron pulled a folded sheet of paper out of his pocket. "But he's also offered to help with the dog if Luca can't make it. Colt and Brady too. I've set up a schedule with everyone's availability on it."

Of course he had. It was colour-coded too.

"You're a freak, did anyone ever tell you that?"

"All the time. But I'm an organised freak. One of us has

to be," he added as he leaned down to kiss me on the cheek. "I need to finish packing, scatterbrain. See you in two weeks."

"Don't call me that," I yelled at his retreating back.

The only answer was the door slamming behind him.

I DIDN'T COVER my yawn as I stumbled around the kitchen on Thursday morning. Why bother? I was alone apart from Vega, and it was his fault I was so tired. He'd woken me up with his barking in the middle of the night, and then I couldn't get back to sleep, not when every time I closed my eyes white lilies danced in front of them. Now Vega was whining at the door again, but Luca wasn't due to arrive for another half hour. And it was definitely an "I'm excited" whine, not an "I need the bathroom" scratch. Even though we'd only been together for a short time, I'd learned there was a difference.

"Oh, *now* you want to chase squirrels? You'll have to wait, goof. You're not allowed."

Whine.

"Or chipmunks. Come and eat your breakfast, okay?"

I tipped doggie kibble into a bowl and made a mental note to pick up another bag the next time I went to the grocery store. Or I could drive a quarter-mile farther to the feed store and save a buck, plus Hal would carry the bag to my car for me. It wasn't as if I was short of time. Now that I'd moved back to Baldwin's Shore, my social life was practically non-existent. Paulo kept trying to get me to go out with him and his friends, but even the thought of trying to keep up with those party animals made me tired. Brooke 1.0 had wanted to be one of those people—you know the kind. They were all over Instagram, drinks in hand, make-up perfect, always smiling and surrounded by friends. The good-time girls. The social butterflies. The Adelines of this world. And when I'd moved to Coos Bay, Addy had welcomed me into her circle and invited me to every event going.

I'd dressed up, gone out, giggled, flirted, and even mastered the perfect smoky eye. But I'd always felt like an impostor. And after the disaster that sent me running back to my childhood home, I'd decided that crochet was more my thing. Paulo's birthday dinner would be the first time I'd had a lively evening out in months.

While Vega crunched up his breakfast, I taped a baggie of candles to the top of the plastic box containing Paulo's cake and checked the lid was secure. If I put it in the car now, that would save time when Luca arrived. I felt guilty enough for monopolising his day already, without him waiting around while I made trips backward and forward.

At least the sky was blue this morning. Yesterday had been gloomy and grey, and—

The cake went flying as I tripped over something on the landing outside, the box bump-bump-bumping all the way down the steps to the bottom. Each time plastic hit concrete, it felt like a punch to the chest. Dammit, dammit, *dammit*! I'd spent hours making that freaking cake. And what had I tripped over? I sure as heck hadn't left anything in the way.

Frustration turned to fear as I caught sight of the box of chocolates—expensive-looking, tied with a fancy ribbon—and worse, the card stuck to the top. I recognised that writing. Skinny block capitals with a slight slant. One word. *BROOKE.*

My heart thudded against my ribcage as I tore open the

envelope, read the one-line message and saw the cupid's heart.

NOTHING TASTES AS GOOD AS YOU.

It took a second for the words to sink in. For the horror in their meaning to become clear. That snake had tasted me. His slimy, disgusting tongue had touched my skin, maybe *more* than my skin, and now he was revelling in my distress. Had he planned this all along? Known when he assaulted me that he'd torment me later?

That sick freak.

And the nightmarish revelations continued, like peeling an onion, if onions were made of molten lava mixed with sulphuric acid. Every layer drew more tears out of me.

There was no postage on the box. No address label. The man who'd given me the worst night of my life had hand-delivered his vile package in the early hours. Had he poisoned the candies? Drugged them? I picked up the box and hurled it as far as I could. It hit the side of Mrs. Crowe's summer house and split open, spilling the contents everywhere. Vega flinched, and another sob burst out of me because not only had I scared my dog, my protector, but I'd also have to clean up the mess. I hated that man. *Hated him.* Nonna always said that love and hate were two sides of the same emotion, that you couldn't have one without the other, but I knew now that she'd lied. Or maybe there were two kinds of hate? Either way, I wanted to douse my stalker in gasoline and roast marshmallows as he burned.

I sank down onto the top step and buried my face in Vega's fur as he let me hug him for the first time.

"I'm so sorry, goof. You tried to warn me, didn't you? You knew he was outside."

Vega just licked my face.

I had a sudden panic that Cupid might still be out there, watching, but as I scrambled to my feet, I realised that Vega was quiet. He'd bark again, wouldn't he? Like a furry burglar alarm?

Maybe I should install an actual burglar alarm as well? What if I went out with Vega one day and when I came back, Cupid was waiting for me? Should I get a gun? I'd never been keen on them, but now I was beginning to see the attraction.

I needed a hug. I needed my brother. And...and... More lava bubbled up. What did the timing mean? Aaron was on his way to the airport right now. Did my stalker know that? Was he that close? Had he picked this morning to deliver his "gift" knowing that I'd have a tiny window of time in which to decide whether I should ruin my brother's vacation or handle the problem alone?

He wasn't just a stalker and a rapist; he was also a sadist.

I wiped my face with my sleeve, ruing the day I'd decided to come back to Baldwin's Shore. Had my stalker followed me here? Suddenly, the number of new faces in town took on a more sinister meaning. They weren't only potential friends and customers, they could be the enemy too.

"Hell, what should I do?" I asked, and Vega slurped my face again.

As if in answer, the sound of an engine reminded me that I wasn't completely alone. My brother's Toyota rounded the corner with Luca driving, and I sagged in relief. Luca wouldn't let anybody near me.

Would he?

He *was* new in town. Kind of.

Dammit, Brooke, have you lost your mind? This was Luca.

I'd known him for as long as I'd known my own name. Luca wouldn't hurt me. But where had he been on March twelfth last year?

Luca unfolded himself from the driver's side of the Camry, and of course he spotted the spilled candy right away.

"Bad morning?"

"Something like that."

I couldn't stop Aaron from going to Cabo. I just couldn't. Luca or Colt or Deck or Brady would come to my apartment every day, first thing in the morning and last thing at night, and the rest of the time, I could drag the couch in front of the door. Vega would alert me to prowlers, and I'd make sure I slept with the phone in my hand. I'd survive.

Or perhaps I could sleep at the store? The couch in the break room was really comfortable.

"Want me to clean this up?" Luca stopped in front of the remains of the cake. "Ouch. Was that a chocolate sponge?"

I nodded, and another tear trickled down my cheek. "Paulo's birthday gift. I should throw it in the trash."

"It's still edible."

"It's ruined."

"Your cakes always taste great." Luca climbed the steps two at a time and raised my chin with a finger. "He's a guy. Trust me, he'll eat it with a spoon."

I sobbed out a laugh. When he wasn't being an asshole, Luca always had a way of making me feel better.

"You really think so?"

"I'll put it in the trunk."

He did that while I fixed my face and fetched my purse. The stalker's card I'd just tucked away in there burned at the faux leather, a reminder of past stupidity and bad decisions. Maybe I should pass it to Colt? He was the sheriff's deputy in Baldwin's Shore, after all. But then he'd call my brother, and Aaron would fly back from Cabo, and...

Two weeks. I only had to last for two weeks.

When Aaron came back, I'd tell him everything, and Colt too. In the meantime, I just needed to avoid any situations where my stalker could catch me alone. As long as I had Vega by my side, or Darla, or Paulo, or one of the other guys, the freak couldn't touch me.

Luca carried Vega to the car, and I locked the door to my apartment. Double-checked it was secure. Triple-checked. A touch of paranoia was a healthy thing, right? Given the situation, I mean. The chocolates strewn on the grass by the summer house were a stark reminder of that. I'd have to pick them up later. Should I keep the box? Would the freak have left any fingerprints? Somehow, I couldn't imagine him doing that. He'd been careful so far. The only traces of him had been the messages he wanted me to see.

"Ready?" Luca asked. "Or do you want to check the door a fourth time?"

"I just don't want to get burgled."

"Not being funny, but your lock's a piece of shit. Any self-respecting burglar would get past it in thirty seconds."

As if I wasn't scared enough already. "Thanks, that makes me feel so much better."

"If you're worried, I can get a new lock installed. Although you probably need a new door too. The one you have is barely a step up from cardboard."

Maybe I should book a motel room? In, say, London? Okay, perhaps fleeing the country was slightly drastic, but when it came down to the choice of fight or flight, running like hell won every time. Was the new hotel in Baldwin's Shore pet-friendly? The Peninsula Resort and Spa had opened a year ago to great fanfare, and although many of the locals despised the place—Addy's parents called it a blight on the landscape—it had a doorman and a security patrol. I could hide away inside for two weeks. Order room service. Just come out for work and Vega's bathroom breaks. Oh, and also end up bankrupt because that place was *obscenely* expensive.

"Do you want me to call someone?" Luca asked.

"Huh?"

"To change your door?"

"How much do you think it would cost?"

Were we talking hundreds? A thousand? It wouldn't only be the cost of materials but labour as well. And if I put that money into my new apartment at Deals on Wheels, I'd be able to move out faster. Sharing a building with my brother had never looked more attractive.

"The cost doesn't matter," Luca said.

"Actually, it does."

"I'll pay Deck to do it."

It was a kind offer, but Luca's caveman attitude grated, even when he opened the car door for me like a perfect gentleman. Although if I cared to unpack my feelings, which I didn't, I was probably as annoyed at myself for ending up in this predicament as I was at Luca. Yes, he might have been a little on the alpha side, but he was still too good to be true. Always had been, despite being brought up by an abusive alcoholic who'd done his best to break his son's spirit.

"You don't have to do that. I can pay for my own door."

"Yeah, I know I don't have to, but I'm still doing it. Deck can take a day away from your brother's cabinets to make your place safe."

The way Luca said that... It was almost as if he knew what was going on. He couldn't... Could he? I glanced across as he started the engine and pulled away, just in time to see him cover his yawn with a hand. He was tired? Why?

He hadn't been making a nocturnal delivery, had he?

"Late night?"

"Early morning. I had to call some people, and Djibouti's eleven hours ahead of Oregon."

"You're going to Djibouti?"

"It's a possibility."

"Is it dangerous?"

"I'm a security contractor. Danger is my middle name."

"Your middle name is Rey," I said, then immediately regretted it because Rey was also Luca's dad's name, and he hated to be reminded of that awful man. "Seriously, could you get hurt?"

"There's always a chance I could get hurt. But I'm good at what I do, and I don't take unnecessary risks. Brooke, I'm not some macho idiot."

"I know you're not." Luca was tough, but nobody could ever describe him as stupid. "Why did you leave the army? I thought you'd signed up for life."

"So did I in the beginning. But having to fight other people's battles wears thin after a while, you know? In the army, I couldn't decline an order, and when the time came to decide whether I wanted to re-enlist, I figured I'd try the private sector instead. At least this way, I can pick and choose which jobs to take."

"How long ago did you leave the army? I remember Aaron mentioning it early last year."

Dammit, my mouth was doing its own thing, and now I was going on a fishing expedition. A part of me hated myself for not trusting Luca, but the other part hoped that a definitive answer with regard to his whereabouts in March would rule him out as a suspect once and for all.

"I got out at the end of May."

"And where were you before that? I mean, did you have a tough assignment?"

"I was stationed in the Middle East for six months." He cut his gaze sideways for a second. "Kuwait, but you didn't hear that from me. And all of the assignments were tough."

"That's great." *Brooke, you idiot, that might be great for your suspect list, but it sure isn't great for Luca.* "Great that you got a lot of practice at...tough things. And Kuwait's sunny, right?"

"Right."

Luca wasn't smiling. In fact, he looked slightly irritated.

"Sorry, I'm babbling. I'll stop talking now."

"Brooke, are you okay?"

"Fine, totally fine. A bit tired."

"It's just that there was candy all over your lawn, and you seemed kind of upset when I arrived."

When in trouble, blame PMS. "Uh, it's the wrong time of the month? And I don't like that flavour much."

"Okaaaaaay. In that case, I'll stop talking too."

10

LUCA

Out of the corner of my eye, I saw Darla check out my ass as I loaded the dog into the car, and I wasn't saying that to brag. Okay, maybe I was, but I didn't do two hundred squats every day for nothing. Or a hundred push-ups. Or fifty chin-ups. And women dug the glutes even more than the six-pack.

But when I straightened, Brooke's boss had disappeared inside, and Paulo had taken her place. He checked out *everything*. Then licked his lips.

"Do you want some cake? There's plenty left."

"The cake Brooke made?"

"Yes, although it's not so much a cake now as a dessert. It had a tiny accident, so we added strawberries and called it Baldwin's mess. You know, like Eton mess?"

"Like what?"

"Eton mess. It's a dessert they eat in England. Smashed-up meringues, strawberries, and cream."

"Never heard of it, but I wouldn't say no to a slice."

"Bowlful." He turned on his heel and marched inside. "Brooke! Your boyfriend's here."

"I'm not—"

"Do you want extra cream? Of course you do. Cream contains calcium, so it's practically a health food, and those muscles won't fuel themselves."

Brooke skidded into the break room, sparkling. Literally sparkling. Red, green, and gold glitter covered her from head to toe. What had she done, rolled in the stuff?

"Paulo, he's not my boyfriend!" She turned to me, arms out, helpless. Glitter flaked onto the tile. "I've told him that a hundred times, but he just won't listen."

"But you'd be so perfect together. Look at you—Sleeping Beauty and Prince Charming."

As if on cue, Brooke yawned. "Aaron would kill me. Luca's his best friend."

Not quite right. "Actually, he'd kill *me*."

"Yeah, right. He's a lawyer and you're a commando."

Aaron had a mean left hook when the need arose. "I think you underestimate him."

Paulo pouted. "Aw, c'mon, guys. I crashed and burned last night, so at least let me live vicariously through somebody else. Darla never dates. She's so *boring*."

"I heard that," Darla called from the other room. "Go open your Tinder—"

"Grindr."

"Go open your Grindr and stop harassing Brooke."

"See? Bor-ing."

The bickering was all in jest, and it reminded me of my days in the Rangers, although my brothers in arms would have included at least three curses in every sentence. Plus the food was better here. Paulo spooned cake into a bowl, decorated it with not just strawberries but raspberries too, and squirted cream from a can over the whole concoction. The presentation could have used work, but I'd give Brooke ten out of ten for the taste. Vega whined from the car, and she went out to pet him.

"He's been begging for cake all day, but he's not allowed any," Paulo said. "Did you know chocolate's poisonous for dogs? But Darla bought him a rotisserie chicken for lunch, so there's no need to call the ASPCA."

"Should've been a dog," I muttered. Not least because Vega got to go home with Brooke every night. Would he share her bed once his leg recovered? Fuck, I was jealous of a damn mutt.

"Oh, totally. Dogs have my dream life. Sleeping all day, long walks on the beach, eating without putting on weight... Plus you could lick your own balls."

The cake I'd just forked into my mouth stuck in my throat, and I began coughing. Cake spluttered all over the floor. Paulo thumped me on the back, and he was surprisingly strong for a little guy.

Brooke ran back inside. "What happened? Do you need water?"

"I wouldn't"—*cough*—"say no."

Brooke thrust a glass of water in my direction, and then the cat showed up and tried to eat the cake crumbs. It seemed that chocolate wasn't good for felines either because Paulo shrieked and carried it through to the store. This place was a damn circus.

"Are you okay?" Brooke asked softly.

"Fine." Embarrassed because I'd spit cake everywhere, but okay. "I should clear this up."

"Paulo can do it. I'm sure whatever happened, it was his fault."

"I heard that," Paulo shouted.

Fuck my life. How was Brooke still sane?

Finally, we all made it out to the car, and I headed for

the Crowe property. I still had two more weeks of this, and I couldn't even hate it because it let me get my Brooke fix before I headed overseas again. Who knew when I'd be back? I'd become a nomad—no roots, no home, no concrete plans for the future. Maybe it was genetic? Romi was living out of a hotel room in Paris this month. Yeah, my father was still in Baldwin's Shore, but that was only because he was too poor to leave and too drunk to care, and nobody knew where the hell my mother was. She hadn't sent so much as a postcard since she walked out on us two decades ago.

"I'm sorry about Paulo," Brooke said. "What did he say?"

"He wants to be reincarnated as a dog so he can lick his own balls."

Brooke clapped both hands over her mouth, but a giggle still escaped. "Are you serious?"

"Unfortunately."

"He has no filter."

"Yeah, I got that. But he seems like a good friend to you."

"He's the best. Darla too. When I moved back into town, I was worried about finding a job here, but I got lucky."

"I'm happy that you're happy."

And I meant it. The last time I'd left Baldwin's Shore, Brooke had been hurting, and I wasn't sure I could walk away and leave her miserable a second time, not without trying to fix things first. Twenty-year-old me had taken the easy way out, but the army had taught me there was no place in this world for chickens. A lesson it had taken me far too long to learn.

Brooke gave a quiet snort, and I couldn't blame her. I didn't exactly have a great track record when it came to caring about her feelings. I should have made the effort to call her. Or emailed when the time difference was unkind. I missed the friendship we used to have, and this pilgrimage back to Oregon was showing me just how much.

"Key." I held out my hand when we got back to her place. "I'll get the front door while you walk Vega around the yard."

She handed it over without a word, and I lifted the dog out of the car. Fuck, everything was covered in glitter, including me. I'd have to get the car detailed before Aaron came back. Was the car wash behind the gas station on the outskirts of Coos Bay still open? A couple of Mexican guys used to run it, father and son, but the father would be about seventy by now.

I jogged up the steps and nearly tripped over the box at the top. Looked like a gift from Mrs. Crowe. Her barely legible, spidery handwriting hadn't changed. I remembered Addy trying to forge it for school permission slips, and the teachers always shrugged and nodded because they couldn't read a word Mrs. Crowe wrote either.

"Hey, Brooke—you got a package."

I thought she'd be pleased, but she froze. She fucking froze, and all the colour drained out of her face. What the hell? I scanned the yard in case Brooke had seen something I'd missed, like a bear or a mountain lion. One hand went to my gun, and I prepared to fire a warning shot, but there was nothing. Nothing apart from the remains of the spilled candy, still scattered beside the summer house. Some creature had been helping itself—half of the chocolates were missing, and paw prints criss-crossed back and forth. A fox, maybe, or a large cat.

"Brooke? You okay?"

Vega whined and nudged her leg with his nose as I ran down the steps, keeping an eye out for potential threats as I went. Brooke was already tearing up when I reached her, and I wrapped an arm around her waist as her knees buckled.

"What's wrong? Do you need to go to the hospital?"

She shook her head, and the tears spilled down her cheeks. Ah, shit. She'd gone from happy to distraught in the space of thirty seconds, and I didn't have the first fucking clue as to why. What a day for Aaron to pick for the start of his vacation.

"You want me to call someone? Addy? Paulo? Darla?" Brooke bit her lip, and the dog licked her hand. "Aaron?"

"No!"

"Brooke, you gotta talk to me. I'm out of my depth here."

"W-w-where did the package come from? Is there an address label?"

"Mrs. Crowe left it there."

Brooke sagged in my arms, and I shifted my grip to hold her up.

"Are you sure?"

"Ninety percent? Your name's almost unreadable, so I'd say it's a fair assumption."

"Thank goodness." The words escaped on an exhale, so quiet I was barely able to hear them.

"Who did you think sent the package?"

And why had that left her so upset?

"It doesn't matter. It wasn't him." Another gulped breath. "It wasn't him," she repeated, almost to herself.

"Wasn't who?"

Which asshole did I need to send to the emergency room? Because if the prick had caused Brooke's distress, then he needed to be informed of the error of his ways. When Brooke didn't answer, I scooped her up in my arms and carried her back to the apartment. Vega ambled along beside us, taking the drama in his stride.

"Can you climb up the steps, Brooke? Because unless I sling you over my shoulder, I can't carry you and the dog at the same time."

"I-I-I can manage."

I set her onto her feet and nudged her in front of me. That way, if she fell, I'd act as a backstop. Then I picked up the dog and followed Brooke up the stairs, still in the dark about what the hell was going on but getting more worried by the minute. It was a different kind of fear than I usually felt. In a war zone, there was a baseline level of apprehension, the knowledge that the unexpected could and probably would happen. But I'd trained for that. My skills had been honed over the years until I didn't have to think, I just reacted.

But today? Today, I was lost.

Inside, I set the dog in his bed, guided Brooke to the couch, and secured her piece-of-shit door. Pulled the drapes closed. Then it was time to get some answers.

"Brooke?"

Her lips trembled in a poor attempt at a smile. "I'm fine. It's just been a long day, that's all."

"Bullshit."

She dragged her gaze up to mine. "Thank you for bringing me home. I'll see you later?"

"Sure. You'll see me later. And I'll bring a sleeping bag and a pillow because unless you tell me what's going on, I'm spending the night on your couch."

"Oh, no. No, no, no."

"Then talk. Right now."

What the fuck was the problem?

11

LUCA

Brooke curled up as small as she could get, knees drawn up to her chin with her arms wrapped around her legs.

"Someone's been sending me weird packages. I thought that was another one."

"The chocolates? The flowers?"

She looked up sharply. "How do you know about the flowers?"

"I watched you take them inside, and then I saw them in the trash."

"Oh."

"What else has he sent you, Brooke?"

And it had to be a guy, surely? She'd referred to "him," plus she wouldn't get worked up if a chick was sending her candy.

"Only a card."

"A card?"

She nodded.

"Where's the card now?"

"I threw it a-a-away. I thought it was just a sick j-j-joke."

"What did it say?"

"I c-c-can't…" Brooke gave a shuddering sniffle, and I didn't know whether to hug her or squeeze her hand or stay the hell back. This was outside my area of expertise. I did one-night stands, not relationships, and if those women ever cried, then I wasn't there to see it. "I can't say."

"Can't or won't?"

"Y-y-you'll freak out and call Aaron, and he's on vacation."

"I'm already freaked the hell out, sweetheart. And if you don't give me the facts, I won't have a lot of choice about calling your brother because I don't know how to help you myself."

Brooke's anguish was tough to watch. This hadn't built up over a few days or even a few weeks, had it? The pain ran far deeper.

Screw boundaries. Screw the carefully constructed rules I'd imposed on myself. I gathered Brooke onto my lap and she clung to me as she crumbled, her tears soaking my shirt, her heart beating against my chest. I hoped that if I held her close enough, I could take some of the agony away. What had she been going through? And why hadn't she told anyone? If Aaron had an inkling of Brooke's secret, he'd sure as hell have warned me before he left the country.

"Brooke, talk to me. What did the card say?"

"It…it was an anniversary card. It said 'Do you remember me? Because I remember you.' I can't get the words out of my head. At night… I can't sleep."

"Who sent it? *Do* you remember him?"

"I don't know! I don't know who he is, but I'll never forget what he did to me."

That motherfucker.

A chill ran through me, quickly followed by a burst of

white-hot fury. Some piece of shit had hurt Brooke? He was a dead man.

"What did he do?"

I didn't want to know the answer, but I had to know what we were dealing with.

"I think... I think he r-r-raped me."

Once, I'd been angry all the time. Teenage Luca Rey Mendez had been liberal with his threats and wild with his fists. The army had shown me how to channel that anger, how to hone it to a razor-sharp point and punch it through the enemy. But right now, I wanted to punch the damn wall. I had to put Brooke down and walk. Pace the damn apartment while the anger hissed and slithered inside of me.

Back and forth, back and forth, back and forth...

Something in my jaw cracked, and I forced myself to unclench my teeth.

"You *think* he raped you?"

Wasn't that the kind of thing a woman would know?

"I was at Addy's birthday party. I got drunk. And maybe somebody put something in my drink, I'm not sure. I was s-s-so stupid."

"Don't ever say you're stupid, Brooke. You're anything but stupid. If some motherfucker assaulted you, that's on him. You didn't report this?"

Brooke shook her head, wretched. "I don't remember anything apart from waking up the next morning and feeling sore, like, like... Do I have to freaking spell it out?"

"You're certain you didn't consent?"

Now Brooke's eyes flashed with the same anger I felt, except hers was directed at me.

"And next you'll want to know *why* I didn't file a report. I already said I don't remember. I don't remember *anything*. I don't remember talking to a guy. I don't remember leaving the party. I don't remember going home. And I sure as heck don't remember having sex."

"What did Addy say? Did she see you with anybody?"

Brooke focused on her lap.

"Shit, you didn't even tell Addy?"

"Not everything. I said a guy had been bothering me, but she didn't remember seeing me with anyone in particular. Just a few minutes here, a few minutes there. A social...a social caterpillar."

"A what?"

"She was the butterfly, I was the caterpillar."

"Addy called you a caterpillar?"

Brooke wasn't a fuckin' caterpillar. She was a hummingbird—beautiful and delicate.

"It was a joke between us. I was the one who started it."

Should've dodged the government soldiers and stayed in Eritrea. Life on the run would've been easier than dealing with this mess. But fuck, then Brooke would be on her own. And Aaron was like a brother to me. Although Brooke definitely wasn't like a sister. If I thought about my own flesh and blood the way I thought about Brooke, I'd be arrested, and rightly so.

Although prison was still a possibility because when I got my hands on the motherfucker who stole what Brooke hadn't freely given, I'd take the death penalty over letting him walk away. Did Aaron have experience with defending murder one? If not, he needed to brush up on his statutes.

"You're not a damn caterpillar." I brushed away the hair stuck to Brooke's cheek and wiped her tears with the bottom of my shirt. "Don't come out with that bullshit again."

"But—"

"Brooke..." My voice held a warning, and she fell silent,

then burrowed against me like a scared puppy. "No caterpillars. And you gotta tell Aaron."

"When he gets back from his vacation."

"You know he'd leave Cabo in a heartbeat if he thought you were in trouble."

"Yes, I do know, and that's exactly why I didn't tell him. He's been working so hard lately. You might not have noticed how tired he is, but I did."

She wasn't wrong, and I had noticed. Aaron hadn't taken a vacation in years, and since he moved back to Baldwin's Shore, he'd spent every waking minute either building up the law firm he hoped to run once Asa Phillips retired or remodelling the derelict building he wanted to call home. Even when he lived in New York, he'd worked two jobs so he could send money home to Brooke and Nonna and keep his student loans to a minimum. Bartending, plus legal work when he could get it and a stint interning at the NYPD. I'd sent money to Nonna too, and so had Romi, but being sick was expensive, and Aaron's pride meant we couldn't do as much as we'd wanted. But toward the end, Romi had come to an arrangement with the hospital so Aaron never even got to see most of the medical bills. Despite my sister's tarnished reputation, she had a good heart.

As did Brooke.

Nobody would hurt Brooke over the next two weeks, not on my watch. Was it really necessary to call Aaron right away? Yeah, he'd be upset that we kept him in the dark, but even if he came home tomorrow, there wasn't much he'd be able to do. He wasn't a detective.

"Fine. But we have to report this to Colt so he can start an investigation."

"No! Please, no."

"Why the hell not?"

"Because Colt will have to get others involved, and I don't trust anyone with a dick, okay? Well, except Aaron and Paulo. And Colt. And you."

Never thought I'd be so happy to make it into a select group with Paulo, but these were strange days.

"Thank you for trusting me."

"I know you weren't there at the time."

And then it hit me. Her questions this morning about when I'd transitioned out of the Rangers. She hadn't been certain I was innocent, had she? We'd known each other since we were kids, and she hadn't been fucking certain. That was a punch to the gut.

But I swallowed my disappointment because acting pissy wouldn't help Brooke.

"Did you keep the notes?"

"Only today's." Shit. Her brother was a lawyer, and she didn't understand the value of evidence? "I just... I just wanted to pretend it hadn't happened. That's what I've been doing for the last year—pretending."

"You can't pretend anymore, sweetheart, and you need to talk to Colt."

"I—"

"You might not trust the process, but we need his help on this."

"I'm so..." Her voice had dropped to a whisper. "I'm so ashamed of it all."

"There's nothing to be ashamed of. You didn't cause any of this."

She didn't believe me, I could tell, and I hated that she felt that way. Hated that a man, a motherfucker with a dick and an ego, had made her feel ashamed that she'd gone to her best friend's birthday party and had a drink.

"You won't call Aaron?" she asked.

"I won't call Aaron on one condition."

"What condition?"

"For the next two weeks, unless you're at work, you're by my side."

Brooke opened her mouth to disagree, but I cut her off. Right now, her safety came before any stupid arguments she might have.

"No ifs, no buts. I'm your shadow. Either I'm moving in here, or you're sleeping at Deals on Wheels. Preferably the second option since your door isn't fit for purpose."

"Deals on Wheels is a building site."

"The room I borrowed is habitable, and the building's got decent doors. Solid. You can take the bed..." Okay, so it was a mattress, but it was still better than staying in a stalker's paradise. "And I'll sleep outside the door on a cot."

Plus that would save me from driving to the Crowes' place four times a day to let Vega out, but Brooke's sour expression said she hated the idea.

"Think of it as an adventure. You can bring your dog and your tchotchkes, and I'll buy a camping stove and bug spray."

"There are bugs?"

"It was a joke. There are no bugs."

Just the occasional spider, but I wasn't about to tell her that.

"Maybe I could try staying there for a night?"

"Pack up your shit, Brooke. I'll call Colt."

12

BROOKE

If Luca thought sleeping at Deals on Wheels would help, he was wrong. I didn't sleep a wink. For the past year, my life had been falling apart in slow motion, but now I'd hit the downhill section and things were rapidly hurtling toward disaster.

Firstly, there was the obvious problem—my stalker. Secondly, there was no avoiding the fact that I had to spill my secrets to Aaron in less than two weeks. Thirdly, I'd never be able to look Colt in the eye again after what I'd told him last night. My statement was filled with words like "vagina," "penetration," and "naked," and if dying from mortification had been an option, I'd have gladly taken it. Luca had stayed with me the whole time, his expression growing darker and darker, and when Colt asked if I might possibly have dreamed the entire event—a question I'd asked myself many times—I feared Luca might take a swing at him.

"Brooke doesn't make shit up, asshole."

I'd laid a hand on his arm, the cords of muscle tight under my fingers.

"There was the note. I didn't write the note."

Colt's tone was apologetic. "I have to ask. Wouldn't be doing my job if I didn't."

"I understand. And until I received the card this year, I wasn't a hundred percent sure that I hadn't consented and then blanked it out. But these gifts... They're just sinister."

"Yeah, I have to agree. If the guy was on the up and up, he'd have signed the notes."

And last, but by no means least, I had to spend two weeks living with Luca, and I was so messed up inside that I couldn't decide whether I wanted to whack him with a leftover piece of two-by-four or crawl into bed beside him. The sensible part of me, the part that was hanging onto my sanity by one thin thread, understood that both options were out of the question, but if that thread snapped...

Perhaps I *should* have taken a flight to London.

Vega woof-growled in his sleep, his legs twitching as if he were chasing squirrels in his dreams. Moonlight filtered in through the huge windows, and I pulled the quilt tighter around me. There were no drapes, no blinds. Nothing to stop my stalker from turning into a peeping Tom. Was he close? Did he live on the same street? Shop at the same stores?

At this hour, there was no traffic outside, and if I listened hard enough, I could hear Luca's quiet breathing. He hadn't been kidding about sleeping right outside the door. Since there was nowhere open to buy a cot today, he'd folded a couple of blankets in half, added a pillow, and crawled under a spare quilt. He'd slept in far worse places, he assured me, but that still didn't make the situation okay.

Nothing could make the situation okay.

This room would be one of the guest bedrooms when Aaron's home was finished, but even so, it was the size of my entire rented apartment. Aaron's bedroom wasn't finished yet—it had wires hanging out of the ceiling because Brady was still working—but it would be even bigger, with a dressing room as well as an en suite. After living in a New York studio for years, my brother had craved space, and Jackson Pettit, who'd run the car dealership until he had a heart attack at the age of sixty-three, had offered the building for a steal on the condition that Aaron mowed his lawn every week the way he had when he was a teenager. An opportunity too good to turn down. Aaron hadn't wanted to take advantage of the old man, but Jackson was friends with Asa, and Asa let slip that Jackson had terminal cancer and just wanted the place to go to someone who'd restore it rather than knocking it down. So Aaron got two cavernous floors plus a roof terrace, a smaller service building that would one day house the law firm, and a falling-down shed.

Amazing how small fifteen thousand feet could feel when I was sharing it with Luca Mendez.

But at least he made coffee. There was a microwave in the half-built kitchen, and Luca knocked on my door at eight o'clock the next morning with a steaming mug.

"You dressed?" he called.

"Yes."

Mainly because I hadn't gotten *un*dressed.

"Hope you still take cream and sugar because that's what I put in it."

"I do."

I'd decreased from two spoonfuls to one, but when I'd tried cutting the sugar out completely, it was the worst week of my life. Of course, that had been before last March. I'd since learned that all things were relative.

"How are you feeling? I left you to sleep as long as I

could, but if you're planning to go to work, then you need to get up. Plus I need to use the bathroom."

Ah, yes. The awkwardness of sharing one bathroom, a bathroom whose door happened to be in the room I was sleeping in. The nasty staff restroom had been demolished now, ready to be overhauled in the next block of plumbing work. The plumber slotted us in during his slow weeks at a discounted rate. At first, there'd been a backup bathroom in Aaron's trailer, but something had gone wrong with a pipe not so long ago—he did tell me the details, but my eyes had glazed over while he was talking—and he'd had to decide whether to invest money in fixing it or in finishing a nicer bathroom inside. He'd picked the latter, much to Clarissa's disgust. Oh, she liked the idea of living in a giant, luxurious home, but the interim stage where everything was difficult and a bit icky meant that she and my brother spent most of their time together at her apartment in Coos Bay. I'd been there a handful of times, and it was soulless, just like her.

Brooke! Okay, scratch that final thought from the record.

"Sure, sure. I'll take Vega outside while you, uh..."

"Shit, shower, and shave." Sometimes, I forgot just how blunt Luca could be. "But you're not taking Vega outside alone. Have you forgotten everything we talked about last night?"

"No, but—"

"I'm your fuckin' shadow. Give me ten minutes."

Ten minutes was barely enough time to drink my coffee. I still had a mouthful left when Luca walked out of the bathroom wearing nothing but a towel, and I nearly spluttered it everywhere. Holy heck. He'd always had muscles as a teenager, but this was taking things to a whole other level. That body... It was as if a master craftsman had sculpted every curve and sinew out of marble, inch by painstaking inch, then stretched skin over the top. And Luca had a tattoo? That was new. Ink curved across his chest, over his shoulder, and down his left arm. I took a step forward for a closer look, then quickly stopped myself and screwed my eyes shut. Backed away. Tripped over Vega.

My arms windmilled as I tried and failed to get my balance, then my stomach lurched as I waited for the inevitable thud of klutz meeting concrete. But it didn't happen. Instead, I got to experience the damp squish of dimwit meeting divine being. When I finally plucked up the courage to open my eyes, Luca's face was an inch from mine, his tattooed arm around my back like a steel band.

"Th-th-thanks," I stuttered.

"You okay?"

Absolutely not. My heart was careening around my chest like a bowling ball tossed by an uncoordinated toddler. But at least I didn't have any bruises.

"I am now."

Luca grinned, and it wasn't a "thank goodness Brooke isn't splattered across the floor" grin, it was a lazy, sexy, "I'm so awesome" grin. Then he seemed to catch himself, and his expression quickly turned serious again.

"You need to watch where you're going. Neither of us wants to explain an emergency room visit to your brother as well as everything else."

"Thanks for that stunning piece of advice. I'd never have thought of it myself."

He chuckled as he set me back onto my feet.

"Still the same old snarky Brooke."

Could you blame me? Snark was one of the few defences I had against Luca's charms. I tried to change the subject, but because my brain didn't fully function at that early hour, I changed it to something even worse.

"You got a tattoo?"

Up close, I saw how detailed it was. The intricate design made it look as if his skin had been peeled back, and underneath were cogs and gears and linkages, steampunk style. I spotted a compass and a clock lurking among the metalwork. The hands were set to ten past six, and the compass pointed west. Was that significant?

Before I could stop myself, I reached out and traced the largest cog. Luca stepped back in a heartbeat.

Dammit, could I act any more inappropriate?

"Sorry," I muttered.

"Yeah, I got a tattoo."

"I'd better take a shower."

Before I managed to do anything else stupid, I ran into the bathroom, then snorted out a laugh because Luca had drawn a smiley face in the steam on the mirror. I'd almost forgotten how he used to do that. Whenever I was feeling down, I'd find his messages lurking—a Post-it inside my locker door, a doodle on my notepad, and one morning, his footprints in the snow outside my bedroom window.

How I missed the easy camaraderie we used to have. All that remained was awkwardness plus embarrassment on my part.

I'd left my blow-dryer at home, so once I'd showered, I towel-dried my hair and twisted it back into a lumpy bun. Did it look okay? It would have to do. Luca had closed the bedroom door on his way out, thank goodness, and he'd taken Vega with him as well. The sound of power tools told me Decker had shown up for work, so I threw on a pair of jeans and a sweater and steeled myself to answer his questions about why I was sleeping in Luca's bed instead of my perfectly nice apartment. Oh, hell—Deck wouldn't think

Luca had been in it with me, would he? Because that would take some explaining.

When I got out into the great room, I found not only Deck but Brady too, both busy working.

"Hey, Brooke." Deck saw me and raised a hand in greeting. "Sleep well?"

"Not really."

"Hearing the pitter-patter of tiny feet in your dreams?"

"Huh? What feet?"

Deck chuckled. "Denial's the best policy, huh? Luca told us all about your mouse problem." Oh he did, did he? "I had squirrels in the attic a couple years ago. Trapped the critters, but they just kept coming back."

Brady was balancing on top of a ladder with a pair of pliers in his hand. Wires sprouted out of the ceiling like mutant vines. My brother had decided to go for the semi-industrial look in the great room—exposed ducting, bare light bulbs with decorative filaments, a red brick feature wall with posters of old cars and motoring memorabilia in a nod to the building's past. His coffee table was made from an old engine block he'd cleaned up, and he'd rescued a bench seat from a 1954 Buick Skylark to use as a couch.

"Don't tell Brooke your rodent horror stories," Brady said to Deck. "Or she won't sleep tonight either. You finished with that saw? I need to shut off the power again."

"I need fifteen more minutes. Luca asked me to make a holding pen for the dog, and I gotta finish cutting the uprights for the frame."

Just then, Luca walked in with Vega. He'd put on a T-shirt now, which was both a crying shame and a welcome relief.

"Ready to go to the store?" he asked.

"I'll just grab my purse." Outside in the car, I raised an eyebrow. "Rodents?"

"Figured it would be easier to explain a mouse infestation than a stalker."

"You didn't tell them?"

"Tell one person in a town this size, and everyone'll know by the time the bars close. I don't want the asshole lying low and then coming back in a month or a year when I'm gone. But I did ask Brady to fit a security camera over at your apartment, and Deck's gonna replace your front door. I'll set up a bunch of mousetraps to make the cover story look convincing."

"But I can't afford—"

Luca held up a hand. "You don't have to."

"That's—"

"I'll save you the trouble of coming up with some bullshit argument by telling you right now that I'm gonna ignore it."

Luca was Schrödinger's Asshole—both sweet and frustrating at the same time. Past experience told me it would be pointless trying to reason with him, but that didn't make me feel any less guilty for upending his life and ruining his downtime.

13

BROOKE

"Happy birthday to me, happy birthday to me, happy birthday dear Paulo, happy birthday to meeeeeeeeee."

The rest of us were singing too, but Paulo's voice eclipsed all sixteen of ours. He was winning in the drinking stakes as well, and as he waved his glass around, half of his cocktail splashed onto the floor of the private dining room. Luckily, it was tiled. A waiter hovered in the background with napkins in his hand and a pained expression on his face.

Unlike some of the town's long-term residents, Paulo didn't bear any grudges toward the Peninsula Resort, and that was where he'd decided to hold his birthday party, partly because the view across the beach was fantastic, but mostly, I suspected, because the cocktail list stretched to three pages. He'd started at the top, and halfway down the first page, he showed no signs of slowing.

Luca muttered skyward as Paulo tripped over thin air and fell backward onto his chair.

"Is he always like this?"

"Yup. I already booked him a cab home."

I'd also swapped shifts with him tomorrow so he could stay in bed and nurse his hangover—he always got a headache after too many cocktails, but he never changed his ways—so I'd limited myself to two cocktails and then switched to water. That wasn't a bad thing because the prices were eye-watering. And admittedly justified. The Peninsula Resort was the epitome of luxury, all dark wood and marble and chrome with a spa, three restaurants, a business centre, two swimming pools, lush grounds, a private beach, tennis courts, a nine-hole golf course, and staff that catered to your every need. Vacationers would stay for two weeks and never leave the resort, which was one reason the locals hated it so much. Not many of those tourist dollars trickled into the local economy. Add in the fact that the private beach had been open to the public under the old owner of the property, an eccentric millionaire who'd only visited once a year to paint watercolour landscapes, plus the fact that the mysterious new owner—who rumour said was an actual billionaire—kept to himself, and a great deal of resentment had built up.

Old suspicions died hard.

But Paulo loved cocktails, and he said we only lived once, so I'd dressed up—in smart pants, not a skirt, because even with Luca by my side, I wasn't feeling that brave—and come with an open mind. And the place *was* beautiful.

Paulo had been only too happy for me to bring Luca along, and now we huddled at the far end of the table with Darla, watching in horror as the paper streamers draped around Paulo's neck dangled perilously close to his birthday candles. He'd just turned twenty-seven, but he approached the event with the glee of an eight-year-old. Darla glanced toward the fire extinguisher tucked discreetly in the corner. Would Paulo live to see twenty-eight?

"Make a wish!" Annie from the hair salon shouted. Paulo was one of her best customers.

"Okay, I wish—"

"Shh, shh! You're not supposed to tell us."

He blew out the candles, and everyone who was still vaguely sober let out a collective sigh of relief. Luca and Darla were drinking water too—Darla was teetotal, and Luca said he needed to stay alert. Although the evening was fast heading toward raucous, it *had* provided a welcome respite from my troubles. Maybe too much of a respite. I'd enjoyed the evening with Luca far more than I had a right to. Yes, he still had that dark, dangerous energy lurking under the surface, but the exterior was more polished now, like a stick of dynamite channelling George Clooney. He'd even worn a dress shirt. An *ironed* dress shirt.

"Five bucks says he wished for a bottle of Advil," Darla said.

"Nobody who's known Paulo for longer than five minutes would ever take that bet."

"Too bad. What do you think of this place?"

"I'm scared to touch anything in case I leave fingerprint smudges, but it was worth coming just for the view." On the other side of the floor-to-ceiling windows, the sun was setting in a blaze of pinks and purples and oranges. A lone couple walked on the sand, and the girl threw back her head and laughed at something, wild hair blowing behind her in the breeze. "Maybe I could use sunsets as a theme for next week's craft classes? Painting for the adults and collage for the kids?"

Darla grimaced. "Please, no glitter."

"I promise I'll hide every tube. Think Paulo would mind if I snuck outside to take some pictures?"

"I doubt he'll even notice. His vision has to be blurred by now."

"I'll be back in time for coffee."

Of course, Luca shadowed me, one hand on the small of my back as he guided me through the door to the beach. The manners were new too, and I felt an irrational stab of jealousy as I wondered where he'd learned them. Who he'd learned them with.

"There aren't many things I miss about Baldwin's Shore, but this view is one of them," Luca said. "I've gone weeks where the only water I saw was in the canteen on my belt."

"I love the sound of the sea. Before all this...this *stuff* happened, I used to like visiting the beach in the mornings. Not this beach, obviously, but the one to the north near Turtle Rock."

I'd take off my shoes and walk barefoot through the sand, scrunching it between my toes. In summer, I'd paddle in the waves that rolled onto the shore or take a bathing suit and swim. Not all the way to Turtle Rock—I wasn't that brave—just back and forth where a spit curved out to form a sheltered lagoon. When I was a teenager, I'd always wanted to climb the rock with my brother and Luca, but neither of them would let me and I'd probably have chickened out anyway. After all, the turtle was my spirit animal—when life got uncomfortable, I tended to hide away rather than sticking my neck out to face danger.

"We can walk on the beach in the morning if you want."

That was unexpectedly sweet, but it didn't solve the long-term problem.

"You'll be gone in two weeks. If the stalker's still out there, then a spur-of-the-moment stroll is out of the question."

"We'll catch him. Colt's speaking to the detectives in the

Investigation Section, and Brady's installed a camera outside your apartment."

True, and he'd also set the lights on a timer so it looked as if I were home. The camera was a motion-activated wireless model that hooked into my Wi-Fi, and when I received an alert, I could log in through an app on my phone to see the feed in real time. I dreaded to think how much that set-up had cost Luca.

"I'm trying to stay positive, but..." I trailed off. How did I explain that I just wasn't that lucky? "This is a good spot for the photos."

I only had my phone camera, but it was good enough to capture some half-decent shots of the blazing sky with the waves breaking in the foreground. I might also have snapped a few pictures of Luca when he wasn't looking. Who knew when he'd show his face in Baldwin's Shore again? Those images might have to last me for the next eight years.

The wind whipped through my hair, and I shivered from its sudden bite. My sweater was still hanging over the back of my chair in the restaurant.

"Cold?" Luca asked.

"A little."

"Want to head back inside?"

"Just a couple more minutes."

"I'd offer you a sweater if I was wearing one. You could have my shirt if you want, but then I'd get kicked out of this place for breaching the dress code."

No matter how bad things seemed, Luca always managed to make me smile. That was one of his special skills, along with soldiering, being stubborn, and looking good in shorts.

"Nah, they'd probably give you a job as a lifeguard."

"How about I act as a windbreak instead?"

He positioned himself behind me, close enough that I could feel his body heat radiating against my back but not so close that we were touching. And suddenly, I felt much warmer. Quite hot, in fact. And most of that heat had pooled between my thighs.

At that moment, I knew the next two weeks were going to be hell, although if I'd realised we were talking the ninth circle rather than the second, I'd have retreated back into my shell and prayed for the horrors to be over. But for now, I was living in blissful ignorance, so I steadied my phone and snapped half a dozen more pictures.

"Hey, what's that?"

"What's what?"

Luca turned me to face west, his hands on my shoulders. "Did you see the splash? Looked like a dolphin."

No matter how many times I saw dolphins jumping off the coast, it never got old. The creature leaped again, silhouetted against the sun's dying halo, a dolphin or perhaps a porpoise, and I couldn't keep the smile off my face. Nonna used to tell me that seeing a dolphin jump was lucky, and I hoped she'd been right because I could really use some good vibes right now.

The dolphin treated us to one final flick of its tail before it disappeared, and I realised Luca still had his hands on me. For a whole year, I'd avoided accidental contact with men because the slightest touch made me shudder, but somehow, Luca didn't have the same effect. Having him close felt nice. Kind of like the old days before I'd destroyed our friendship.

As we turned back to the hotel, two hands turned into one arm across my shoulders, and I couldn't bring myself to shrug it away. Purely because of the warmth factor, you understand. I wanted to avoid catching a chill. In fact, what I really wanted—other than Luca—was hot chocolate with cream and marshmallows the way Nonna used to make it. Nonna's hot chocolate had been my second favourite thing in the world.

"You want to stick around?" he asked. "Or make an excuse and split?"

"Is there any hot chocolate at home? I mean, at Deals on Wheels?"

"Why do I get the impression we're having two completely separate conversations?"

"I have a craving for hot chocolate, that's all. Well, not quite all—I want cream and marshmallows too."

"There's coffee at home, and that's it, but we can stop at the 7-Eleven if you want." Really? But the 7-Eleven was over in Coos Bay. "Or at the bar here. Seems like the type of place that'd have marshmallows."

Of course the Peninsula Resort had marshmallows. When I asked, the bartender acted as if the mere suggestion that they might not have marshmallows, fresh whipped cream, and chocolate sprinkles was a personal insult.

"We also use the finest Belgian chocolate," he snootily informed me. "Would you prefer milk or dark?"

"Uh..." Heck, don't ask me to make a decision. "Uh, could you mix them?"

"As you wish."

Beside me, Luca snickered. "Where did they dredge that guy up? *Downton Abbey*?"

"Hold on—you watch *Downton Abbey*?"

"Yeah, so?"

"I just never pictured you as a fan."

"We used to stream it on base, okay?"

The idea of a bunch of Rangers taking pleasure in the

dramas of the British aristocracy made me giggle. I couldn't help it.

"It's not fuckin' funny."

"It is." Even the businessman drinking red wine on the other side of Luca was smiling. "Can you do the accents?"

"Stop talking, Brooke."

"No, I think this is a subject that needs to be explored."

But we wouldn't be doing the exploring that evening. Before I could tease Luca about wearing a bow tie, a newcomer slid onto the stool beside me.

"Decided to take a step up in the world, Brooke?" I could smell the man's whisky breath before I turned, and judging by Luca's dark expression, I didn't want to put a face to the odour. "Clearly, I'm talking about the location, not the company. I'm surprised they let that Neanderthal through the door."

Easton Baldwin. Ugh. You'd think he'd know better than to goad Luca given the fact that Luca had left him with more than one black eye in the past, but firstly, Easton was drunk, and secondly, he'd never been one to learn from his mistakes. He'd never been one to learn, period. He'd gotten his high school diploma by the skin of his teeth and—if rumour was to be believed—bribery, then quit college in favour of bumming around Europe. Now he was back and as obnoxious as always. Was his brother around? They often hung out together. Parker was the smart one, and he tended to stop Easton from doing anything monumentally stupid.

But I couldn't see him this evening.

"Leave us alone, Easton."

"Aw, he needs a woman to do the talking?"

Luca was on his feet now, and in my peripheral vision, I saw his hands curl into fists.

"You want my knuckles to do the talking instead?"

"What are you doing with him, Brooke? The brute hasn't changed at all. Apple didn't fall far from the tree, did it?"

I gripped Luca's arm because I couldn't cover the security amount to get him out of jail and Aaron was still in freaking Cabo. Easton deserved to lose his teeth, but if blood was shed at the Peninsula Resort, I could kiss any future cocktails goodbye. Why did he always act like this? Oh, who was I kidding? The answer was clear—his surname and his money. Easton was the eldest great-great-grandson of Milton Baldwin, the construction-worker-turned-property-developer who'd founded Baldwin's Shore. The Great Depression hadn't been kind to the family, but they still owned at least two dozen rental properties around town, plus an estate on the outskirts and several more buildings in Coos Bay.

Easton had been acting like a prick for as long as I could remember. He'd bullied me all through high school, then after I'd had my braces removed and lost my puppy fat, he'd asked me to be his date for senior prom and had the gall to act surprised when I told him where to stick his invite.

"Luca, don't. He's winding you up. Trying to provoke a reaction."

"Yeah, I know." And Luca did something else he never used to do. He relaxed. "He uses big words to make up for his tiny dick."

Unfortunately, Easton didn't relax. He lurched off his stool and made a grab for Luca, missed, and ended up jabbing me in the chest instead. Half a second later, Luca was in front of me, an impenetrable wall of muscle, and I'm ashamed to admit that I closed my eyes because I didn't want to see what came next. How bad would it be?

"I think you should leave."

Wait. I didn't recognise that voice. I cracked one eyelid

open and found the stranger with the red wine had decided to join the party, and surprisingly, his words were aimed at Easton rather than Luca. Usually, Easton's privilege meant he got to stay while Luca or anyone else unfortunate enough to cross paths with the Baldwin spite got escorted to the door.

"What did you just shay?"

Uh-oh. Now he was slurring.

"I said you should leave. You're drunk."

Easton snorted, and whisky spittle landed on the stranger's cheek. Yeuch.

"What, do you think you own the place or something?"

"Yes, actually, I do." The man's voice was quiet, measured, but a hard edge had crept into it. Sitting down, he hadn't seemed like much, but now that he'd stood up, power curled around him like smoke, expanding outward, cloying and potentially deadly. "And you're disturbing my guests."

Seconds later, two security men in suits materialised on either side of Easton, and the bluster belched out of him as he realised he was both outgunned and out-moneyed. But he did have one parting gift. I jumped back as Easton vomited on the floor, exactly as he used to do in high school. He never could hold his liquor.

The stranger lifted his chin toward the door—a barely perceptible motion, but his security team understood exactly what it meant. The sight of Easton Baldwin being dragged out the exit by his elbows was glorious.

"Don't let the door hit ya where the Good Lord split ya," Luca murmured. He'd gotten that from Nonna, and I had to smile even though a magical evening had been ruined.

"My apologies," the stranger said, holding out a hand. I couldn't quite place his accent. Was it Russian? "That shouldn't have happened. Nico Belinsky."

Seriously? *This* was the resort's owner? Not the guy's son or something? Nico couldn't have been more than thirty, and he had the looks to go with the money. Short dark hair, high cheekbones, almost delicate features. I always thought billionaires were old, Mark Zuckerberg excepted. And Jeff Bezos. And that guy with the electric cars. Okay, so maybe I'd been a little judgmental.

We shook hands, and Nico held onto mine for a beat too long as he studied me. I might have felt uncomfortable, but I'd noticed he did the same with Luca.

"Thanks for helping out there," I said. "Easton's been bearing a grudge since Luca dumped him on his ass in high school."

Nico smiled faintly. "He strikes me as the type of man who deserved it."

"Oh, yes, he did. He definitely did."

A click of Nico's fingers brought the bartender running. "Pour these folks a drink on the house. Now, if you'll excuse me, I'm needed elsewhere. Enjoy the rest of your party."

He disappeared without another word, skirting around the cleaner who'd arrived with a mop and bucket and leaving his half-full glass of wine on the bar. I understood now where he'd gotten the "mysterious" tag and also why the town's gossip mill said he was aloof and unsociable.

"Interesting guy," Luca murmured.

"Isn't he?"

"He always that chatty?"

"Who knows? I've never met him before, and neither has anyone else I've spoken to. At least he threw Easton out."

"If he has any sense, he'll bar him permanently." Luca gave my arm a light squeeze. "You okay?"

"Peachy. On a scale of one to stalker, Easton barely rates a three."

"Ready to go back to the party?"

"Somebody has to make sure Paulo doesn't break an ankle dancing on the table, and there aren't many sober people left."

Luca looked slightly alarmed. "Darla can help out with that, right?"

"Sure, but if someone needs to lift him down…"

"Okay, okay. Let me get those drinks, and we'll go play chaperone."

14

BROOKE

"Thanks for your help yesterday," I said to Darla as we went over the orders that had come in overnight. "I can't believe Paulo lost his shoes."

Darla had found them out in the hotel grounds, half-hidden under a bush. Quite why Paulo had decided to walk barefoot across the grass in the dark I wasn't sure, and by that point, he hadn't been able to articulate his thoughts on the matter.

"I can believe it. I'm more surprised that the whole group of us didn't get thrown out of the hotel."

"Most of the noise was contained in the private dining room, I guess, and we *did* spend a lot of money. Plus the owner seemed quite laid back about the whole thing. Like, he told us to enjoy the party."

Darla glanced up, pen in hand. "You met the owner? But nobody ever meets the owner. Annie's sister works there as a housekeeper, and she doesn't even know his name. Apparently, he manages the place from a distance and his minions do all the work."

"He was there in the bar last night."

"You're sure? It wasn't just some guy making up stories to impress you?"

I thought back to the way the bartender and the security guards had leaped at his command. "I'm sure. He said his name was Nico Belinsky."

Darla's eyebrows winged up in surprise. She looked almost…shocked?

"Nico Belinsky?"

"You know him?"

"Some secretive billionaire? Of course not. But darn it, I had a bet with Annie that Bill Gates had bought the place. That's five bucks gone." Darla clicked the computer mouse. "Wow, a lady in Wisconsin just ordered forty balls of yarn. We're gonna need a really big box."

"Forty? What's she planning to knit? A blanket the size of Texas?"

"Aw, she left a comment in the box—she said she knits sweaters for rescue dogs. Put an extra half-dozen balls in with her order, okay?"

"I'll do it after I've finished with Paulo's class."

Thankfully, it was his Sunday watercolour class and not his Monday macramé class because Darla would have had to step in otherwise. Whenever I tried macramé, I spent more time unpicking knots and cursing than producing art, and today I couldn't focus on *anything*.

Which was all Luca's fault.

This morning, I'd rolled over and kept my eyes firmly closed when he tiptoed through my—his—bedroom to the shower, then tried not to picture him standing under the water, naked, shampoo bubbles sliding over that tattoo and down toward his… *Brooke!* I'd failed, obviously, but he hadn't been able to see my blushes so I thought I'd dodged a bullet.

I'd been wrong.

Deck and Brady didn't work Sundays, so when I stumbled out into the great room a half hour later, still groggy from lack of sleep, it took my eyes a few seconds to register Luca standing in front of the portable gas burner that substituted for a stove.

Shirtless.

In sweatpants.

Oh, holy hell. He looked *edible*. And of course my gaze had strayed downward—an uncontrollable reflex when faced with such delicious man candy—and locked on the biggest dick print I'd ever seen.

"How do you like your eggs?"

No way. He did *not* just ask that. The worst pickup line in the world popped into my head, and only the distraction of Vega licking my hand stopped me from blurting out, "Fertilised."

"Uh, scrambled?"

Exactly like my brain.

"Toast?"

"Yes, please. And you need to put a shirt on."

Dammit, I did *not* just say that.

"Why? It's warm today, and I didn't want to turn on the AC and jack up Aaron's electricity bill."

Why? A good question. And if I'd been thinking straight, I could have come up with a sensible answer. Told him I was worried about grease spitting onto bare skin or whatever. But since I was suffering from a brain-to-mouth malfunction at that moment, I managed, "Because you're distracting."

Luca's cat-that-got-the-cream smile made me want to throw something at him. Like the frying pan. Or possibly myself.

"Distracting?"

My cheeks burned. "You know perfectly well what I'm talking about."

"No, I think you need to explain."

"Maybe I'll skip breakfast."

I turned to walk away, but Luca caught my arm, suddenly serious, his dimples gone.

"Don't run, Brooke. I'll put a shirt on. Just watch the eggs, okay?"

Why did this man have me so unbalanced? Life had turned into a roller coaster of emotions, not only fear but frustration and confusion and uncertainty too. And desire. But I'd already crashed and burned when it came to lusting after Luca, and in the background, a clock ticked down to his inevitable departure.

I poked at the eggs with a spatula.

He came back in a ribbed tank top, which was almost as bad as no shirt at all—it did everything for his muscles and nothing for the dick print. But I couldn't complain when he'd made the effort. Plus he finished cooking the eggs, buttered my toast, and poured me a glass of orange juice. Nobody had made me breakfast since Nonna in the days before her first stroke, and watching Luca move around the makeshift kitchen, knowing that he was taking care of me, set off a strange tingling sensation in my scalp that felt good in a weird way.

And even when I got to work, I couldn't stop thinking about him.

That feeling lasted until ten thirty when one of the Baldwins walked in. Not *that* Baldwin, thank goodness, but Sara. The youngest of the clan, and technically she was a cousin rather than a sibling, which was perhaps the only reason I didn't run out the back door and keep going until I hit water.

Instead, I pasted on a fake smile.

"How can I help?"

"I'd like to learn to paint. I mean, I heard there was a class?"

Hadn't I already exceeded my dose of Baldwins for the week? Definitely, but this was work, and we didn't turn customers away.

"Sure. It starts at eleven." I waved a hand at the tables set up at the back of the store. Before Darla rented the place, it had been a restaurant, and the tables had been there when she moved in. "We supply all the materials you need, but some people like to bring their own paints and brushes."

Sara fiddled with her silver necklace. "I think maybe I'll start by borrowing yours."

"Do you want a drink while you wait? Coffee? Soda?"

"Just water is fine."

I brought her a bottle of mineral water and a glass, then sighed with relief when the old-fashioned bell over the door jingled and another customer meandered in. I recognised Nelly Scott, the town's realtor. Her husband was some big shot at a marketing firm in Portland, and he mostly stayed in the city from Monday to Friday and came back on the weekends. Nelly could talk about crochet patterns for hours, which was boring on a normal day but more enjoyable than making small talk with Sara Baldwin. What was she even doing here? Couldn't she use some of her family's fortune to hire a private painting tutor?

Easton couldn't have sent her to spy on me, could he? I wouldn't have put it past him. He was a vindictive snake, and he'd no doubt blamed Luca and me for him getting tossed out of the town's fanciest bar last night. From what I remembered, there'd been no love lost between him and Sara, but blood ran thicker than water in the Baldwin family.

The universe really hated me this week, didn't it? And I still had to call Addy later, something I was dreading because she'd be hurt that I hadn't told her the whole truth about what happened after her party last year.

But first, painting. Nine people showed up for Paulo's class. The theme this week was flowers, and he'd asked everyone to bring a picture they wanted to paint, either a photo they'd taken or one they'd clipped from a magazine or printed from the internet. All the regulars had managed that, except for Marjorie Hallett, who brought an actual potted plant—an orchid in full bloom. She always had done things her own way, but at eighty-four, she wasn't going to change. Since Sara hadn't known the topic in advance, I handed her the folder of backup pictures that Paulo kept for precisely that purpose.

"I'm sure you'll find something you like in there."

She did.

A vase of lilies.

Stargazers rather than the white ones like my stalker had sent, but they still gave me the creeps. It felt as if the cosmos were trying to send me a message, and Easton and Sara Baldwin were two of the messengers.

Still, I smiled politely and tried to keep the quake out of my hands as I critiqued line drawings and talked about light and shade. And Sara seemed friendly, if a little quiet. Did she know what had happened between me and Luca and her cousin last night? Her presence here was unnerving, but this was my job, and I couldn't hide in the break room or make a fuss.

But I did shed a tear in the bathroom at lunchtime. All

these changes in the past two weeks—Luca's return, my stalker's resurgence, the run-in with Easton... It felt as though I was losing control of my own life. When I was a teenager, I used to complain about being bored. Now I longed for monotony.

15

BROOKE

"What the heck?" Addy half yelled. "You waited a year to tell me this? No, no, more than a year. Are you crazy? That sick freak should be in jail getting his ass stretched every time he bends over to pick up the damn soap. And you say you don't know who he is? What about fingerprints? There might have been fingerprints! Wow. I can't believe this. I'm sending virtual hugs. No, no, I'm coming over."

"Addy, it's seven o'clock on Sunday evening. Don't you have work tomorrow?"

"Who cares? You're more important than emails, and my new boss is a jerk anyway. I'll be there in, like, an hour."

"Honestly, there's no need—"

But it was too late. Addy had hung up, and I slumped back onto the Buick bench seat Luca had dragged in front of the TV.

"That didn't go well, I take it?" he said, holding out a glass of wine.

I grabbed it and poured half down my throat. Some of it went the wrong way, and in between coughing and Luca thumping me on the back, I managed to splutter, "About as well as I expected."

"She's coming over?"

"You heard?"

"She was shrieking so loud she didn't even need the phone." Luca muttered a prayer to the heavens. "I should order pizza. Neither of us is gonna feel like cooking tonight."

"I'm not gonna feel like eating either."

Luca ignored me and ordered three pizzas, which meant we had six pizzas because Addy had the same idea.

"Great minds think alike," she said, dumping her boxes onto the plywood counter and shrugging out of her jacket.

Luca took a calming breath, retrieved her jacket from the floor, and draped it over Deck's workbench. Sighed long and hard. It wasn't that he disliked Addy, more that she was a whirlwind of energy and he valued his peace.

"Nah, they don't. Great minds think differently. If they all thought the same, the world would be a boring fucking place."

"When did you get so wise? Did they teach philosophy in the army?"

"Some guy in a bar told me that. The army just taught me how to shoot."

"What are you doing here, anyway? I thought when you left town, we'd never see you again."

"When I left town, *I* thought you'd never see me again. But time changes a man."

"He came to visit Aaron," I explained. "Luca used to stay with him in New York, but now Aaron's back, so..."

"Where *is* Aaron tonight? I thought he'd be here freaking out."

"He went to Cabo with Clarissa. I'll tell him when he gets home."

Addy's eyes widened. "Wait, Aaron doesn't know either? Wow. He is *not* going to take this well."

"Please don't. I'm trying not to think about it."

"I'm still trying to understand why you kept this a secret. We would have supported you—you know that."

"I wasn't exactly rational at the time. The very next morning, there was a news segment about the backlog of rape kits, and Sammi at work didn't think it was a big deal."

"You told Sammi?"

Great, now Addy was even more hurt.

"Only because she found me crying. And...and I was embarrassed. Ashamed. I let my guard down, and a man took advantage of it. You'd never screw up like that."

All through our school days, trouble had rolled off Addy like cell phones off a car roof. And can you guess whose cell phones they were? That's right: mine. I'd lost three that way. After the third, Addy had attached its replacement to one end of a piece of cord and my wallet to the other and threaded them through my sleeves like mittens.

"Oh, you think? A year after we graduated high school, I drank way too much at one of Tania Fry's parties and ended up naked with Mike Benton."

"What?" My eyes bugged out. "Are you kidding?"

Mike Benton had always been odd, and that was an understatement. He spent every recess shucking ears of corn and eating them raw while writing out pi to, like, a million decimal places on sheets of paper. He filed each sheet in a binder, and I heard that by the time we graduated, he had thirty-seven files neatly organised on shelves in his bedroom. Oh, and in eighth grade, he'd gotten suspended for bringing a live chicken to class in his backpack.

Addy made a face. "Unfortunately, no. But you know what was weird?"

"Weirder than wanting to get to the end of pi?"

"Kind of. He had a huge dick. *Massive*. And I guess he must've watched a lot of porn when he wasn't doing the pi thing because he sure knew what to do with it."

Did I mention that, like Paulo, Addy had no filter? If Paulo hadn't been gay, they'd have made the perfect couple.

Luca stuck his fingers in his ears. "Adeline, please."

"What? I'm trying to make Brooke feel better here. If you want to help, pour her a glass of wine."

"Already did that three times."

"Bravo. If you pour a fourth, you'll get the full set of steak knives."

"Bullshit."

But Luca poured us drinks anyway—a large glass of white for me, a small glass for Addy because she was driving, and water for him because he was still doing the *alert* thing.

"So, you didn't consider seeing Mike again?" I asked, curiosity getting the better of me.

"Ugh, no. He kept his socks on, and afterward...afterward..."

"He rolled over and went to sleep?"

"No..." Addy turned red, which was notable because she had no shame. Or so I thought. "He checked his watch and said we could cuddle for seventeen minutes if I wanted, but then would I mind leaving because his Dungeons and Dragons group was coming over and explaining my presence would be onerous. That was the word he used. Onerous."

"Whoa. I really don't know what to say."

"Now do you see why I didn't tell you?"

I caught the corner of Luca's mouth twitching and shot

him a warning glare. He had a lifetime's experience of being inappropriate.

"I'm so sorry that happened." I put my wine down to give Addy a hug. Due to the present company, I skipped the traditional "all men are jerks" speech and stuck with specifics instead. "Mike may be book smart, but he has the common sense of a pocket calculator."

"Probably used to his girlfriends coming with a foot pump," Luca offered. "What happened to him, anyway? Is he still in town?"

"He moved to DC to work for NASA. His mom mentions it in every single conversation."

"Brooke!" Addy put her hands on her hips. "Stop changing the subject. This evening's about your past, not mine."

"And that's the problem—it's not so much in the past." I needed every sip of the wine as I told the whole story again for Addy's benefit. Her face morphed through shock and fear and finally to anger. "And that's why a detective's going to be contacting you. A colleague of Colt's."

Addy reached over to Brady's toolbox, pulled out a pair of pliers, and waved them menacingly.

"When I get my hands on him, I'm gonna chop off his balls."

"You'll have to fight me for the honour," Luca said.

"Maybe it's best if the sheriff's department handles it." Sweet though it was for Addy and Luca to offer bloodshed on my behalf, I didn't want either of them to get arrested. "Jail is the best place for him."

"Ohmigosh!" Addy clapped her hands to her cheeks. "Do you think he was at my birthday party *this* year? You said you got the card right after? And on CSI, the perps often return to the scene of the crime. I'm so sorry—if I'd known what happened, I'd have cancelled."

"That's another reason I didn't say anything. I hated the thought of ruining your birthday year after year." I'd forced myself to go to this year's party rather than hiding in bed the way I wanted to. Even though I took a cab there and back and spent the whole evening stuck to Addy like glue, I'd still wanted to puke the entire time. "And besides, I checked the envelope—the card was mailed the morning before the party. That much I do recall."

"I'll start making a list of everyone I remember being there. But I'd been drinking Prosecco, and some people brought friends, and a few neighbours showed up uninvited, and probably a bunch of others crashed too because I'm generally pretty relaxed about that." Her mouth hardened into a thin line. "But not anymore. Not anymore."

"Start the list, and hopefully other people will be able to add to it," Luca said. "In terms of suspects, we're looking for a man who knows his way around Baldwin's Shore. Maybe somebody who lived here and then moved to Coos Bay or vice versa. Or who travels between the two places regularly."

"That's half the people I know," Addy said. "The street I live on is nicknamed Shoreside because so many people from Baldwin's Shore rent apartments there. Just in my building, there are three people we went to high school with."

"Then that's a good place to start. What are their names?"

"Okay, so one of them's a girl—Shara Newell. And there's Harry Dents."

"Dents by name and dense by nature," Luca muttered, and I had to agree. I just couldn't imagine Harry acting with the degree of sophistication my stalker seemed to possess.

The man tormenting me was cruel but not careless. Harry had once cheated on a test and gotten caught because he copied the other person's name as one of his answers.

"Plus Marc Preece. But there's no way I invited him because he's a creeper."

"He could have been one of the crashers," Luca pointed out. "He goes on the list. Did you notice anybody paying a little too much attention to Brooke?"

Addy rolled her eyes at that. "Define 'too much.' Have you seen Brooke? *Everyone* pays her attention. Even the girls. I'm not saying I'm gay, but if I was, I totally would."

"Yeah, I've seen Brooke." Luca gave his head a quick shake. "Did you see her talking to any guys? Did anyone hand her a drink?"

"You think she was drugged?"

"It would explain why she can't remember a thing."

Addy didn't recall anyone giving me a drink, and when we worked through the evening in chronological order, it turned out that her memory was barely any better than mine after nine thirty or so. She'd woken the following day with her ex snoring away beside her, which led to a whole different type of regret. And no obvious answers. The only way to get to the bottom of this mess would be to keep picking at threads and see which one unravelled.

In the meantime, I had Luca. And while his presence left me hot and bothered, at least I felt safe with him around.

16

BROOKE

"Why do you keep looking at me?" Luca asked. "Do I have something on my shirt?"

"That's not a shirt."

Monday morning, and he was back in a tank top again. Today's was white and possibly tighter than yesterday's. Muscles rippled in his back as he stretched as far as he could reach from the ladder to paint the next strip of wall.

Now he looked puzzled. "Yeah, it's a shirt."

"A shirt has sleeves. Usually buttons too."

"This is what I wear in the gym, and it counts as a shirt under army rules. No shoes, no shirt, no training session."

"Well, this isn't a gym and it isn't the army, so their rules are invalid."

Luca placed his roller in the tray and turned to eyeball me.

"Why? Are you *distracted* again?"

Maybe a tiny bit. The glint in Luca's eye said he knew exactly what I meant and that he was playing me. And there was only one way to win this battle: fight fire with fire.

Earlier when we went out to buy paint, we'd stopped at

my apartment on the way back. Luca had checked the mail because I couldn't bring myself to do it, and I'd stuffed armfuls of clothing into Luca's duffel bag plus a small suitcase of my own and brought the whole lot to Deals on Wheels. And if I recalled correctly, that clothing had included a push-up bra and the hot-pink camisole I wore to yoga classes, although I hadn't been for weeks.

Luckily, Brady was upstairs working on my apartment today, and Deck had driven his elderly neighbour into the city for a hospital appointment. Luca was singing softly to a Dolly Parton song playing through his phone when I emerged from the bedroom. He always had been a fan of the oldies, and he had a surprisingly good voice, although he rarely used it. How long would it take him to notice my outfit?

"Coffee?" I asked.

"I'll never say no to coffee."

I hummed along with Dolly as she sang "9 to 5," although we'd started work at eight this morning. Did that mean we could finish at four? After the painting, we planned to take a trip to the second-hand furniture emporium in North Bend because I wanted a bed frame to go with the mattress I was currently sleeping on. Luca might be perfectly happy with a fold-up cot he'd bought online, but sleep was hard enough for me at the moment without an uncomfortable bed adding to the problem.

"Coffee's on the workbench."

"Thanks." A pause. "What the fuck happened to your shirt?"

"Huh?" I feigned surprise. My cleavage did look good, even if I said so myself. "I don't understand what you mean."

"Five minutes ago, you were wearing a shirt."

"I'm still wearing a shirt."

"That's not a damn shirt."

"Sure it is. And it's perfectly acceptable in my yoga classes."

Ah, now Luca got it. He glanced down at his own "shirt," then fixed his eyes on my boobs again.

"My face is up here."

He dragged his gaze skyward. "Sweetheart, you play dirty." And then he grinned. "I like that. How do I sign up for yoga classes?"

Gah.

Alma's Furniture Emporium was housed in a huge warehouse just off Route 101. Many years ago, the building had been home to a stock-car racing team, but that had gone bust years ago, although the logo was still faded into the paintwork outside. Nobody knew who Alma was. The couple who ran the place were named Ed and Betty.

Inside, couches and tables and beds and chairs and bookshelves stretched as far as the eye could see, each item with a neon price label attached. Either Ed or Betty—probably Betty—had been on a bargain-basement marketing course, because they'd added helpful snippets of information such as "Free matching sweater pattern" on a particularly ugly couch and "Would look great in a castle" on a table that seated sixteen. If you wanted knick-knacks, those were upstairs on the mezzanine level, a trove of pre-loved books and vases and cardboard boxes filled with junk from estate sales.

The whole place smelled of dust and old leather, and every time I set foot inside, I felt an almost uncontrollable urge to sneeze. But the prices were great, and if you looked hard enough, you'd find hidden gems among the trash.

Betty was sitting by the register in an armchair, watching an *I Love Lucy* rerun, and she waved when she recognised me.

"Got some nice couches in this week," she called. "Nearly new."

"Thanks, I'll take a look."

"This place is like a black hole," Luca muttered, and then he sneezed.

"Bless you."

"Blessing me isn't enough. We're gonna need an exorcist."

"It's not that bad."

"Sweetheart, I shop on the internet for a reason. This is my worst nightmare."

"I'll admit the lighting could be better, but when you're on a budget, it's a great place to pick up furniture, plus Ed will deliver anything you want for twenty bucks."

"You haven't tried eBay?"

"Yes, I did." Unwelcome colour rose in my cheeks. "It didn't work out."

"What happened?"

"Hey, what do you think of this table?"

"Brooke, what happened?"

"I bought a rug for twenty bucks and it turned out to be for a dollhouse, okay? And it's not funny," I added because I knew he'd laugh otherwise.

"Absolutely not." The corner of his lips twitched. "Maybe you could buy two and strap one to each foot?"

I grabbed one of Betty's neon labels and threw it at him like a frisbee. It failed to hit the target. Story of my life.

"Be serious."

"Okay, okay." He bent to pick up the label and stuck it back onto the table. "You ever see the movie *Downsizing*?"

Sigh. This was going to be a really long afternoon, wasn't it?

But at least Betty hadn't been kidding about the couches. Right at the back of the store, I found a beautiful pale-grey leather three-seater and two matching armchairs, and the price was a snip at two hundred bucks.

"These look as if they've never been sat on."

"Where d'you figure they got this stuff? A millionaire's yard sale?"

"I don't know, and I don't care. I'm buying them for my new apartment."

"I thought we came for a bed?"

"We did, but you're the one who won't let me spend my money on Vega's medical bill. And would you rather watch TV sitting on a couch or a Buick seat?"

"A couch," Luca conceded.

"Well, there you go." Did I look smug? Maybe a little. I got my bearings and pointed to the other side of the warehouse. "I'll tell Betty we're taking the couch and chairs, and then I'll meet you by the beds."

Was it weird to be bed-shopping with the teenage crush whose rejection I'd never quite gotten over? Probably, but over the past two weeks, I'd grown comfortable with Luca again. Perhaps even more than comfortable now that some of his rough edges had been smoothed away. Underneath, he was still the same boy I'd grown up with, with the same charms and the same twisted sense of humour, and most importantly, he made me feel protected. For the last year, I'd carefully arranged my life to avoid being alone with any man but my brother or Colt or Paulo, but now I dreaded the thought of sharing the time I had left with Luca with anyone.

There was only one bed frame I liked that was the right size, an old-fashioned iron frame that might have been an antique. Ivy and roses twisted through the metalwork at the foot, and a brass finial topped each corner. It wasn't quite what I'd envisioned for my apartment—I'd been planning something more modern—but it *was* beautiful. I could make it work. Plus it was only a hundred bucks.

"What do you think?" I asked Luca. "Do you like it?"

He gave it a good shake. "Solid. I'd say it has its pros and its cons."

"Which are?"

Uh-oh. That dirty smile sent my heart skittering.

"If you're into kink, there are plenty of tie-down points, but if your head hits those iron bars in the throes of passion, it's gonna hurt like fuck."

My jaw dropped, and I clenched my thighs together as heat rushed between them. The smirk said he knew he was being totally inappropriate, and I should have been annoyed, but before my brain caught up with my mouth, I blurted, "That's what pillows are for."

His turn to gape, and I hurriedly back-pedalled.

"But it's irrelevant anyway, since I don't intend to get into any passionate throes ever again."

Cockiness turned to curiosity. "Why not?"

"You know why not."

"You mean you haven't…? Not since…?"

"Of course not! How can I? Even the thought makes me sick."

"So you're gonna abstain for the rest of your life?"

"Probably."

"The right man would work things out with you."

"Can we just not talk about this?"

Luca shoved his hands into his pockets and pretended to look at a closet. And I knew he was pretending because the closet was hideous and chipped around the edges. Reluctant as I was to admit it, Luca did have reasonable taste.

A tear rolled down my cheek, and I hated that I'd let myself get emotional in a furniture store of all places. I suppose until that moment, I'd focused on getting through one day at a time and avoided thinking too much about the future. But the thought of spending the rest of my life alone... I sank onto the edge of the bed frame and forced myself to breathe.

"Bottling this up isn't good for you, sweetheart." The metal creaked as Luca sat beside me. "If you don't want to talk to me, you should talk to somebody."

"You mean a therapist?"

"If that's what it takes."

"I don't have the money for a therapist. The apartment—"

"Is not as important as your mental health. What about a support group?"

"A support group? There's no support group." Without thinking, I laid my head on his shoulder. "And where would I even start? I've been on one date since it happened—a double date with Addy—and the guy was sweet and polite and funny and I spent the whole of dinner wondering if *he* might be the man who took advantage of me. And when he tried to give me a peck on the cheek at the end of the evening, I ran. Literally ran. Addy thought I'd lost my mind, and maybe I had."

"She knows what happened now. She can help."

"By explaining to every guy I leave in the dust that I was raped so I might be a teensy bit screwed up in the head when it comes to sex?" Luca blanched, and I realised that now I was being the blunt one. "It's just that few men would have the patience to stick around, and even if we could build up that trust between us, I'd still be freaking out in case I freaked out."

"I'd offer up my dick for practice, but that would be a bad idea."

I choked out a laugh along with more tears. Hell, I was a mess. "A terrible idea."

"The worst."

Although I *did* trust Luca. And sure as heck I was attracted to him. No matter how much I tried to kid myself, eight years had done little to cool the heat that sizzled through my veins whenever he came near, and four days of sharing an apartment with him and his stupid non-shirt had only turned up the gas. Another advantage? In two weeks, he'd be gone for half of forever again, so we wouldn't spend the remainder of our lives awkwardly dancing around each other while trying to pretend to my brother that everything was normal.

I turned to face him, and our gazes locked. And his...his was all fire and filth and *what the fuck are we doing?* Which was an excellent question and one I couldn't answer. I couldn't breathe either.

I leaned forward an inch.

He did the same, and his focus shifted to my lips.

"Hun, Ed says he can deliver that couch this afternoon," Betty called. "And did you want to take the bed frame too?"

A low groan came from Luca, and I jolted to my feet.

"Oh, that's terrific." Jumbled thoughts careened around my skull like balls in a lotto machine. "Yes, I'd love to take the bed frame."

One thought tumbled out. *Holy hell, I almost kissed Luca.*

"Want me to help Ed load the truck?" he offered, his voice oddly stiff.

"That's mighty kind of you to offer, but our grandson's helping out after school. You remember Kieran? He just turned fifteen. Ed pays him five bucks a load, and Kieran's saving up for one of those game consoles, so he wouldn't thank you for putting him out of a job."

"I don't suppose he would."

Did he almost kiss me back?

"How d'ya want to pay, sugar pie?"

"I'll—" Luca started, and I held up a hand.

"By debit card."

Did I dodge another bullet?

"That's three hundred and twenty bucks. Can I tempt you with a vase? We got some nice ones in last week. A florist over in Coquille passed away, and her daughter didn't wanna keep none of her stuff."

Ugh, flowers. "I'll pass on the vase."

Or did we miss out on something amazing?

Would we ever find out?

17

LUCA

Fuck.

We hadn't just dodged a bullet, we'd dodged a whole damn minefield.

I'd been a heartbeat away from kissing Brooke, thinking with my little head instead of my big one, when Betty had shuffled to the rescue. *Saved by the septuagenarian saleswoman.*

But damned if I didn't have regrets.

And I also remembered Plunk. That wasn't his real name, obviously, but it was all we ever called him after he fucked up his gun assembly during Basic Combat Training and the magazine fell out as he raised his hand to shoot. *Plunk.* Thankfully, his skills had improved, and we'd gone through Ranger School together, but that still hadn't stopped him from getting shot. Or from charming the panties off the nurse who took care of him in the hospital. They lived in Georgia now, had two kids and a cat that did whatever it damn well pleased.

Plunk's fate was proof that not dodging the bullet

sometimes worked out for the best. Short-term pain for long-term gain.

It was also a reminder that Aaron owned a gun.

In the army, I'd gotten used to making difficult decisions, but they'd been simple life or death, not the judgmental equivalent of crossing a snake pit without knowing which of the slithery little suckers were poisonous. Now I was faced with a choice—should I stick to my original plan, back the hell off, and keep enough space between us that I didn't get tempted to lock lips and other body parts with Brooke before I left? Or do whatever was necessary to help her get over her fears and then lick my wounds afterward?

Brooke seemed to have made her decision. She kept her hands in her lap and stared studiously ahead the whole way back to Baldwin's Shore, not quite giving the silent treatment but definitely not encouraging conversation. I tried a couple of meaningless questions, got one-word answers, and returned to my own thoughts.

Attraction wasn't a problem. I'd been gone for Brooke for half my life. And I hadn't imagined the heat radiating from her in the furniture store. Now I was Icarus, flying too close to the fucking sun.

And I wasn't sure I could change direction, even if I wanted to.

Brady was lying across the Buick seat when we arrived back at the dealership, his messy brown hair visible at one end. The *beep, ping, boop* of whatever game he was playing on his phone broke the silence.

"We're back."

He sat up, stretching his arms above his head. "Deck had a date, so I stayed with the dog. Get what you wanted?"

Partially. Got the furniture, didn't get the girl. "Brooke bought a couch and a bed frame. You ever been to that furniture emporium over in North Bend? Weird place."

"Nah, I never stay put long enough to need my own furniture."

Neither had I in the past, but for the first time in my life, I wondered whether it might not be so bad to put down roots.

"Thanks for watching Vega. You got much left to do here?"

"Couple more weeks. Maybe three, seeing as I took time out to install that camera system you wanted."

"Thanks for that too. Just let me know what I owe you."

Brady waved a hand. "No problem. You already bought the hardware, so call it fifty bucks for the installation?"

I'd have paid triple. Brooke's security was my most important consideration right now, and I was damn grateful that Brady had dropped everything to help out. Electronics had never been my forte—there was a good reason I hadn't become an EOD operator. Give me a red wire and a green wire and I might as well have been colour-blind.

"Does cash work?"

"Folding drinking vouchers? My favourite method of payment."

By the time I'd paid Brady and heard his truck pull away outside, Brooke had disappeared into the bedroom. Was she planning to hide in there all night?

"Hungry?" I called.

"Not really."

Well, damn.

A brush-off. And also a lie. We'd eaten nothing but

potato chips for lunch, and I'd heard Brooke's stomach grumbling on the ride back from the furniture store. But what was I meant to do? Barge into her bedroom? No way.

"I'm gonna order pizza anyhow. I'll get you something in case you change your mind."

My phone was on the kitchen counter—Deck had been busy this afternoon because the grey countertop hadn't been there at lunchtime—but I'd barely gotten halfway to it when the door clicked open behind me.

"I think we need to talk."

I froze. Almost ducked. *We need to talk.* The four worst words in the English language. They couldn't have been more terrifying if Brooke had fired them from a semiautomatic.

Pew pew pew pew.

My talking skills were on a par with my electronics know-how. I'd always been more of a doer.

"Talk?"

"Or are you going to run away again?"

"We both knew I'd signed up to join the army."

"You avoided me for two whole weeks before you left town."

True. Okay, so I probably deserved the barb.

"I'm not running this time." If war had taught me one lesson, it was to stand my ground. To fight when possible, to carry out the mission, and to only engage in strategic retreat when necessary. "We can talk."

Brooke opened her mouth. Closed it again. Stood for a long while staring at her feet.

"Uh, so it turns out I don't really know what to say."

"Then how about I start? Brooke, you know I like you. I've always liked you."

"Like? Or *like*?"

"The second one."

"Then why did you tell me you didn't?"

Shit.

I'd asked myself that question many times over the years, and I didn't like the answers. I'd been scared. Scared that if I admitted the truth, if I gave in to my feelings and started a relationship with Brooke, I'd lose everything. Scared that Aaron would never forgive me for breaking our pact and fucking around with his sister. He'd been my best friend for years. His family had given me the security my own parents never had.

And speaking of my parents, I'd been scared of turning into my father. Easton Baldwin's words still echoed in my ears: *the apple didn't fall far from the tree*. If I had a dollar for every time I'd heard that line over the years, I could be a rich jerk like him and spend my whole damn life going to parties.

And I'd been scared that Brooke would become my mother. That she'd get sick of me and vanish overnight. So I'd decided to pre-empt future disaster, rip out my own damn heart, and hightail it out of Baldwin's Shore. Now that decision had come back to bite me on the ass.

I shrugged. "It seemed like the best option all around."

"You hurt me," she whispered, and it turned out that I hadn't ripped out my whole heart, because her words still made my chest ache.

"I'm sorry, sweetheart. I only ever meant to hurt myself."

Brooke walked away. Instinct screamed at me to go after her, on my knees if necessary, but reason told me she needed space. I'd give her that. As long as she didn't try to leave the damn building.

Vega whined, so I let myself into his pen and took a seat

on the floor while he crawled closer to get his head scritched.

"Bet you don't know how much trouble you caused, do you, boy?"

Although if he hadn't injured himself, then Brooke would still be trying to deal with her problems on her own, which wasn't a scenario I cared to think about. The mutt didn't acknowledge the question, just flopped onto his belly and rested his head on my leg. Pain in the ass or not, I'd miss the farting furball when I left.

Not in the all-consuming way I'd miss Brooke, but yeah, there'd be a gap.

Soft footsteps approached, and Vega pricked up his ears. I would have too, if I'd been a dog.

"Did you mean it?" she asked, quiet, hesitant.

"Did I mean what?"

"What you said earlier? I think you were joking, but sometimes I can't tell."

"Sweetheart, you're gonna have to back up here."

I turned, and Brooke's blush spread from her neck to the tips of her ears.

"Don't do that."

"Do what?"

"Look at me. It's hard enough without you looking at me."

Slowly, I swivelled back. This conversation, this whole day, had taken a really weird fucking turn. The dog looked as confused as I felt, but at least he was allowed to make eye contact.

"What you said..." Brooke swallowed hard. "What you said about your dick."

Someone made a choking noise. Right, that was me. My tongue felt too big for my mouth, and at Brooke's words, my dick rapidly grew too big for my pants, even though this moment was a clusterfuck of everything I'd been trying to avoid.

"Sweetheart, you're my best friend's kid sister."

"I'm twenty-six, and he's not here."

"This isn't a good—"

"It's actually perfect. You said yourself there wasn't a problem with you being attracted to me. Aaron's gone for almost two more weeks, and after that, you'll be flying off to the other side of the world and you probably won't be back for years. And I do trust you not to hurt me physically, even if you can be kind of a jerk sometimes. Actually, forget that last part. I shouldn't call you a jerk when I'm asking for a favour."

A favour?

A fucking favour?

She thought sex with her would be a *favour*?

Brooke might have lost her mind, but damn, she'd really thought this through, hadn't she? And I had to concede that her points were valid. I sure as hell was attracted to her, I'd be leaving, and I was also a jerk.

Which was perhaps why I was considering taking her up on the offer.

"Brooke, I—"

"I promise I won't get upset when you go. If nothing else, you leaving the first time taught me how to guard my heart."

Ouch.

But what about *my* heart? The fissures were already beginning to appear in the last remaining ventricle.

"Please, Luca. There's nobody else I can ask, and I don't want to spend the rest of my life celibate."

Could I do it? Could I spend a week making love to

Brooke and then put her back on the shelf for some other man to pick up at his leisure?

"Please?"

The chance to have her in my arms, even temporarily, was too much of a temptation to turn down.

"Okay. Okay, I'll do whatever you want."

And deal with the aftermath when the time came.

18

A FEW WORDS FROM CUPID...

He watched as Brooke and Luca danced around each other, a mating ritual he'd never quite felt comfortable with. When they kissed, little flames of anger licked up his insides, but he paused and took stock of the situation. Tamped down the sparks. His self-control was excellent—every daring move was rehearsed in advance and executed with precision. He was a magician. An escape artist. The Magnificent Pretender!

This was why he hadn't been caught.

Oh, they'd come close once, *they* being the fools on the school disciplinary board. A bunch of stiffs who probably fucked their tight-assed wives in the missionary position monthly on a schedule. But it turned out that colleges really didn't like scandal, so the whole affair got swept under the proverbial carpet and he moved on.

Coos Bay made a surprisingly good hunting ground.

He'd tried various cities, states, countries, but there was something about rural Oregon... The prey was so trusting, so guileless, and even if one of the girls had reported their suspicions, the Coos County sheriff was a bumbling idiot who should have retired years ago. But the voters kept electing the man, which didn't say much for their IQs either.

Probably why it had been so easy to keep up the act. People around here took you at face value, what you saw was what you got. And what they got was a wolf in sheep's clothing.

Sure, he'd tried dating the traditional way, had no problem getting women to sleep with him. But where was the fun in that? For him, the thrill came in the chase. The game. Take Brooke, for example... The first time with her, he'd acted on impulse—she'd strayed into his territory, an innocent lamb, standing outside Adeline's apartment building with a drink in her hand as she gazed up at the night sky. She just needed some air, she said. They'd chatted —Brooke a little distant but unfailingly polite, him hiding behind a veneer of charm.

She hadn't even noticed when he slipped the roofie into her drink.

And when she began feeling tired, she'd been grateful for his offer to walk her home, her mind already short-circuiting.

Fools.

All of them.

But this time... This time would be different. This time, he'd experienced the build-up. The slow burn. Watching, waiting as Brooke grew more and more skittish. Nervous enough to move out of her apartment.

This affair with Luca was a setback, but nothing more. He had patience. Luca would be gone soon. Everyone said how much he hated Baldwin's Shore, hated his father, and he'd already left once. He'd leave again.

And then Brooke would be ripe for the taking.

19

BROOKE

Luca sure knew how to kiss. I hadn't doubted for a moment that he did, but until last night, I'd never experienced the magic for myself. It was everything I'd imagined. Everything I'd dreamed of. Everything I could never have, not permanently. My insides had heated and clenched until I was basically one giant ovary with good hair and a glazed expression.

And I couldn't stop replaying it over in my mind.

The way he'd turned and agreed to a suggestion I'd felt sick about even making. Desperate people do desperate things, okay? The way we'd both paused before moving toward each other, hesitant, neither of us wanting to make the first move. The way his lips had touched mine, the little sparks that had zapped across my skin as he deepened the kiss and wrapped his arms around my waist. I'd waited for the nerves to wash over me, for my fight-or-flight response to kick in the way I'd always feared it would, but all I felt was a delicious apprehension about what was to come. My fingers reached for the hem of his T-shirt, and I lifted it an inch, enough to feel the hard muscle and smattering of hair underneath, but he'd stopped me with a shake of his head.

"Not tonight, sweetheart," he murmured against my lips. "There's no hurry."

"Actually, we *are* on a time limit."

His groan sent ripples of need through my core.

"Don't remind me. But you're not some quick fuck, Brooke. You're a goddess, and that's how I'm going to treat you. Hmm... You can be Aphrodite. I'm sure she wore nothing but a sheet at one point."

"Does that make you Adonis? Where did you learn about Greek mythology, anyway?"

"We had downtime on tour. When I ran out of porn magazines, a buddy lent me Homer's *Iliad*."

Only Luca could make me laugh in the middle of something so awkward. "Be serious."

"You don't think I read *The Iliad*?"

Was he serious? He sounded kind of hurt, and the last thing I wanted to do was upset him.

"I thought you hated English lessons at school?"

And *The Iliad* was heavy. I'd tried reading it myself once, but I'd only made it a quarter of the way through before Netflix won out.

"No, I hated Mrs. Gibson. When I was in eighth grade, she told me I'd never amount to much, and she prejudged every assignment I ever submitted."

"I didn't realise..."

"One time, I did Aaron's English homework and he did mine. Who do you think got the higher mark?"

Luca might have offered to be my temporary lover, but above all, he was my friend. And even though years had passed since he left high school, I figured a hug might help. Our new arrangement meant I didn't worry about squashing myself against him and nuzzling his neck. He smelled nice. A hint of woodsy cologne, and underneath, the musky scent that was all Luca.

"I'm so sorry. If it helps, Mr. Gibson doesn't like her much either. I heard they got divorced recently."

Luca's turn to chuckle. "Why are we even talking about this?" He wrapped a fist in my hair and tilted my head to the side, then feathered soft kisses along my jaw. "I've got better things to do with my mouth."

And he'd been serious about that, too. My toes curled just from thinking of it.

"Earth to Brooke." Darla snapped her fingers in front of me. "You okay, hun? You look kinda…stunned?"

Dammit, I'd broken my "no daydreaming at work" rule. How long had I been holding this ball of yarn? I hastily shoved it onto the shelf as I tried to gather scattered thoughts.

"Uh, yes? I mean, I think I'm okay."

"You've been smiling to yourself for the past half hour. Did something happen with Thor?"

"Thor?"

"Darn, I've been spending too much time with Paulo. Luca. I meant Luca."

"Why does Paulo call him Thor?"

"No reason."

Oh, there was definitely a reason. Paulo had nicknames for all sorts of people, and there was always a story behind the moniker. He called Elmira Fairbanks "Olympic," for example, because she always wore a lot of rings. And also because she could bitch for America. Colt was "Concrete" because Paulo had accidentally walked into him once and said it was like hitting a wall, and Mary from the coffee house was "Monet" because she liked to stencil little cocoa pictures onto everyone's cappuccino foam.

"Spill. And don't tell me it's because Luca reminds him of Chris Hemsworth—they look nothing like each other."

Darla huffed out a sigh. "Fine. It's because Paulo says he has a magnificent hammer."

"A magnificent…? Hey! That's totally objectifying."

"I'm making no comment." Darla mimed zipping her lips and tossing the key over her shoulder. "So, *did* something happen?"

"Maybe."

She raised an eyebrow.

"It's complicated. You can't tell anyone, okay?"

"Not even Paulo?"

"Not even Paulo." Because if Paulo knew, then Aaron would find out in three and a half seconds. Darla, on the other hand, was more of a sponge. She absorbed secrets rather than sprinkling them around town like confetti. And despite what I'd once thought, sharing my problems with the right people had eased the burden rather than making it heavier. "I've been having some trouble with a guy following me."

"What guy?"

"I don't know who he is, but I think…" I paused, but talking about this was getting easier now. "I think, no, I *know* he's the same man who hurt me last year."

"Gosh darn. Did he hurt you bad?"

I nodded, and thankfully Darla didn't ask for more details because I wouldn't have been able to hold back my tears.

"I'm always here if you want to talk."

"I appreciate that so much. Really. Anyhow, he left a package at my apartment, so Luca insisted I move into Deals on Wheels. And then I lost my mind and we made this...I guess you could call it an arrangement. For ten days, and it ends when my brother gets home from his vacation."

"A no-strings fling? Gosh, I didn't think you were the type." Darla sighed. "Which means I'll lose five bucks to Paulo if he finds out, so you definitely can't tell him."

"You were betting on my love life?"

"Love? I thought you said it was just a short-term thing?"

Heat rose up my cheeks. "Of course, yes, that's all it is. But he's been really sweet. When we were at the Peninsula Resort, Easton Baldwin was being an asshole to me, and Luca planted himself right between us. I honestly thought he was going to swing a punch, but then Mr. Belinsky stepped in and threw Easton out."

"Easton was being an a-hole? Easton the Third?"

I nodded.

"That doesn't surprise me one bit."

Darla's own run-in with Easton the Third—Paulo called him Easton the Turd, or just "the Turd" for short—had come two years ago. Easton the First had left her a house in his will, a thank-you for taking care of him in his twilight years, and the Turd didn't like that one bit. He'd contested the will, but it had been drafted by Aaron's boss and ultimately proved to be watertight. So Darla had gotten to stay in her home, and she'd also made enemies out of the remaining Baldwins.

"I was surprised when Sara Baldwin showed up here the other day."

"So was I, a little. I'm mostly surprised she has the time to paint. Those cousins of hers usually keep her busy doing their scutwork the whole day, the girls especially. Back when I cared for East, Lillian and Kayleigh used to nag her from dawn until dusk."

"I thought they ran a party planning company?"

Darla snorted. "Sure, they 'run' it. More like Sara does the planning, and they show up at the parties." And Darla should know. She'd spent far more time with the Baldwins than I had. "I don't mind Sara—she was the only one who used to visit with East when he couldn't move around so well—but if the other girls show their faces in here, I'll run them right out."

The thought of Darla running anyone out of the store made me giggle—she didn't have a nasty bone in her body. But I had to admit that I shared the sentiment. Maybe Paulo could do the honours?

And at least we'd changed the subject away from Luca.

"Speaking of running, should I go to the grocery store and pick up more milk? We're down to the last drops."

"No, you finish stocking the shelves with the new yarn colours. I'll go."

Two minutes after Darla left, the bell over the door jingled, and a half-dozen ladies walked in, ooh-ing and aah-ing at the beadwork samples and the variety of embroidery floss. Judging by the expensive clothes and the New York accents, they'd escaped from the Peninsula Resort. Then the Snyder family showed up—Mom, Dad, and twelve-year-old Sophie—and I knew this was the start of a busy day.

At a quarter to six, I sagged back against the counter and surveyed the rainbow of chaos that only a group of finger-painting five-year-olds could create. I even had paint in my hair. How did it get into my hair?

"Where do I start?" I muttered, half to myself and half to Darla.

"With donuts. They're on special at the grocery store. I was trying to stay healthy, but this calls for sprinkles. Back in ten."

I texted Luca to let him know I'd be slightly late getting home, but not to worry. Since Vega was staying at Deals on Wheels in the daytime now, with Brady and Deck sharing the dog-sitting duties, Luca had let me drive myself to work on the condition that I didn't stop anywhere on the way. But now, with Darla gone and the store empty, I began to feel a tiny bit twitchy. What if Cupid was out there watching me? Had Darla locked the door on her way out? No, so I quickly turned the key, then checked the rear door was secure too. We usually kept it locked, but one couldn't be too careful.

Then I started scrubbing.

And daydreaming.

How far would things go with Luca tonight? He'd promised to take it slow, but we only had nine nights left together, and after waiting for a whole freaking decade, I wanted to make the most of them. What time did Deck and Brady plan to leave? Brady in particular sometimes worked into the evenings, and while his dedication had to be admired, I really hoped he'd start clock-watching.

Although if this red paint wouldn't come off the table, I might be here into the night myself.

"I got chocolate as well as the donuts," Darla called twenty minutes later. "Did you know you have a note on your car? I hope nobody bumped it."

Every nerve fibre stiffened. "A-a-a note?"

"Tucked under the windshield wiper. You okay? You've gone white as a ghost."

"I'm sure it's just a flyer or something." But deep down, I knew it wasn't. Cupid had found out where I worked, and the knowledge left me cold. “Did you see anyone by my car today?”

“No, but Deon had his cargo van parked in the way for most of the afternoon.”

Deon made deliveries for the grocery store along the street, and since our parking lot was bigger than theirs, Darla let him borrow a space when he needed to. Dammit, I should have caught a ride with Luca this morning. He’d offered, but I hated losing my independence. *Hated* it. I didn’t want to be on my own all the time, but nor did I want to be reliant on others if I felt like popping out to the grocery store.

Darla watched from the window as I hurried out to my car. Out of nosiness or concern, I wasn’t sure, but I was grateful.

The sight of Cupid’s block letters turned my stomach, slashes of dark red on the white envelope. I wanted to tear it open and burn the contents, but at the same time, I couldn’t bear to be anywhere near it. Whatever, I’d learned my lesson about ruining the evidence. With shaking hands, I dialled Luca.

20

LUCA

So much for a cosy dinner.

I'd wanted to do something nice for Brooke, but when she called to say her stalker had left another note on her car, I'd had to cancel our reservations at the Italian restaurant in Coquille. Cupid, she called him. More like stupid. And also dead, when I got my hands on that motherfucker.

Or maybe the latest incident was just fate stepping in with size-thirteen shitkickers? I hadn't been sure how Brooke would react to a date, not with our new "arrangement," as she'd termed it. *Arrangement.* As if I could distill what I felt for her down into a handful of calendar entries and a ticking clock.

"*We should be together*," Colt read. He'd put on a pair of gloves and slit open the envelope with a penknife before sliding out the note. "And he signed off with that creepy little heart again. A declaration of love? Or an intention of harm?"

"No idea, but he's not getting anywhere near Brooke. How's the investigation going?"

Colt glanced toward the Craft Cabin, which was a misnomer because the place was massive, but Brooke said Darla had started the enterprise in a smaller building that it quickly outgrew, and the name stuck. The two of them watched us from the window, out of earshot. Brooke hadn't been happy when Colt sent her inside, but she also hadn't argued, which was one reason I knew how upset she was.

"It's going slower than I'd like," Colt admitted. "The department's short of manpower. We've lost two deputies this year—one retired and the other moved to San Diego—and there aren't many folks interested in moving to this little corner of paradise to replace them. A group of us are trying to convince Sheriff Newman to offer a relocation package, but he's thinking on it. Been thinking on it for six damn months."

"Sheriff Newman? He's still in charge? He must be seventy by now."

"Sixty-nine, and he doesn't look a day over eighty."

"And he keeps getting re-elected?"

"You know the way things are around here—the natives don't like change, and the newcomers wouldn't want anyone competent looking at their business too close. Sheriff Newman's more interested in photo ops and the annual summer cookout than stirring up trouble, and the rest of us don't have the time."

"I'm surprised the *Coos Bay Chronicle* doesn't have something to say about that."

"The sheriff's daughter is the editor now. They put together an eight-page colour special on the cookout."

The whole fucking world was being sent to try me.

"So what *has* been done?"

"An investigator spoke to Addy, and he passed me a list of everyone she remembers being at the party. So far, I've spoken to three of them, but apart from a few extra names, they didn't recall anything useful. And I'm trying to get ahold of a list of the tenants in Addy's building, but the Baldwins are stonewalling."

"What do the Baldwins have to do with this?"

"They own half of that block. EJ's insisting on a warrant, but the paperwork's stuck in the system. And the lab's backed up, as usual, so we're still waiting on forensics for the note and the candy." Colt raked a hand through his hair. "Sometimes, I wonder why I do this job."

"Because you're a fan of justice?"

"Yeah." He sighed. "I'll book this note into evidence, and then I gotta pick Kiki up from the sitter."

I couldn't argue with that. Being a single dad was tough, and Colt still hadn't gotten over the death of his wife. Probably never would. Hannah had been his high-school sweetheart, the woman he'd declared at fifteen years old he was going to marry. Me and Aaron thought he was kidding, but no, we'd ended up as groomsmen with matching suits and buttonholes. Kiki had come along soon after I left town, the apple of her father's eye. And now, a constant reminder of what Colt had lost. I'd seen pictures of her, and at seven years old, Kinsley Hannah Haines looked so much like her mom it was uncanny.

"You want me to talk to some of these people?"

"You've got no legal standing."

"No, but I know how to ask questions, and I recognise a bunch of the names."

The women, mostly.

"Oh yeah? How many of their hearts did you break?"

"Hey, I never made them any promises."

I'd always been completely up front about my lack of commitment. And when those girls got me for a night, they got *all* of me—my dick, my tongue, my hands, my attention. Hell, I even brought them breakfast in the morning. Nine times out of ten, we parted on good terms, and I could leave the remaining ten percent for Colt.

"Officially, I can't condone that, but unofficially, if you think you can obtain the information we need without getting kicked in the nuts, then I'm not gonna say no to the assistance."

"I'll start making calls tomorrow." Tonight, I had other things on my mind. "What's the best restaurant around here that delivers?"

"You want to treat Brooke?"

"Nah, man, I'm gonna sit at home and eat lobster while she watches."

"Relax, buddy. No need to act all defensive. It's obvious you like her."

Fuck. "We've been friends for a long time."

Colt gave me a "do you think I'm stupid?" look. Double fuck.

"Just watch your step. Aaron's been taking boxing lessons over in Coos Bay."

"I'm not planning to be his new brother-in-law."

"Didn't think you would be, but if you hurt her again, *I'll* kick your ass."

"Again?"

"How do you think she felt the first time you left? And whose place do you think she was crying at? Hannah was buying Kleenex in bulk for months."

Ah, hell. I knew I'd hurt Brooke, but we were both young. I figured she'd move on to better things rather than wasting her thoughts on yours truly. Had she been hung up on me the way I'd been hung up on her? Colt was right—I did have to tread carefully.

"You may be like a brother to me, but Brooke's like a sister," Colt carried on. "And Hannah's not here to pick up the pieces this time. Neither is Brooke's grandma. Right now, Addy and Paulo are a big part of Brook's support network, and if you screw her over, I wouldn't want to be in your position when they take their revenge. You want glitter in your eyes? Your balls set on fire?"

"Message understood," I ground out through gritted teeth. "I'm not planning to hurt her, but I'm also not gonna stand back and let this motherfucker and his sick notes ruin her life. If the sheriff's office can't do its job, then somebody has to keep her safe."

Colt's expression darkened. "Yeah, I get the message too. I'll do everything I can, but that asshole's careful, and I bet there are no fingerprints or DNA on this." He waved the note, now safely tucked into an evidence bag. "The Mexican place in Coos Bay delivers, and Brooke likes everything on the menu. Go take care of her."

I intended to, in every way possible.

Only time would tell if I'd live to regret it.

Or whether I'd dig myself into an early grave.

21

BROOKE

"Pillows? You bought more pillows?" I asked Luca.

Eight more pillows, to be precise, four in cream satin cases, four in navy blue, all stacked neatly onto my new bed. Ed had delivered it yesterday evening along with the couch and chairs, which had at least given my lips a break from Luca's kisses. Thanks to his five o'clock shadow, my skin felt decidedly chafed today. And it wasn't just pillows that had magically appeared—yesterday, the windows had been bare in the bedroom, but now he'd hung drapes and laid a matching rug on the concrete floor.

"The pillows were your idea."

"My id— Oh." My traitorous cheeks burned, and I momentarily forgot how annoyed I was at Luca. "You really think that's necessary?"

Was Luca *that* good in bed? I very much suspected the answer might be yes, something that both thrilled me and made me extremely nervous.

"Yeah, it's definitely necessary." That unapologetic smirk made me clench my thighs together. "But before we test out the bed, we need to eat." He took a step closer, and I was proud I didn't back away. Sometimes Luca could be… overwhelming. "Brooke, are you okay? After what happened earlier, I mean."

"You mean when you sent Darla and me back inside? When you left me out of a discussion about my own problems?"

"Technically, it was Colt who told you to go inside."

"You didn't argue with him."

"Because I didn't want you to get upset," Luca muttered, his smirk gone.

"Newsflash: I was more upset by you thinking I couldn't handle it. I've *been* handling it. On my own. For a year."

"And I'm so fucking sorry, sweetheart. Sorry I pushed you away. Sorry I gave the impression I didn't trust you. But most of all, I'm sorry I wasn't here and that you had to deal with this alone."

And that was why I'd never been able to stay mad at Luca for long. Even when we were kids, if he'd done wrong —a regular occurrence—he held his hands up and admitted it. Took the punishment. Looking back, the inability to apologise was one of the biggest faults my only two serious boyfriends had shared. Dale had simply avoided me in the aftermath of arguments—the bigger the fight, the longer he disappeared for. Then he'd send flowers and show up a day or a week later as if nothing had happened. And Steve, he'd said the words, but he always twisted them to make things my fault. *I'm sorry you feel that way. I'm sorry you can't see things from my perspective.*

Luca, he spoke from the heart.

"I'm sorry I flew off the handle."

"Nothing to be sorry for. If I don't know how you're feeling, I can't fix it. This situation isn't one I've had much experience with."

"What, spending more than a single night in a woman's company?"

I hated myself the moment the sentence left my mouth. Luca didn't deserve that dig. He'd never hidden who he was. Yet he flinched, and I realised that despite his size and his strength, despite his muscles and his "don't fuck with me" attitude, I had the power to hurt him. A decade had worn away the swagger he'd once used as armour, let his emotions run closer to the surface. He stepped back. Opened up the distance between us again.

"No, having to watch someone I care deeply about being tormented by a stranger while I'm powerless to stop it." His voice dropped to a whisper. "I don't want to fight with you, Brooke."

"I don't want to fight either." Especially when we had so little time together. "Truce?"

"Truce."

"But I still want to know what you discussed with Colt. What did the note say?"

"It said 'we should be together.'" Luca wrapped his arms around me as I shuddered. "But I won't let him near you. I promise. Colt's doing what he can, and I'm going to give him a hand by talking to some of the people on Addy's list tomorrow. But tonight, we're going to forget about all that."

"I'm not sure I can."

"Try. Don't give this motherfucker your headspace. That's what he wants. If he can't have you in person, he wants you thinking about him, obsessing over him. He feeds off your fear."

Like the monster that lives in the closet. When I was little, Aaron used to check in there every night before I went to sleep, and under my bed too. He'd grumbled, but he'd always done it.

"Y-y-you think he's watching me?"

"I want to say no, but I'm not gonna lie to you. I think there's a chance."

Little puzzle pieces clicked into place. "That's why you bought the drapes, isn't it?"

And they weren't only in the bedroom. Every window in the living area was covered too. Filmy floor-length drapes in shades of grey with thick white blinds behind them for extra protection. He must have roped in Brady and Deck to help. There was no way one man could have done all that on his own in a day.

"Partly."

"Partly?"

"The number of windows was making me twitchy."

"Why?"

"Because..." His sigh told me that every word I uttered was making this conversation harder. "Because a friend of mine got shot by a sniper. One minute, we were talking to a guy about his missing son, and the next, Nathan was bleeding out in my arms."

"He died?"

"At least it was fast."

"I'm so sorry." Words were inadequate. Instinct took over and I hugged Luca tighter, as if I could squeeze out some of his pain. Take it from him. Divide it equally. "You were close?"

"We went through Ranger School together. Shared a CHU."

"A choo? I don't understand."

"A containerised housing unit. We were roommates. And yeah, his death hit me hard. Not only because I'd lost a buddy, but because I'd gotten a stark reminder of my own mortality. If I'd been standing four inches to the left, I'd have been in a casket too."

"Don't talk like that."

"It's true. But anyway, I got out. Figured if I'm gonna die doing dangerous shit, I might as well do it on my own terms."

I glanced around the cavernous space, at the elegant drapes I'd thought were so beautiful just a few minutes ago. Now I saw them as shields.

"You don't seriously think...?"

"That there's a sniper in Baldwin's Shore?" Luca barked out a laugh. "Nah, sweetheart. But like I said, I'm twitchy. Humour me, okay?" He kissed my hair, such a small thing but also huge. "We should find plates. Dinner'll be here soon."

Mexican. He'd ordered Mexican. An entire freaking menu's worth of Mexican and paid extra for delivery. Nachos and tacos and burritos and quesadillas plus a token salad. We still didn't have a dining table, so we dragged Deck's workbench over as a substitute. Vega flumped down beside it, ready to catch any morsels we dropped.

"I take you to all the best places," Luca kidded. His voice had lost its earlier sombreness, and I decided to steer clear of any army- or stalker-related conversation for the rest of the evening.

"The company's more important than the ambience. Although..." I spotted Aaron's Bluetooth speaker on the kitchen counter. "I could put some music on."

While Luca laid out the food, I set a "Latin love songs" playlist to stream. Yes, I knew it wasn't a date, but was there any harm in wanting it to feel like one? *Nine days...* I didn't want to waste any of them. Would anything happen tonight?

Luca seemed to be in no hurry to strip me naked, although I wouldn't have complained if he did.

I'd have been hellishly nervous, but I wouldn't have complained.

"Beer? Wine? Tequila?" He wrinkled his nose. "Water?"

Tonight? I needed all the courage I could get.

"Tequila."

It didn't matter if I got drunk. Didn't matter if I let my guard down. With Luca, I was safe. And it seemed he was off duty for once because he filled two shot glasses and held one out to me.

"*Sláinte.*"

"Don't you mean *salud*? You spent too much time in the Cave."

"Nobody drinks like the Irish. Except maybe the Russians. Before I went to Eritrea, I spent a couple of months in Sudan, and there were a bunch of Russians on the team. I always thought I could hold my liquor, but those motherfuckers drank me under the table. Brewed their own vodka too."

"What did you do in Sudan?"

"Even if I could tell you, you wouldn't want to know."

The burn of the tequila in my throat eclipsed the chills that ran through me. Luca was right; I probably didn't want to know. Especially not tonight. Not when we were on our first—and possibly last—non-date.

"Then let's eat."

Sharing Mexican food with any other man would have left me taking dainty little bites and trying not to make a mess. But this was Luca. I'd eaten dinner with him a hundred times before, even if we were usually with my brother or his sister or a group of other people, so I dug in.

Sauce squished out. But he'd brought napkins, so that was okay.

"What are you smiling about?" he asked.

"Just thinking about the time I went on a date and the guy took me to La Cantina and ate tacos with a knife and fork. Which meant *I* had to eat tacos with a knife and fork, and that was super awkward."

"Soft-shell tacos?"

"Crisp tacos."

"The man was a monster."

"Exactly. Like, who does that? They broke, and the filling went everywhere, and I was trying to scoop pieces into my mouth and plan my escape at the same time."

"I had the opposite problem once—I took a girl for rice and curry in New York, and she ate it with her fingers. Said she'd backpacked around Sri Lanka when she was younger, and that was the local custom, so she stuck with it when she came home because it felt more authentic."

"Tell me she washed her hands first?"

"Her immune system must've run on rocket fuel. You want more tequila?"

"Sure, why not?"

What was the worst that could happen? I'd get drunk and fall asleep on the couch?

No, as it turned out. I'd get drunk, drop cookie-dough ice cream down my cleavage, then fall over my own feet when I tried to get up and rectify the problem. Oh, and land in Luca's lap. With my face smushed into...you get the picture.

"Ah, sh...sugar."

My arms had stopped working. Why had my arms stopped working?

"Babe, if you were hungry for cock rather than ice cream, you only had to say so."

"I-I... Just get it off! Out! Whatever! It's so freaking cold!"

I grabbed the hem of my sweater and pulled, but it got stuck over my head and then I couldn't see either. My arms flailed as I stumbled back, and I winced, already preparing myself for a hard landing.

Which never came.

"I got ya, sweetheart."

Luca's words vibrated an inch from my ear, his arms tight around my waist as he dipped me backward like a ballroom dancer at the end of a particularly dirty tango. Except I was a terrible dancer. And as if to rub that little factoid in, the Macarena started playing in the background.

Freaking heck. *Please, somebody kill me now.*

But not my stalker.

I didn't want to give him the pleasure.

"I'm such a mess," I mumbled through an alcoholic haze and a layer of merino wool.

Slowly, deliberately, Luca licked the ice cream from between my boobs, and I just about melted.

"Not anymore."

I kind of expected him to do the gentlemanly thing and help me out of my sweater so I could see again, but who was I kidding? This was Luca. Half a second later, my bra popped open—he'd clearly had practice at *that* move—and then his tongue was *everywhere*. I didn't have time to get nervous. The tip circled my nipples, trailed up my neck, snaked across one shoulder, leaving a cool trail and goosebumps in its wake. With my arms trapped and my eyes blindfolded, every other sensation was heightened, and the rasp of Luca's breathing told me he was as affected by this as I was. Good thing he was holding me because my knees would have buckled otherwise.

"I want to see you," I whispered.

My feet left the floor as he lifted me, and I wrapped my legs around his waist on instinct. Holy hell, he was hard. And huge. And mine, for tonight at least.

My ass met the leather couch, and he gently tugged the sweater free, kneeling in front of me so our eyes were level.

"I've gotta change this fuckin' music," he said, and I burst out laughing.

The doubt, the dread, all the fears I'd lain awake turning over in my mind for the last year, he held them at bay with a little fun and a lot of filth. I stared unashamedly at his ass as he bent to snatch my phone off the workbench and picked out a more appropriate track. And for "more appropriate," read "dirtier." I hadn't heard it before, but a breathy woman was singing about sapphires and moonlight and tequila sunrises.

Luca turned, a secret smile tugging at the corners of his lips as he strode toward me. Then he paused. Took a step back. Picked up the tub of melting ice cream and a spoon. Was he going to feed me ice cream? I'd seen that in the movies. Swooned over it.

"Lie back, sweetheart."

I did as instructed. Closed my eyes and opened my mouth, waiting. Then gasped as the ice cream hit my chest.

"What the heck…?"

My eyes flew open to see the gleam in Luca's.

"That was fun. Thought we'd do it again. Don't worry; you'll get your turn. Good things come to those who wait."

"You're such an asshole."

"So I've been told." He grinned, quirked an eyebrow. "I've also been told I'm a massive dick. Care to verify?"

Best not to confess that I already knew that. When he was sixteen, he'd run the whole way down Main Street in a pair of Speedos for a bet, and I hadn't been able to take my eyes off him, back or front. I'd positioned myself halfway so I'd get an excellent view of him coming *and* going. My photos had come out blurry, but Addy's hands had been steadier than mine, and she'd been kind enough to send me a copy of the video. I must have watched it a hundred times.

But now my gaze strayed downward, and I swallowed hard. That was one heck of a bulge.

"Maybe?"

Luca laughed. "Well, while you make up your mind, I'm gonna enjoy dessert." He flicked another spoonful of ice cream, and it splattered across my chest. "Chill."

Was it possible to love someone and want to throttle them at the same time? Absolutely. Luca was living proof of that, but when he treated me to another helping of that magic tongue, I decided I didn't care about the negatives. I also realised in that moment that no matter what happened in what was left of my life, no matter who I spent the years with or where I ended up, I'd always love Luca Mendez. Even if these nine days were all we'd ever have together, a part of my heart would be his forever. That ache of a memory would be with me for the rest of my days.

"Fuck. Sweetheart, why are you crying?"

"I..." Crying? I put a finger to my cheek, and it came away wet. "I didn't realise."

"It was a joke. I only meant it as a joke." He held out the tub as I processed the note of panic in his voice. "Throw the whole damn thing at me if you want."

"No, no, it's..." I could hardly tell him I was miserable over the future, could I? Getting emotional about a lack of commitment was the surest way to send a man running for the hills, at least if those self-help articles on the internet were any indication. "Just bad memories, that's all."

"Want me to stop?"

"No, I want you to take the memories away. Bury them beneath new ones."

"With or without ice cream?"

"Uh, with?"

Luca's mouth curved into a dirty smile, and I knew I'd never look at a tub of Häagen-Dazs in the same way again. But who cared? Luca skimmed a hand over my body, light, almost reverent, then unbuttoned my jeans and slid them off.

"These need to go too," he muttered as he dragged my panties down my legs and tossed them over his shoulder.

"Hey, you're still dressed."

"Yeah, yeah, we'll get to that, but I've been waiting ten damn years to taste you, so don't spoil my fun."

Nothing tastes as good as you.

The words from Cupid's note played on my mind, and I shivered, but luckily at the same instant Luca spooned ice cream over me, so I managed to hide my momentary freak-out. Wait a second... He wasn't going to...? Oh, yes, he was. Luca buried his head between my legs and sucked, and stars burst behind my eyes as I arched off the couch. Based on my past experiences with other men, I thought he'd give a couple of licks, shuck his jeans, and get his rocks off, but no, he kept going. His hands were everywhere, and that tongue...it was magic. I honestly hadn't realised it was quite so long. Like an anteater's, except obviously there were no ants, and... *Shut up, Brooke.* Sometimes, my inner monologue took on a life of its own. But then Luca added his fingers to the mix and even background-Brooke was at a loss for words.

I came on a long moan, tasted myself as Luca kissed me. I was wrecked. Ruined. How could he expect me to go back to my old life after that?

"Worth the wait," he whispered, leaning his forehead against mine.

Another tear rolled down my cheek, and I hastily wiped it away. "Ignore that. I'm just happy, that's all."

"You cry when you're happy?"

"Yes. I mean, I suppose. I've never felt quite like this before."

"Then I guess that makes two of us. You want to move this into the bedroom?"

I nodded. The fear was gone, but I was secretly concerned that my legs would never work again. And perhaps Luca knew that because after he'd taken Vega out and settled him into his pen for the night, he picked me up and carried me to bed.

And it turned out we needed every single one of those pillows.

22

LUCA

"You're sure Brooke was at the party? I don't remember seeing her there."

Marnie Simcox—now Marnie Pettigrew—was the second of the names on Colt's list. The first—Lydia Fairbanks—I'd skipped over because, according to Brooke, she still lived at home with her parents, and Elmira Fairbanks wasn't my biggest fan. Not because I'd ever upset her personally, more because my reputation as a teenager had preceded me and she didn't want me anywhere near her daughter. I couldn't imagine she'd changed much over the years.

Neither had Marnie. Despite being only two years older than me, she'd been married three times and divorced twice since I saw her last, and judging by the way she was eyeing me up, divorce number three would be in the cards soon. Still, she seemed to have done well out of her chosen path. Her home on the outskirts of Coos Bay had to be six thousand square feet, and I spotted a swimming pool through the open terrace door. The shirtless guy cleaning it watched me suspiciously. Checking out the competition?

The row of trophies on a shelf in the living room suggested Marnie's current husband liked golf—I couldn't imagine her playing—and the framed certificates on the wall told me he was a doctor. A cosmetic surgeon? Her boobs had definitely gotten bigger since I'd seen them last. Trust me—a guy remembered these things. Her lips were plumper too. And her hair had grown. She wore it piled on her head in an elaborate style that defied gravity, apart from a few chestnut strands that floated around her chin like spider silk on a breeze.

"Yeah, Brooke was there. I'm surprised *you* were too—I don't remember you and Addy being close at school."

"Oh, we weren't. But when Addy moved to Coos Bay, she worked as my second hubby's executive assistant, and we became friends." Marnie gave a little huff. "I ended up speaking to her more than I spoke to him. The party really wasn't my thing—I'm more of a champagne girl—but of course I wanted to drop off a gift for Addy."

"What time did you arrive?"

"Maybe eight thirty?"

Brooke had been there until at least nine thirty, so Marnie wasn't very observant.

"How long did you stay?"

"Ten minutes? Fifteen? Not long."

Okay, so Brooke could have been in the bathroom or somewhere.

"Who else *do* you recall seeing?"

"What's this all about? Did something happen to Brooke?"

I went with the half-truth Colt, Brooke, and I had agreed on, both to protect her privacy and to avoid tipping off the perpetrator about how much we knew.

"She's been getting weird notes and anonymous gifts

sent to her home. The first one came right after the party, so we figured a guest might be sending them."

"Gifts? What kind of gifts?"

"Candy and flowers."

"Aw, that's so sweet."

"It's creeping her out."

"Each to their own." Marnie shrugged. Receiving unsolicited gifts was probably nothing unusual in her life. "I saw Lydia Fairbanks talking to Addy. Tannis Winfield was there too. You remember Tannis?" Marnie didn't wait for an answer. "She went to college in Boston, and now she works in the shoe store near Walmart. Shara Newell had her tongue stuck into a man's mouth, as usual, and Easton Baldwin was pouring beer down his throat in the kitchen."

My ears pricked up. "Easton Baldwin was there?"

"I don't suppose Addy invited him, but her door was open and he probably sniffed out the liquor. That man has a serious drinking problem."

I didn't doubt that Easton's morals would allow him to fuck an unconscious woman, but I'd seen him drunk plenty of times, most recently last week. Between whisky dick and a lack of coordination, would he have been able to pull it off? I wasn't convinced, and nor did I believe he had the finesse to place those notes without either bragging about it or being seen. Tongues wagged when Easton was around.

"Anyone else?"

"It was a year ago. I've been to a hundred parties since then." Marnie reached out and straightened my collar. I'd figured a dress shirt would be appropriate today, since this was semi-official business. The jeans stayed, though. "Are you and Brooke a thing now?"

"Me and Brooke? Nah." It physically hurt to deny it, but I had no other choice. "Colt's snowed with other cases, so I said I'd help out by talking to a few people. Informally, you know? He'll follow up if I hear anything important."

"You're a good friend. I always said people misjudged you." Marnie's hand moved from my collar to my cheek. "So if you're footloose and fancy-free, how about you come back later?"

Ah, fuck. "I thought you were married?"

"A woman still has needs."

No, she hadn't changed at all. "I have a kitchen to install before Aaron gets back. A guy's gotta earn his keep."

"Too bad."

I jerked a thumb in the pool guy's direction. "Looks as if Ken out there might be interested."

A slow smile spread over Marnie's face. "Oh, he is. He most certainly is."

LIKE MARNIE, Shara Newell remembered Addy's twenty-fifth birthday party. And like Brooke, she'd never forget the aftermath.

It, or rather he, was sleeping in a crib beside her in the studio apartment she called home. Every surface in the room was piled high with baby stuff, junk mail, takeout cartons, or balled-up laundry. Her parents had moved to Coquille after she graduated high school, and she'd followed six months ago because—in her words—childcare was a bitch. Seemed housekeeping wasn't much easier.

"That jerk takes no responsibility at all. None! Like it was *my* fault the condom broke. He was the one who invited me over to his place, at least, I'm almost certain he did—it's hazy, you know?—and it definitely took two to tango. What is it with men?"

She seemed to expect an answer, so I shrugged and said, "We're assholes."

"Right. And he's meant to pay child support, but he lost his job again so he figures that lets him off the hook. How am I meant to buy diapers? Do you know how many diapers a baby goes through? Like, hundreds. All they do is shit and eat. Which is all Harry does too, that and watch TV, because he sure doesn't lift a finger to help. I can't even drive, and he has a truck, but..."

I tuned out Shara's tirade about men in general and one man in particular and let my mind wander. How did Colt do this every day? I'd rather tiptoe across a live minefield with the Taliban on my tail. And every moment I spent with Marnie and Shara and their ilk was one less I'd be able to spend with Brooke.

Brooke.

Now that I'd finally gotten her into my bed—and also the double-width shower stall she'd had the foresight to pick out on her brother's behalf—I never wanted to sleep alone again. In the past, I'd thought of spending the night with a woman as a necessary evil, something to be endured because I figured I owed them, but with Brooke, it had been no chore to wrap her up in my arms as we drifted off. Nor had I minded when I woke in the early hours, hot, too hot, with her legs tangled in mine and her head on my chest. I'd be her pillow any day.

And deep down, I wouldn't even mind if the condom broke, which was a fucking terrifying thought.

Because we only had eight days left.

"...and I'm gonna join a convent. Do they let nuns bring kids? Like, if they have them already?"

"Uh..." It wasn't a question I'd spent much time considering. "Maybe you could call and ask?"

"Yeah, I'll do that. Anyhow, sorry I don't remember anything else about the party."

"No problem. Good luck, okay?"

The despair in her eyes as she glanced across at the crib said she'd need it. So would I, but at least we could cross Harry Dents off the list now.

PHOEBE GILMORE WAS NEXT UP, but she'd have to wait until tomorrow because today I needed to fit locks to Aaron's windows. Understandably, securing the perimeter hadn't been highest on his list of priorities—who wanted to break into a half-finished building?—but with Brooke sleeping there now, the task had taken on a new urgency. I planned to stop at the hardware store in Coquille before I headed back. If I needed anything more, I could drop by the Lowe's in Roseburg when I went to visit Phoebe.

But the smaller store was surprisingly well-stocked, and I'd installed the locks by the time Brooke finished work. Since Deck and Brady were getting ready to leave, I took the dog for a ride in Aaron's car. He seemed to like hanging his head out the window. The dog, not Aaron.

"Hey."

I couldn't kiss Brooke the way I wanted to, not in public, but I reached over to squeeze her thigh. She laced her fingers in mine and laughed as Vega leaned between the seats to lick her face. Lucky mutt.

"Thanks for picking me up."

"It's not exactly a hardship."

"Can I smell food?"

"Maybe." I figured since we couldn't travel together, I'd

take her on a culinary tour of the world. Mexico yesterday, China tonight. "Tell me you like kung pao chicken?"

"I'll eat anything."

The little glance toward my crotch as she said that... That tiny flick of the tongue... Did she even realise she'd done it? Either way, I hardened in a second, and I no longer gave a fuck about dinner.

"Noted."

I floored it out of the parking lot, and Brooke grabbed the handle above the door. I glanced in the rear-view mirror. The dog was wearing his harness, and I'd clipped it to the seat belt so he didn't slide around.

"Hey, slow down!"

"And waste a moment of our time together? I don't think so."

"You'll get a speeding ticket."

"From who? Colt? There's no traffic anyway."

Brooke didn't say another word, just reached over to my belt and began to unbuckle it. No way. She wasn't going to...? She fucking was. A second later, she had my fly undone as well, and my dick sprang free. I hadn't bothered to put on underwear. Another barrier to Brooke had seemed like overkill when I got dressed this morning, and I hated doing laundry.

"Is this a good—" I started, lifting my foot off the gas.

"Yes."

The rest of the question stuck in my throat when Brooke sucked my dick into hers. The woman was a natural. Either that or she'd had a hell of a lot of practice, which wasn't a possibility I wanted to consider. Fuuuuuck. The dog watching felt weird at first, but I soon tuned Vega out and focused on the road instead. The road and Brooke's mouth.

Brady waved as he drove in the other direction, and I

managed to raise a hand back. The thrill of passing people who recognised me, of knowing they didn't have a clue what Brooke was doing to me at that moment, was a turn-on I'd never expected, and my balls tightened.

"Sweetheart, I'm gonna come," I choked out.

She didn't stop. No, she cupped my balls in her hands and massaged gently. Holy fuck, I'd struck gold. This woman, she was everything, and I wasn't saying that just because she was sucking me off. I loved everything about her. The added filth was an unexpected bonus.

I nearly missed the turn for Deals on Wheels as I pulsed into her mouth, perhaps harder than I'd ever come in my life. She swallowed every damn drop, then turned to me wide-eyed, her lips smirking their way into a smile.

"I can't believe you did that."

"Neither can I." Her grin turned smug. "But I got you to slow down, didn't I?"

23

LUCA

If I'd had to put money on anyone in high school joining a convent, it would've been Phoebe Gilmore, not Shara. The address Addy had given me was over in Roseburg, but driving ninety miles was still preferable to speaking with Lydia Fairbanks, even if it was a waste of time. The Phoebe I remembered would have been in bed by eight thirty every night, definitely not a party girl, but she'd agreed to talk to me at two p.m. on account of how she'd been out until the early hours. And Colt said it was better to speak face to face because body language told you what words couldn't. Had he ever been propositioned by Marnie Simcox? Was that where he'd come up with that gem of advice?

Phoebe lived in a good-sized family home in a nice neighbourhood, just the type of place I'd have expected her to live, but there was only one car in the driveway, a new Honda with an "if you can read this, you're too close" sticker in the rear window. No kiddie seat. The front yard was small but neat, with a freshly mowed lawn and purple flowers exploding from pots lined up in front of the porch. Violets? Pansies? Not roses, that much I knew.

I rang the bell. Waited. No barking, no music, no sound at all until the door swung open. Phoebe hadn't changed much. She'd always been tall and thin in an athletic sort of way, but her hair was longer now. Blonder too.

"Luca?"

I didn't think I'd changed much either, but I nodded anyway. "Good to see you again, Phoebe."

She didn't seem to share the sentiment, but she opened the door wider and took a hesitant step back.

"Won't you come in? Please excuse the mess—I've only just gotten up."

What mess? The place was spotless.

"You work the night shift?"

"Yes, I do. The hours are antisocial, but I love to dance, and my colleagues are wonderful. I've made so many friends since I moved here."

"You took ballet lessons, right?"

In school, she always used to be in a hurry after classes finished. Her mom picked her up every day and drove her to some fancy dance academy miles away. Probably why I didn't remember much about her. She hadn't socialised much, although she'd obviously made friends with Addy. Then again, Addy made friends with everyone. If only she hadn't, this case would have been infinitely easier to solve.

"Oh, yes. That was a lifetime ago."

"There's a theatre in Roseburg?"

I should buy tickets for the show. Take Brooke. She'd probably like *Swan Lake* or *The Nutcracker* or whatever it was that ballerinas danced to nowadays.

"A small theatre, over on West Harvard Avenue. They're

performing a musical production of *Beauty and the Beast* at the moment, evenings with a Saturday matinee. It's really wonderful if you have the time to visit. Please, take a seat in the living room. Can I get you a drink? Coffee? Soda?"

She waved at a door on her right, and I stepped through it. Stopped dead at the sight of the stripper pole set up in the centre of the room. One entire wall was mirrored, and the only other furniture was a couch, a side table, and a TV.

Fuck, couldn't Addy have warned me?

I clamped my mouth shut to stop myself from asking the burning question: does your mama know? When Mrs. Gilmore wasn't shuttling Phoebe backward and forward, she'd taught Sunday school and played the piano in church. I'd never sought out the Baldwin's Shore gossip—although Romi, Brooke, and Addy had kept me well-informed—but these days, I was so far out of the loop I might as well have been slingshotted into Nevada.

Phoebe's tinkly giggle said she knew why I'd stopped. "I always wanted to join one of the big ballet companies, the American Ballet Theatre or the Royal Ballet in London, but thousands of girls share that same dream, and it's not easy for a girl from Oregon to break into those circles. And musical theatre is just as competitive, at least if you want to work on shows that pay enough to live. I moved to New York for a while—did Addy tell you?"

"She must've forgotten to mention it."

"That was a real eye-opener. Everything's *so* expensive there. My apartment didn't even have a kitchen, only a shelf with a tiny refrigerator and a microwave, and there was never any peace, just noise, noise, noise. Really, I didn't want to leave Oregon, but Danny was spending time with Sue Ellen behind my back. He swore they did nothing more than talk, but Lila said she saw Sue Ellen in the pharmacy filling a prescription for birth control, and then my mom moved to Florida with Father Jacob—obviously he's not *Father* Jacob anymore..." Another giggle. "And I guess I just didn't think there was anything left here for me."

There was a hell of a lot to unpack there. Her high-school sweetheart—a boy with the backbone of wilted spinach—had cheated on her with a second-rate cheerleader who'd only gotten onto the squad because she'd bought her own pom-poms? And her mom had corrupted the most pious of the town's three priests?

"But you moved back here?"

"I came on...well, I guess it was a vacation, but then I met Larry at Alcoholics Anonymous."

"Larry?"

Alcoholics Anonymous?

"He owns Edge of Eden. I know what people think, but it's really quite a classy place—no drugs, definitely no funny business, and the security staff look after us real well. Larry makes sure they take us home at the end of each shift, or sometimes he even drives us himself. And we keep all our tips. I could never have afforded to buy this place on a ballerina's salary." Phoebe adjusted the collar of her shirt while I lowered my ass to the edge of the couch. "Did you want a drink?"

"Coffee would be good."

I needed the caffeine with the amount of sleep I hadn't gotten last night. Didn't plan on getting much tonight either.

Phoebe strode gracefully out the door, and yeah, I could imagine men paying her big bucks to dance for them. Not this man, not anymore, but other men.

Some people changed, some people stayed the same. What did the folks in Baldwin's Shore think of me now? Sure, I had a few new scars, a little weathering around my eyes, a tattoo that had been worth every second of the pain it took to ink it onto my skin, but underneath… Underneath, I was still the kid from a broken home. The teenager people whispered about. *Poor Luca—his mom left and his father can be a beast. Do you think that's why he acts the way he does?* The boy angry at having to become a man before he was ready. But I'd served my country and served it well. Surely that must count for something? Oh, who was I kidding—most of the townsfolk were probably just surprised I wasn't in jail.

Phoebe came back with drinks—lumpy purple juice in a glass for her and a steaming mug of coffee for me. She hadn't asked how I took it, but I'd learned in the army that beggars couldn't be choosers. I'd cope with overly milky rather than my usual black.

She didn't take a seat herself, probably because that would have meant sitting next to me. Instead, she leaned against the pole, clasping it with one hand behind her back. Her anchor.

"You said this was about Brooke? And Addy?" Phoebe let go of the pole, and her hand flew to her cheek as I repeated the story about the stalker. "Oh, that's terrible! They're such lovely girls. I remember when I broke a heel during high school and Brooke lent me her sneakers so I wouldn't need to walk around lopsided all day. Really, we don't see enough of each other anymore. Every year, I promise myself that I'm going to get better at keeping in touch, but before I know it, we've gone through spring and summer and I still haven't made those calls. Do you use Facebook? Gosh, without it, I'd have no idea what's happening over in Coos County, and it really isn't far away."

"Nah, I never have."

But maybe I should start an account. Then I might have the faintest fucking clue what was going on.

"I like to check in once a day. Since I work such strange hours, it helps me to feel connected. And we have a private group there for people who work at the club, kind of like a support group, I guess, so if somebody can't make a shift, we ask others to fill in, that sort of thing."

"Back to Addy's party..."

"Oh, yes, of course. That was how I found out about the party—Facebook. She posted a reminder message. And I hadn't checked my mail for several days, so I'd have completely missed the invitation otherwise."

For fuck's sake, Addy. She posted on Facebook? Why hadn't she mentioned that? That increased the pool of potential suspects by anywhere from a few hundred to a few thousand.

"Who could have seen that? Anyone?"

"Uh, I'm not sure. Let me check. I have my phone right here."

Phoebe scrolled. And scrolled and scrolled and scrolled. How much time did Addy spend on social media?

"Here it is. See?" Phoebe passed her phone over. "It was only shared with her friends, but she has over three thousand of those."

Hell, there weren't even three thousand people living in Baldwin's Shore. There had been once, before the paper mill closed down, but when production moved overseas, many of the town's inhabitants had drifted away. Families fractured, but the old mill still stood, a hulking brick shell of a building set on a large lot not too far from Deals on Wheels. At least it gave the local graffiti artists somewhere to practise.

I took the phone from Phoebe and read Addy's post.

Hey, y'all! If you're near Shoreside tonight, don't forget to swing by and help me celebrate (or not, lol) another year on this planet! Eight till late, bring a bottle ;)

"She didn't give out her exact address," I murmured. "That narrows it down a little. Not all of these people would have known which building she lived in, right?"

"Well, really, you only had to listen for the music once you got to Shoreside. It was *very* loud. She had the balcony doors open because it was so hot in her apartment."

"The neighbours didn't complain?"

"I think most of them were at the party. It spilled into several other apartments and out into the street as well. They were mixing cocktails in a bathtub in Addy's living room. I guess someone in the building must have been having renovations done, because the tub wasn't Addy's. She only has a shower, although it's quite a large shower, and she made the whole bathroom seem even bigger with mirrors. Have you been to her apartment? The decor's lovely, all—"

Didn't Phoebe ever stop talking?

"I'm more interested in *who* was at the party. Did you see Brooke with anyone?"

"Addy, of course, and do you remember Tannis Winfield? She left Bayshore High during junior year—our junior year, not yours—when her parents moved here to Roseburg. She goes to the same gym as me, so we see each other from time to time. And then there was Lydia—"

"What about men? Did you see Brooke talking to any men?"

"Gosh, let me think... Well, Steve was there, and I'm sure I saw them speaking."

"Steve?"

"Her ex-boyfriend. I barely saw Brooke during that time,

but Addy told me they were dating, and between you and me, he's kind of a jerk."

My blood boiled in a heartbeat. Cavemen didn't need to invent fire; they could've just cooked over the burning embers of their jealousy. And why was I jealous? Because although I had Brooke this week and Steve didn't, he'd been able to date her openly while I had to skulk around in the shadows.

"It was a bad break-up?"

"Golly, I can't say for sure. But Steve got banned from the club because he kept trying to touch my friend Maddy, and she did absolutely nothing to encourage him. And even before that, he was a terrible tipper."

Steve frequented strip clubs? "When you say 'the club,' you mean Edge of Eden?"

"Yes, that's right."

I'd have paid good money to be the doorman that night.

"Did Brooke look upset when she was speaking to him?"

"Not that I recall, but I only saw them for a moment while I was on my way to get a drink. I'm sorry."

Phoebe's perky smile dropped, and for a moment, she just looked tired.

"Hey, it's okay. This is all useful information. Did you see Brooke again after that? Or Steve?"

"No, I don't recall seeing Steve, but Brooke was there during the Easton drama."

That prick again. "What drama?"

"He got into an argument with another guest. I can't remember what it was about, or whether I even knew, but his lip was bleeding."

"Whose? Easton's?"

"No, the other man's. Two of his friends were holding him back, and more people were trying to calm Easton down. Nobody wanted to tell Addy in case they ruined her birthday, and then someone suggested calling Parker to see if he could take his brother away. Easton never listens to anyone else—I'm sure you already know that—and sometimes he doesn't even listen to Parker."

"Did he listen that night?"

"I don't know. I mean, I imagine he did because I didn't hear of any more trouble, but it was crowded in the kitchen, and horribly hot, so I just grabbed a drink and moved back to the living room to give them space."

"What about Brooke? She stayed?"

"I..." Phoebe screwed her eyes shut for a second, thinking. "I think she went outside. To get some air, you know?"

"Did she come back in?"

"I didn't see her again, but maybe?"

"What time was this?"

"Two minutes before ten o'clock."

"Everything else is hazy, but you remember the exact time?"

"Yes, because Lydia Fairbanks was leaving right then, and her mom was waiting outside to pick her up. And I'm not sure if you remember, but—"

"One minute late, and I'm not gonna wait," I finished. Elmira Fairbanks was famous for the phrase. She'd left Lydia standing at the kerb more than once during our high school years.

"Exactly. So that's how I know the time. Lydia might have seen Brooke outside, if you talk to her? I don't think she'd been drinking much. Mostly soft drinks. She just ate all the chips, and the cookies too. The boys were complaining about it."

"She's on my list to speak with. Does her mom still breathe fire?"

"I'm sorry, but I just don't know." Phoebe lowered her voice, even though we were the only two people in the room. "I've been avoiding Elmira for my whole adult life. I suppose I should wish you luck."

"Thanks. Guess I'll need it."

24

BROOKE

"Close your eyes."

I did, but Luca covered them with his hands for good measure as we shuffled through Deals on Wheels. Probably because he figured I'd peep otherwise—there were pluses and minuses to non-dating someone I'd known for so long. But mostly pluses. I didn't have to pretend around Luca. He'd seen the best of me, and he'd seen the worst of me, and he was still here. I could be myself.

"Where are we going?"

"Up the ramp."

I found my footing as he guided me up the giant concrete ramp that led from the first floor to the second floor. The ramp was one of my favourite things about the building. There was a hidden flight of stairs at the other end too, but the ramp was a feature. A talking point. A convenience when you were tipsy, a godsend when moving furniture, and a potential hazard if I ever had children. What little boy would be able to resist whizzing down it on a skateboard or a bicycle? We'd have to pad an entire wall.

But that was a problem for the future. And who the heck

would I have kids with anyway? If I couldn't have Luca, I'd probably die alone.

My heart was his.

I tried to push thoughts of tomorrow out of my mind and live for today. Today, I had Luca, and as he'd said last night, we shouldn't waste the time we'd been gifted. My cheeks heated as I thought of what I'd done to him in the car. That had been so out of character for me, but since he'd shown up, it was as if I'd become a different person. Brooke the succubus. Brooke the vamp. Brooke the hedonist who sought out pleasure at every opportunity.

I'd managed to behave on the way home from work today, but I still craved the taste of him.

Luca guided me up the ramp, one arm around my waist in case I tripped. The second floor didn't have as much indoor space as the first, only half the amount, although that was still plenty enough for an apartment. The other half formed a roof terrace, a suntrap we planned to turn into a garden since there wasn't so much outside space at ground level, just a concrete apron and a small parking lot to the rear. Aaron wanted a hot tub on the roof. I wanted palm trees and a hammock. In time, we'd have it all.

The door to my apartment, my soon-to-be sanctuary, was on the left at the top of the ramp, but Luca didn't open it. Instead, he stopped in the hallway that led to the roof, and even at this time of day, light streamed through the French doors that opened onto the terrace. I felt the sun's warmth on my skin.

"Okay, you can open your eyes now."

Why was there grass inside? And not only grass but palm trees and flowers as well? I took a step forward and realised the grass was made of plastic, but it looked surprisingly realistic. The trees were in big terracotta pots, the flowers in smaller ones made out of silver metal. Pink and purple and orange and blue. With the red-and-yellow checked blanket on the grass, we had the whole rainbow, and the cerulean sky beyond made the space feel tropical. A tiny corner of paradise.

"What is all this?"

"Women like picnics, right?"

"We're having a picnic? Here?"

"You know how people talk around town. Somebody would've seen us if we sat outside."

"Where did you get this stuff? The grass? The plants?"

"Found the grass over in Roseburg. Borrowed Deck's truck to pick up the rest from Coos Bay." Luca held up a hand. "And before you ask what I told him, I said you'd gotten into feng shui and wanted your air purified."

"Huh? That's not what feng shui is."

"Well, on the basis I have no fucking clue, I figured Deck wouldn't either."

Luca had even brought Vega's bed upstairs, and was that a picnic basket?

The sun might have warmed me, but the realisation that he'd planned all this, spent hours arranging a non-date to make me happy, sent a flood of heat through my veins. It was the nicest thing anyone had ever done for me. But the joy was curbed by the knowledge that it could only be temporary.

"I like this sort of feng shui much better." I twisted in his arms and stood on tiptoe to press a kiss to his lips. "Thank you."

He looked embarrassed, as if he wasn't accustomed to being thanked, or to making grand romantic gestures either.

"Worth it for you, sweetheart. I'll get the dog."

He hadn't bought the food in Baldwin's Shore. If I had to guess, I'd say he'd paid a visit to the fancy Italian deli in Roseburg. Bread, cheese, cured meats, a cold frittata, olives, sun-dried tomatoes, oranges, dainty little pastries. And, of course, wine. A bottle of red and one of white. Why were the good men always so, so far out of my reach? Dale had avoided paying for anything wherever possible—he split restaurant bills with a calculator and I had to leave the whole tip—and Steve had expected me to greet him like a hero returning from war if he managed to stop at the drive-through on the way over.

Luca, well, he was all kinds of sweet wrapped up in a bad-boy package.

And I loved both sides of him.

While he carried Vega up the ramp, I set out the food. He'd even brought plates, and glasses, and cutlery. Cloth napkins too. Once Vega was in his bed, I motioned Luca over to lie on the grass next to me.

"Why?" he asked.

"Because I want to take a picture to remember you by."

"To remember me by? It's not as if we'll never see each other again."

"I know. But it won't be like this, will it?"

He didn't answer—probably because he knew I was right—just lay down and pulled out his phone for a selfie.

"Smile."

I did, but it was bittersweet.

The food was delicious, but without the luxury of time, we couldn't avoid talking about the case, and that made dinner slightly less palatable. I hated hearing about my life via a third party. Why couldn't I remember what had happened that night? The memories I did have were fuzzy, like watching clips of a movie through dirty glass.

"Steve was there? I don't... I don't remember that. I spoke to him?"

"So Phoebe said."

"She could have been mistaken. Did they even know each other? Steve lived in Sutherlin before he moved to Coos Bay."

"Apparently their paths had crossed."

"Really? I can't think where. Steve wasn't religious, and Phoebe's whole life revolved around the church. Oh, and ballet, but Steve wasn't much of a dancer either."

"She knew him in more of a professional capacity." Luca took my wine glass and filled it to the brim. "Here, drink this."

"Why?"

"Because Phoebe made a few adjustments to her lifestyle. She works in a club called the Edge of Eden now."

"The Edge of Eden?" The name was vaguely familiar. Kind of biblical, which was fitting for Phoebe. Had Addy suggested going there? She was always trying to get me to be more sociable. "What's— Oh."

Now I remembered, and it was nothing to do with the book of Genesis, not unless you counted the "no clothes" part anyway. When Addy was organising the paperwork for her boss's expenses, she'd noticed a charge from the club on his credit card statement and looked the place up. Needless to say, she'd been somewhat red-faced and left that particular amount off the reclaim form.

It also explained why Steve had never seemed to have any money despite having a good job.

I sure knew how to pick 'em, didn't I?

"Yeah. Drink the wine, sweetheart."

I poured it down my throat, and it helped a little. What helped more was having Luca with me, sitting on the blanket with one leg bent and the other straight out in front of him as he leaned back on his hands, not quite relaxed but trying. He'd help me to forget all about Steve after the questions were over.

"I'm such an idiot. I even paid for his gas half the time because he said he was short of cash."

"You're not the idiot. Steve's the idiot." Luca brought my hand to his lips. Kissed it. "Your kindness is a strength, sweetheart, not a weakness. But I have to ask—was it a bad break-up? Could you see him spiking your drink and taking advantage?"

"No? I mean, I don't think so, but I'm finding out that I'm not a very good judge of character."

Luca rolled onto his knees, crawled forward and fisted my hair in one hand. Kissed me breathless.

"Everyone has their secrets. Some matter more than others."

"Do yours?"

"Mine are mostly work-related. They matter, but not in this world."

"*Mostly* work-related?"

"You're my biggest secret, Brooke. My filthy, dirty little secret. But we need to finish this conversation before we get to that part of the evening."

The urge to push Luca backward onto the grass and ride him into the sunset was strong, but I tamped it down and nodded.

"Okay." I swallowed the lump in my throat, a lump made of a thousand bad decisions. "The break-up with Steve... It wasn't great. He cheated on me. At least, I think so. I found a condom in his pocket when I washed his jeans, and I'm on the pill, so we weren't..." I closed my eyes and wished I could roll right down the ramp into oblivion. "Anyhow, I had to get tested for everything. My only regret is that I didn't kick him in the balls before I left. It was *horrible.* So while I don't know what I spoke with him about at the party, I can't imagine it was civil."

"I'll pass the information on to Colt."

"Please, no."

I'd never be able to face him again.

"I'll edit the details first, okay?" Luca rested his hand on my thigh. "You're on the pill?"

I should have known he'd pick up on that little point. And yes, I still was. The question was, did I want to strip away that final barrier between Luca and me? Keeping my distance was hard enough without adding extra intimacy, and every time I thought of him leaving Baldwin's Shore again, leaving *me* again, my heart crumpled in my chest.

"Do you get tested?" I asked, stalling, and also because I wasn't *that* naïve. Luca was no saint, and he'd never tried to pretend otherwise.

"Regularly. And I've always used protection in the past. *Always*. But..." He scrubbed a hand over his face, and I realised I wasn't the only one affected. "But you're the one woman I can't get enough of." Now he cupped my cheek. "I wish the circumstances were different."

But they weren't, and no amount of wishing could change that.

"Yes," I whispered. "I'm still on the pill. How many more questions do you have?"

"Just one. Do you remember seeing Easton Baldwin that night? You were there when he had a fight in Addy's kitchen."

How could I have forgotten a freaking fight? "I don't. And don't ask me if I'd have spoken to him because the answer's 'not in a million years.'"

"I thought that's what you'd say. Give me two minutes to put the dog to bed. Do you want anything from downstairs?"

"Tonight, I don't want anything but you."

And he got me.

In more ways than I could count.

As his lips slid over my throat, the last rays of sun kissing my skin and the fragrance from the flowers mingling with his woodsy musk, I began to wonder what life would be like in Africa. Because if Luca was leaving Baldwin's Shore, I wasn't sure I wanted to stay.

Two weeks wasn't enough with Luca. A lifetime wasn't enough.

My skin burned as his caresses left a trail of fire in their wake, and I began to see the downsides of self-restraint. Why shouldn't I make like a cowgirl? I was about to straddle him when he got in first, lowering me until my back hit the grass. A little scratchy, but at least there were no bugs.

"Spread your legs, sweetheart."

"Aren't you the charming one tonight?"

"If by 'charming' you mean 'horny,' then absolutely." His eyes smouldered like active volcanoes. "These pants need to go because I'm gonna make you come before the sun goes down."

He seared me with one more kiss, then unbuttoned my jeans and worked them down my legs. My thighs fell open of their own accord as I craved what he offered. His fingers. His lips. His tongue and the filthy words that rolled off it. I grew slick under his touch, writhing on the blanket as sensation took over. He hadn't been kidding about the sunset part. Orange light bathed us as I arched off the floor, a backdrop for the fireworks that burst behind my eyelids.

"Luca," I gasped.

"Dreamed about you saying my name that way, sweetheart. Next time, you'll scream it."

He told no lies, and I rolled him onto his back. Leaned forward to kiss him again. Straddled him and lowered myself onto his bare cock with a long, drawn-out moan of pleasure. He felt so good. So right. So patient as he let me set the pace, building, building up to another orgasm. At the last moment, he flipped me and thrust his hips, pistoning until we crested at the same moment.

And yes, I gave him what he wanted.

"Luca," I cried.

This man was everything.

Everything.

Breathing heavy, he supported himself on his elbows and gazed down at me, a sheen of sweat gleaming in the dying light. This was what *I'd* dreamed of. Luca looking at me as if I was his world. But it was all getting a bit intense, so I gave his ass a squeeze and then giggled. Call it a defence mechanism.

"What?"

"You have Astroturf dimples on your butt cheeks."

"Occupational hazard." He reached out, plucked a purple flower, and tucked it behind my ear. "You're the most beautiful creature on earth, Brooke."

Difficult to believe, but one truth was certain.

I was his.

25

LUCA

The Fairbanks home was as painfully immaculate as I remembered. Vivid green lawns grew on either side of a brick path, and I stretched out a foot to see if they were made from plastic because they sure looked like it. Nope, real. Flowers grew in regimented height order, and bird feeders were arranged in a perfect square around a stone birdbath. Squawks came from nearby trees. Gerald Fairbanks must have spent hours tidying the yard, but I guess if I were married to Elmira, I'd have wanted to get out of the house too. If you looked up the word "henpecked" in the dictionary, his picture would be there, droopy around the jowls and miserable as fuck.

I raised my hand to knock, but Elmira must've seen me coming because the door swung open before my knuckles connected.

"Whatever you're selling, we don't want any."

"I'm actually here to see Lydia."

Elmira looked me up and down, and her mouth tightened into a pissy line. "You most certainly are not."

"Mom, Mom, it's okay." Feet thundered down the stairs,

and Lydia appeared. She'd gone for the casual look in a cotton-candy-pink velvet tracksuit with matching lips, eyes, and hair bow. Kind of like Barbie, if Barbie had the physique of Jupiter. "Luca called me. You remember Luca?"

Elmira turned that laser gaze on me again, and the prissiness twisted into a sneer.

"I thought you ran off with your tail between your legs."

Years of training at the hands of commanding officers whose egos were bigger than the chip on Elmira's shoulder meant the insult rolled off me.

"I was fighting for my country, ma'am."

"Why did you stop? Are you a quitter?"

"I moved into the private sector." My words were forced through gritted teeth and a smile that meant I wanted to snap her neck like a Christmas turkey's.

"What does that mean? The private sector? Are you part of one of those militias?"

"No, I—"

"Mom, please." Lydia giggled. "He's just here to ask a few questions about Addy's birthday party."

"Why? Did something happen? That doesn't surprise me in the least. Girls like her, they invite all the boys over and—"

"We can sit in the dining room." Lydia's tone took on a note of desperation. "Right, Mom?"

"Make sure he takes his boots off." Elmira glared at me again. "Are your feet clean?"

"Yes, ma'am. Freshly bleached this morning."

She didn't pick up on the sarcasm. "Good. Keep your hands off my daughter."

I'd saw them off at the wrists before I touched Lydia Fairbanks, but I bit back the truth and saluted instead. "Message received, ma'am. Loud and clear."

I was surprised she didn't pass out plastic booties like the ones cops wore at crime scenes, but having said her piece, Elmira backed away. Colt always said her bark was worse than her bite, but her bite was still fucking rabid. Next time, he could speak with Lydia.

I followed her ass into the dining room and took a seat while she fussed with pouring a glass of water I wouldn't drink. I didn't want to delay my escape by even a second.

"Isn't Addy the sweetest?" Lydia said. "Mom says she's trashy, but she always invites me to her parties, even though nobody else does."

Can't think why that might be. Sane people tended to stay off Elmira's radar, and that meant giving Lydia a wide berth too.

"Addy's got a heart of gold, all right."

"She went with a Mexican theme this year. There were piñatas and tacos and that beer with the lime in it. What questions did you want to ask? You were real vague on the phone."

"I'm more interested in last year's party."

"*Last* year's? But that was forever ago. You said this is something to do with the sheriff's office?"

"Yes, but Colt's trying to keep it quiet so the perp doesn't get tipped off."

"The *perp*? Oh my gosh! There was, like, a crime?"

Once again, I went through the stalker story, and I ended with another warning. "But you can't tell anyone. We want to catch this asshole, not scare him off temporarily so he can pop up again in the future."

He'd already proven he had patience. If he came after Brooke when I wasn't there...

"I won't say a word."

"Not even to your mom."

The guilty look said that had been exactly what Lydia planned to do. "But what am I gonna tell her? She'll want to know why you were here."

"Make something up. Say we're planning the theme for next year's party."

"Really? You think I'll get invited again?"

"If you keep your mouth shut, I'll make sure of it."

"I promise. I totally promise. But what is it that you want to know?"

"I heard you left at the same time Brooke went outside to get some air. Around ten p.m.? Nobody remembers seeing her after that."

"I did? I mean, yes, I left at ten—I have a curfew—but I don't remember seeing Brooke. Or really anything else." Lydia giggled. "I might have had some liquor, but not too much because..." She jerked her head toward the hallway. "You know. *Mom*."

Yeah, I remembered Elmira didn't much like alcohol either. Gerald probably kept his whisky in the shed—I didn't see how he could function without it.

"It would have been not long after Easton Baldwin got into a fight. Did you hear about that?"

"Oh, yes! The *fight*. Sure, sure, I heard the shouting. Easton's a jerk when he's sober, but when he's drunk? Whew."

"So let's walk through that scene. Where were you when you heard the shouting?"

"Uh, in the living room? Near the vestibule? I wasn't sure whether to go get help, but then someone said they were gonna call Parker, and I figured it was under control."

"You're certain about that? If he had to drive all the way from Baldwin's Shore, Easton would've had time for round two."

"Parker wasn't in Baldwin's Shore. He arrived, like, five minutes later. Oh, oh! I remember Brooke was there. She left the apartment, and she had a glass in her hand, which was kind of weird because it was Addy's glass and I didn't think we were meant to take them home with us."

"What made you think she was going home?"

"I… I can't remember."

"Was she wearing a coat? Did she say goodbye to anyone?"

"A coat. She was wearing a coat. A pretty blue coat. Bright blue, like the eye of a peacock feather. And… Yes!" Lydia beamed at me. "Now I recall—I saw her outside. At least, I think it was her. The guy with her was blocking my view, but I'm almost sure it was the same coat."

"A guy?" Anger crackled through my veins. Maybe a thrill too. From the chase. From what I'd do to that motherfucker when I got my hands on him. Not just *on* him, but around his damn throat. "Who was he?"

"I only saw him from behind. But Mom drove a ways up the road to turn the car around, and when we drove back, they were farther along the sidewalk. Like they were going to a vehicle? You really think he started stalking her? Because that's super freaky. What if it had been me?"

Yeah, no, that was unlikely. If a stalker showed up with a vase of flowers, Elmira would be lying in wait to give him a lecture on colour choices, probably with a shotgun at her side. He'd run a fucking mile. Though Lydia would've been grateful if he sent candy.

"Tell me everything you remember. What colour was the guy's hair? His skin?"

"Uh, dark hair? Like, brown, I think, not black. They passed under a street light and it seemed lighter on top, you know? And he was white."

"Was the hair long? Short?"

"Short at the sides, and maybe a little longer on top?"

"Good, that's good. How tall was he?"

"Taller than Brooke."

That wasn't difficult. "How much taller? My height?"

"No, shorter. And not so..." Lydia put her fists on her hips in a muscle pose. "Not so big. Just a regular guy. I really didn't pay much attention."

"Can you remember what he was wearing?"

Blonde curls bounced as Lydia shook her head. That hairstyle belonged on a kid, not a grown woman.

"Maybe a jacket? Jeans? Nothing special. I don't know."

"Was he carrying anything?"

She spread her hands, helpless. "It was a *year* ago, and I'd been drinking...well, I'm not certain exactly what it was, but there was a lot of it. Some cocktail."

"It's okay. You've been very helpful." And if she was right about the hair, it ruled out Easton Baldwin, which was almost disappointing. He wore his dirty-blond hair slicked back like a used-car salesman. What colour hair did Steve have? "Colt might want to speak to you later in the week."

"Oh, sure, I'm always available when I'm not at work."

Even as I jogged toward the gate, I could feel Elmira's gaze burning into the back of my head. Lydia was definitely Colt's problem now. I'd gotten everything I could.

And I also needed to spend time with Brooke. Six days left. Six nights. And then... Fuck knew what I was gonna do. My job had never looked less attractive, and the thought of moving to the other side of the world without my girl... Maybe I should talk to Aaron when he came back? Confess I had feelings for his sister, explain how much she meant to me. We could rewind, start dating the old-fashioned way. If I proved I wanted Brooke for more than sex—an admittedly foreign concept when it came to me and women—he might come around to the idea of the two of us being a couple.

When it came down to it, I didn't want to lose either of them.

I just wasn't sure I could have both.

26

BROOKE

I loved Addy, don't get me wrong, but tonight, I couldn't help wishing she were anywhere but Aaron's half-finished kitchen. When she'd invited herself over for dinner, complete with food from my favourite Italian restaurant in Coos Bay, I couldn't come up with an excuse fast enough to stop her. Telling the truth—that I wanted to spend the entire evening naked with Luca—obviously wasn't an option. Addy just wasn't great at keeping secrets. Oh, she tried, but they had a habit of slipping out of her mouth at the most inopportune moments.

So here we were. Fully clothed and getting ready to eat black truffle and pecorino triangoli—which seemed to be triangular ravioli rather than square—that she'd reheated in the microwave.

"Steve?" she said. "You really think it could have been *Steve*? I always thought he was a bit of an ass, but...wow. I'm surprised he showed up at the party at all. Sure, I invited him, but that was before you broke up, and then I forgot to uninvite him, and..." Addy's grip on the bottle of wine she was holding tightened until her knuckles turned white. "I'm gonna chop off his balls with a rusty knife."

"We don't know for sure it was him."

And we wouldn't find out more until Colt questioned him next week. His roommate said he'd gone away for the weekend. A boys' trip to Seattle, but he didn't know precisely where Steve was staying or when he'd be back, and Colt didn't want to call and give him enough time to concoct a story. The roommate had promised not to tip Steve off, and according to Colt, he didn't seem to have a high opinion of Steve either.

And Addy was right—why *had* Steve shown up at the party? He must have known I'd be there.

"Why didn't you tell me he was an ass?" I asked. "We dated for six months. It would've saved a whole bunch of trouble."

"Well, you seemed happy at the time. That was also why I kept my lips zipped about Dale."

"You didn't like Dale either?"

"Oh, please. If Dale was here, he'd be counting how many pieces of triangoli each person ate so he didn't pay more than his share. And don't forget frat-boy Cody."

"The thing with Cody wasn't serious. We only went out four times."

"Which was three and a half times too many. Brooke, he clipped his toenails in my living room." Addy finished pouring the wine and put an arm around my shoulders. "You're a real catch, but we have to face up to facts: you've got questionable taste in men."

Thanks, Addy. I wanted to sink through the floor because Luca was standing right *there*. I couldn't look at him. I didn't dare. And Addy wasn't wrong—apart from Luca, every man

I'd ever gotten involved with had either hurt me or shafted me or both. Or worse.

"I got unlucky, that's all."

"Naw, sweetie, there's a theme. Friends are always honest, right? And it's time to tackle this head-on. We need to fix your dating mojo so that once Steve gets arrested, you don't end up with another dud."

"Can we drop this? Luca's here, and dinner's getting cold."

"Hey, maybe Luca can help?" She turned to face him. "Can you give Brooke some tips on how not to fall for a womaniser like you?"

"Addy!"

"Hey, it's not as if he tries to hide it."

"Just fucking drop it," Luca practically growled.

"What's got your goat? I'm only trying to help here."

"Don't."

"But—" Addy looked from Luca to me, then back to Luca, and her eyes suddenly widened with understanding. "Ohmigosh. Ohmigosh, ohmigosh, ohmigosh! Are you two...? You are, aren't you? I totally didn't mean any of the stuff I just said. Uh, let me put the food on the table."

A string of curses slipped out as I hurried after her. "Addy, it's not like that."

"Like what?"

"We're not dating."

"I'm not stupid. I saw the way he looked at you right then."

"We're... Uh, it's complicated."

"Brooke's just using me for sex." Luca spoke from behind us, and if death were a painless option, I'd have taken it right then. "It's nothing. I'll be gone in a week." His voice hardened. "And Aaron *does not* need to know."

Addy blanched at his tone. Easy-going Luca was gone. "Right, absolutely. I won't say a word, I swear. You can count on me." She held up a hand, palm facing me. "But high-five, sweetie. That's a boss move."

I obliged because what else could I do? Inside, I felt sick. Luca's words had been so flat, so emotionless. *It's nothing.* Was that how he really felt? His actions of the past week said differently, but he sure had sounded convincing.

The food lost its appeal, and I picked at my pasta. Forced down a portion of tiramisu. When Addy hugged me at the end of the night and told me to, "Go jump Luca's bones," I managed a wan smile while I held back tears.

Five days left, and one of them had just been ruined.

ON TUESDAY MORNING, I was back to daydreaming. On Sunday, Luca had told me the three little words I needed to hear. No, not *those* words—"I love you" was a mere pipe dream—but, "You're *not* nothing." He'd followed up with, "You're everything," and then spent the rest of the day womanising me.

Monday was a little less intimate because Brady and Deck were back, so we had to wear clothes, but we got what would someday be my bedroom painted, and in the evening, our culinary tour of the world continued with a trip to India. Well, Little India. Luca picked out the restaurant and drove us north to Reedsport so we could eat dinner together at an actual table. And then he paid the check while I was in the bathroom even though we'd agreed to split it because he hadn't managed to ditch his "asshole" persona altogether.

Secretly, I kind of liked it.

But now we had two days left together, and I wished I'd

taken the day off because the Craft Cabin was quiet and Luca was waiting.

"Still thinking about your man, hun?" Darla asked.

"He's not my man. That's the whole problem. But yes."

"You like him, and he obviously likes you. That doesn't seem like such a big problem to me."

Who else did I have to confide in? Addy had her own notions about Luca, although I still didn't understand why he was branded a womaniser if he had a no-strings fling while I was a "boss" for doing the same. Paulo would run his mouth, and I didn't have any other close friends.

"I think this 'ten days' thing is going to be the death of me." I told Darla part of the truth—that I didn't want Luca to leave but couldn't ask him to stay, about Aaron coming back and his overprotectiveness. The fact that I'd been stupid to think I could wish my feelings away. "Whatever I do, somebody's going to get hurt."

"You want to know what I think?"

"Yes."

"I think you should stop trying so hard to make everyone else happy, because in the end, you'll only make yourself unhappy. Even if Luca's overseas for a while, a long-distance relationship isn't impossible."

"That doesn't help with the Aaron situation."

"Your brother might be more understanding than you think, if you break the news to him tactfully."

"Really?"

Darla had met Aaron once or twice, and unlike me, she was usually a good judge of character. Wise beyond her years, Nonna would have said.

"Introduce the idea slowly. Don't rub it in his face. I've seen how close you two are—above all, your brother's scared of losing you, and he's probably scared of losing Luca too if they're good friends. Make sure he knows he won't be pushed out."

"Three's such an awkward number."

Darla gave a heavy sigh. "Don't I know it."

Before I could ask what she meant, the bell over the door rang and two ladies from the local knitting circle ambled in.

"Why don't you take the rest of the afternoon off?" Darla asked. "I can manage here."

"Are you sure?"

"It's dead in town today, and we've already mailed out the online orders. Go. Enjoy your time with Luca."

Sometimes, dreams did come true.

AND SOMETIMES, nightmares did too.

I'd been home for five minutes when Brady walked in with a potted plant. A pink kalanchoe that matched the ones Luca had bought for me.

"Hey, Brooke. Looks like you have an admirer."

All my happiness drained through my feet and puddled out across the floor. I'd already spotted the envelope, but just in case, I glanced at Luca. He'd broken off his conversation with Deck when Brady walked in, and he gave his head a barely noticeable shake. No, he hadn't been responsible for the plant.

"Where did you get that?" he asked Brady.

"On the step outside. I almost tripped over it when I went to get more 3-core from my truck."

"Did you see who left it? A person? A vehicle?"

"Nah, I didn't see anybody." He glanced between us. Paused on my ashen face. "Why? Is there a problem?"

"Some motherfucker's been sending Brooke unwanted gifts. Put it down. Did you touch the note?"

"I don't think so." Brady dumped the pot at his feet, still puzzled, and understandably so after the efforts we'd made to keep him and Deck in the dark. My heart sank at the thought of having my dirty laundry aired in public. Luca had told me again and again that what happened wasn't my fault, Colt too, but I still kept thinking about the what-ifs. "It's just a plant."

"It's what the plant represents that's the problem. He's crossing boundaries."

"Boundaries?"

"I need to call Colt."

"The sheriff's department is involved?"

"Yeah. He might want to take your prints for elimination purposes."

"Well, sure, if you think it'll help."

It wouldn't. I was certain of that. There hadn't been any prints on the chocolate box or the note left on my car. The man who loved to torment me was careful. He either wore gloves or wiped everything down, and it was pointless wasting Colt's time. Before Luca could stop me, I grabbed the note and tore it open. Better to know than to wonder.

"Brooke, don't."

"It's addressed to me."

Of course, once I'd opened the card, I regretted it. The neat writing, the cupid's heart, the message, it all turned my stomach. Good thing I hadn't eaten dinner yet.

I'LL SEE YOU AGAIN SOON.

"Oh no," I whispered.

Luca snatched the card from me. "The hell he will. I'll be

sitting outside your bedroom door with a gun. Brady, we need cameras installed here, front and back. Same set-up as at Brooke's apartment."

"The same..." Realisation dawned on Brady. "He went there as well?"

"Yeah. He's stalking her."

Deck leaned in to read the card. "That's creepy as fuck. If you need someone to take shifts with you, I got a gun too."

"I can handle it. Brady, the cameras?"

"Ah, sure. I'm meant to finish here at the end of the week, but I can extend things by a few days. My next job doesn't start until the middle of May. Should I bill you or Aaron?"

"Me. Aaron doesn't know about this yet."

Deck goggled. "You didn't tell him?"

"Not yet. Brooke made a misguided attempt to avoid drama."

Aaaaaaaaand there was the asshole again.

"Hey, don't call me misguided. I just wanted Aaron to enjoy his vacation."

"And you did that by putting yourself in danger."

"You think she's in danger?" Deck asked.

"Yeah, I do."

"Uh, I also have a gun," Brady offered. "Out in my truck. You know, if you need any more help."

"I already said I have it handled where Brooke's concerned. Catching this asshole, that's the problem."

Brady backed away, hands in the air, and I had to concede that Luca looked a teensy bit scary at the moment. "Okay, man. I'll get those cameras ordered."

"Got any ideas who it might be?" Deck asked.

"Maybe. There's an ex of Brooke's who was around when all this started. Colt spoke to him today, and he denied everything, but he fits the description. Plus he's a freelance IT consultant so his schedule's flexible, and he doesn't have alibis for any of the incidents."

"So you have a description?"

"A vague one. White male with brown hair, between five-five and six feet, light to medium build."

"That doesn't narrow it down much. Hell, *I* fit that description, and so do half the men in town."

Luca shrugged. "It's all we have at the moment. Which is why we need the damn cameras."

"Okay, okay." Brady pulled out his phone. "I'll order what I need this afternoon."

But would it be enough? The freak was clearly watching me. He hadn't been back to my apartment since I moved out, and he knew I was at Deals on Wheels now. Like, right now. The timing wasn't a coincidence, I suddenly realised.

"He followed me from the Craft Cabin, didn't he? He knew I finished work early today. Did you see anyone behind us?"

Luca cursed under his breath. "No, but I wasn't checking for a tail. This sick bastard's always one damn step ahead."

I wished Deck and Brady would leave. I really, really needed one of Luca's hugs, but we were still under embargo.

"He's got to make a mistake soon. Right? The more people who are looking for him, the more chance he has of being spotted."

"We'll get him, sweetheart. Nobody can hide forever."

27

LUCA

After Brooke's shitty afternoon, I wanted to take her mind off the latest note, but she had her own ideas of how to do that. Which involved putting on a movie, not watching it, fidgeting, getting up, walking to the bedroom, coming back with a pillow for her knees, and sucking my cock.

I wasn't gonna complain, and I fully intended to repay the favour once she'd finished.

Twofold.

She paused to take a sip of wine, and I took a moment to study her. To burn her features into my memory. The flushed cheeks. The tumbling waterfall of hair. Those twinkling brown eyes. The open shirt hanging from her shoulders. The full breasts straining at a bra I'd be removing pretty damn soon. Who the hell knew if or when I'd get to see her like that again after this week?

"Two fucking days."

I must have said it out loud because she shifted her gaze to mine, slightly unfocused thanks to the bottle of white she'd drunk most of.

"Please don't remind me." Brooke put the glass down and shifted her hands to my knees, raising herself to plant a row of feather-soft kisses on my chest. "I don't want to think of the future, just us here, now." She traced a finger over my tattoo. "Why do you have a clock on your shoulder?"

"A long and painful story." And I didn't mean from the needle. "Do you want to hear it?"

"Only if you want to tell it."

I didn't, not really, but I also didn't want to hold back from Brooke. The tattoo was part of who I was. Who I'd become.

"You remember I told you about Nathan?"

She pinched her lips together, thinking. "Your friend who died?"

I nodded. "We called him Worm, as in 'bookworm,' because no matter where we went, he always had some massive fucking brick of a novel with him. And after about a year, he started carrying a notepad too. He'd stay up at night, scribbling away, even when we were exhausted, and when I asked him why, he'd say he just needed to get the words out. That life was short and he might not get the chance otherwise."

"What was he writing? A journal?"

"Nah, his own novel. Eventually, he let me start reading it, and it was pretty damn good."

"What was it about? War?"

"Victorian sci-fi. Steampunk. The tattoo came from one of his illustrations. I wanted the clock as a reminder not to waste time on unimportant things." And he'd died at ten past six. The compass pointing west? That was for Brooke, my girl on the West Coast, but I didn't want her to realise the depth of my obsession so I kept quiet about that part. "And speaking of not wasting time..."

I pointed at my cock and raised an eyebrow, and Brooke's giggle was a relief in more ways than one. Nathan had never finished his book, and he never would. Talking about him hurt. People thought special forces operators were tough motherfuckers, but we still bled the same as everyone else.

Brooke squeezed my hand. "Thank you for telling me the story."

And then she got back to work.

Damn, this woman was everything. *My* everything. I wanted to tell her that. To tell her that I was in love with her, that I wouldn't, *couldn't*, leave her. The words balanced on the tip of my tongue. Maybe I'd blurt them out when I came. When I lost my damn mind again. Now wasn't the right time, but when was? Nathan was right about—

The overhead lights blinked on.

Vega started barking as I dove for the gun I'd left on the box we were using as a side table, and Brooke screamed. Adrenaline kicked in, but adrenaline could only do so much when my fucking pants were around my ankles. I got the gun. Blinked in the glare as my vision adjusted. Aimed at the figure walking toward us and shoved Brooke onto the floor.

"What. The. Ashuuul. Fuck?" Aaron slurred.

Brooke screamed again, but this time in horror rather than fear, and the bottom and sides slowly fell out of the world I'd tried so hard to protect.

There was no way to fix this. No way to hide what we'd been doing. My rapidly deflating dick was hanging out, Brooke was half-naked, and we both looked guilty as hell. I dropped the gun, got my pants buttoned. Helped Brooke up as she shoved her arms into her shirt. Steeled myself for what was to come.

"I-I-I thought you were in Cabo," Brooke stuttered.

Aaron ignored her. "What the hell were you doing with my sister?"

He might not have been able to walk straight, but his voice had turned low and dangerous. I couldn't blame him. If I'd walked in on him doing with Romi what I'd been doing with Brooke, I'd be getting arrested right about now.

"Shit, buddy, I'm sorry."

"Buddy? Don't you fucking call me buddy."

"Aaron, Luca hasn't done anything wrong. Are you drunk?"

"Not so drunk I can't fucking see." Aaron took a step forward, clutched at the counter for support. "Get away from her."

I took a step sideways, but Brooke followed. I gave my head a surreptitious shake. "Brooke, don't."

"But—"

"Don't."

Fuck, now she looked hurt. But having her take my side in this would only inflame the situation. Emotions were fuelling Aaron right now. And I knew him—he needed to get his anger out before he'd calm down.

Brooke put her hands on her hips, then quickly thought the better of it when her shirt gaped open. I had a vague memory of ripping the buttons off.

A million times fuck.

"Aaron, we're two consenting adults."

He snorted. "Consenting? Luca doesn't have to worry about consent. He whispers shit in Spanish, flexes, and women's panties fall off. It's like a damn magic trick."

"That's... That's not how it was."

Aaron's gaze cut to the bottle of wine on the box. "He got you drunk instead?"

"No! Well, maybe just a little, but—"

"He's a player, Brooke. You think I don't know his game? In New York, he went through a woman a night, sometimes two. I'm not gonna stand by and watch him hurt you." Aaron staggered forward, squared up to me. "You're an asshole. We made a pact."

"A woman *every* night?" Brooke asked. "What pact?"

Perhaps I should've heard the irritation in her voice, but I never had been too good at listening. And this was between me and Aaron.

"I know we had a pact, but I can't say I'm sorry for breaking it. Not when I wouldn't mean it. I care about Brooke too much to minimise everything between us with a fake apology."

"Spare me the bull, bro. Brooke's worth more than a one-night stand."

"It wasn't just one night," she told him, snippy now.

Wrong thing to say.

I'd been half expecting the punch, and alcohol sapped its power, but it still stung like a bitch. I worked my jaw, testing. Nothing felt broken.

"You done?" I asked.

"I'm just getting started."

"I'm not fighting you."

Aaron shrugged. "Suit yourself."

This time, he got me in the stomach, but I'd tensed my abs first, so the blow hurt him more than it hurt me.

"Stop!" Brooke shrieked.

"Chill, sweetheart. We'll sort this out our way. Just stay back."

I dodged a jab, blocked Aaron's cross, but he got me with an uppercut. My head snapped back. Seemed those boxing lessons Colt said he'd been taking were paying off. I tasted blood, but I didn't have time to work out where it was coming from before he swung his fist again. I considered taking him down, could have done it in a second, but he needed this. And hell, I probably deserved it. If a few punches sapped Aaron's fury, transferred some of my guilt to him, then I'd take the beating. I'd had worse. In many ways, my father had prepared me well for life, and sparring in the army gym had only built on those lessons.

And besides, I had a bigger problem. What the hell was I going to do about my future with Brooke?

28

BROOKE

I'd once said my goal in life was to learn the right lessons, but sometimes it seemed I'd learned nothing at all. How had everything gone so wrong?

My fingers trembled as I dialled Colt. I didn't know what else to do. My stupid drunk brother had lost his mind, and so had Luca.

"Brooke? It's nearly ten p.m."

"You need to come. Quickly."

The sleepiness in his voice vanished. "What's happened? The stalker? Is he...?"

"No, it's Aaron. He's trying to kill Luca, and Luca's just letting him."

"Huh? Aaron's in Cabo."

"He's here!" The tears fell, and I couldn't stop them.

"Why's he trying to kill Luca? You're not making any sense."

There'd be two of us dead soon—Luca from Aaron's punches and me from embarrassment.

"I was... We were... I was giving Luca a blow job, okay? And Aaron walked in on us. And now he's furious."

"Whoa. I mean, sheesh."

"P-p-please, just come."

"Kiki's asleep. I'll need to— Shit, I'll be there, okay?"

How had I forgotten about Kiki? If Colt had to find a sitter, Luca would be hospitalised before he showed up. I had to stop Aaron and Luca myself. But how? The pair of them were like two dogs battling to become pack leader, snapping and dancing around each other. Hmm... Dogs... When I was a kid, next door's dachshunds had gotten into a fight in our yard, and Nonna had turned the water hose on them. I didn't have a hose, but Vega had his water in a bucket because I'd taken his bowl to the Craft Cabin, and it was almost full. Anger burning, I heaved it up and threw the whole damn lot over the two idiots.

"Enough!"

They turned to face me, dripping, rivulets of blood running from Luca's nose.

"What the hell are you doing?" I yelled. "Competing to see who's the biggest asshole? Because let me tell you, it's a tie. Are you happy now?"

"Brooke..." Aaron started, flexing his fingers and wincing as he did so. His knuckles were bruised. Good. "Somebody needs to defend your honour."

"Defend my honour? What do you think this is? The eighteenth century? Are you gonna invite Luca outside for a duel next?"

"I care about you."

"If you cared, you'd listen to me." Aaron opened his mouth. Thought the better of that idea and closed it again. "Anything I do with Luca is my business, not yours."

"You're in my apartment. That's my business."

Dammit, I couldn't argue with his logic. "Why are you even here? I thought you were in Cabo until Thursday."

Luca was meant to be picking him up at the airport. I'd seen the flight schedule.

"Yeah, well, I was gonna be until I worked out Clarissa was cheating on me. The beach didn't hold the same appeal after that, so I dumped her ass on the street and flew home."

Clarissa cheated on my brother? That little bitch! I'd rip out her damn highlights by the roots, then I'd scratch out her eyeballs and... No. No, I wouldn't because then I'd be the one getting the bucket of water tossed over me. *Breathe, Brooke.*

"You're sure? I mean, how did you find out?"

"Saw the messages between her and the other guy. She didn't even try to deny it."

"I'm so sorry." I actually wasn't because I didn't like Clarissa, but Aaron didn't deserve the heartache. Okay, maybe he did after the little stunt he just pulled with Luca, but... "You left her in Cabo?"

"Figured she's somebody else's problem now. At least I hadn't given her the ring yet."

"The ring?"

Behind him, Luca grimaced. Yes, that had been a close call. Because if Aaron had married Clarissa, then I'd have had to endure being in bridezilla's wedding party, and probably it was frowned upon for a bridesmaid to stick up her hand when the priest asked if anybody objected.

"It wasn't Mom's ring, if that's what you're wondering. I saved that for you."

Those darn tears came back. How could my brother be so sweet and such an absolute dumbass at the same time? Not that I'd be getting married anytime soon—Luca didn't seem like the marrying kind, and I wasn't even sure where we stood now. He was supposed to be leaving in two days, and he'd be taking my heart with him. Although I couldn't deny my brother's words had cut me. Yes, I'd always known that Luca had played the field, but a different woman every single night?

"Uh, thanks?"

"There any wine left in that bottle?"

"I don't think so."

Aaron scrubbed both hands over his face. "Shit. I need a fucking drink."

"Not sure that's a good idea, buddy," Luca said.

"You being here, that's not a good idea. Just get out of my apartment."

Luca looked at me, and I looked at Luca. I needed him here.

"Can't do that," he said.

Aaron bristled again. "The hell you can't."

"You think I want to stick around to be used as a punching bag? I don't, but Brooke's been having some issues, and you're not in a fit state to protect her."

"Issues?" Aaron huffed. "*You're* the issue."

"I've got a freaking stalker, you jerk."

"What?" It took a moment for the words to fully penetrate Aaron's thick skull. "What stalker? Since when?"

"Since a year ago."

"A year ago? Then why didn't you tell me?"

This was exactly how I hadn't wanted to have the discussion about my assault with Aaron. He'd already been hurt by what he saw as Luca's betrayal tonight, and by Clarissa, and now I was going to twist the knife.

But before I could arrange my thoughts, someone hammered on the door. Luca's gun was in his hand before I could blink.

"Put it down! I think it's Colt."

"Colt? What's he doing here?"

"I called him while you were fighting." Which I now regretted doing. "I'd better let him in."

"Stay there. I'll go."

I slumped onto the couch, my beautiful couch, now damp and spattered with Luca's blood. Though long-term happiness was out of reach, half an hour ago, I'd been happy in the moment. Now, that moment had fast-forwarded me straight to hell. Aaron was upset, Luca was putting definite distance between us, and when Colt walked in, he couldn't even meet my eyes.

"The fight's over? Brooke, you okay?"

"Define 'okay.'"

"Nothing's broken?"

Apart from my heart and my spirit? "No, nothing's broken. I'm sorry I brought you into the middle of this."

"Not a problem." He patted me awkwardly on the shoulder, then straightened. "If I go home, is there gonna be any more trouble?"

Luca shook his head. At least the blood had stopped running now, leaving a dark red crust over his top lip and most of his chin.

"Reckon we're done with our fists. But now we have the other problem to deal with."

"The other problem?"

"Brooke's problem."

"Ah."

Aaron's attention swung between them. "Wait, Colt knows about this too? Am I the only person who doesn't?"

"I didn't find out until last week," Colt said. "After you left for Cabo. How was the vacation?" I shook my head hurriedly, and Colt got the message. "Eh, never mind. So, getting back to Brooke's problem, I can understand why she kept it to herself for so long. Statistically, only around thirty percent of rape cases *are* reported to the authorities, and—"

All the colour drained out of Aaron's face. "Are you... Are you telling me Brooke was *raped*?"

Colt took a couple of steps backward. "I thought..."

"We hadn't got that far," Luca said.

"Well, shit."

Someone had to control the narrative here, and it was *my* story. "It happened after Addy's birthday party last year. I drank a few glasses of wine, and maybe my drink got spiked too because I barely remember a thing. But I had sex with somebody, and I sure as heck didn't consent to it."

"You should have—"

"I didn't report it because everything was jumbled in my mind and I had no idea who did it. I still don't know for sure."

"You don't know for sure? But you have an idea?"

"I—"

"No," Luca said firmly. "We still don't know."

He was right to say that, of course. Telling my hot-headed brother that it might have been Steve would only lead to Steve in the emergency room and Aaron in a jail cell. And although Steve was a grade-A prick, I had to abide by the innocent-until-proven-guilty principle. So did Aaron, seeing as he was a freaking lawyer, but he wasn't thinking straight at the moment.

"And the fucker's leaving Brooke notes, including one that showed up here earlier, hand-delivered. Which is why she needs somebody around who can protect her."

"I can do that."

"You've been drinking."

"Well, you weren't exactly alert earlier."

"I'd still have shot him between the eyes if he'd shown up."

"Hey, hey, relax," Colt said. "I'll stay here with Brooke tonight. I can sleep on the couch."

"What about Kiki?" I asked.

"I dropped her off at the Snyders' on the way, and I'm not gonna wake her up again tonight."

Neither Luca nor Aaron seemed particularly happy with the idea, and quite honestly, I wasn't either, but I wasn't going to fan the flames by suggesting I stay at my apartment with Luca. Colt's offer was a kind one, and at this moment in time, it was the best arrangement for everyone.

"Then I'll find you a blanket." I managed a smile. "Thank you."

THE BED FELT cold and empty when I woke in the morning. Funny how quickly I'd grown used to having Luca beside me, and now I didn't even know where he was. Last night, I'd tried to give him the key to my apartment, but he'd declined, saying that if he stayed there, it would only add kindling to Aaron's fire, and he didn't want to bring the Crowes into our mess either. Then he'd packed his bag and walked out.

I'd cried, I'm not ashamed to admit that. Inside, I was hollow, but now I had to go to work and act as if nothing had happened. I rolled over, checked my phone for messages. Nothing. Should I send one of my own? What if Luca had gone for good? He had nothing keeping him here and every reason to leave.

Me: Are you okay? xxx

I wasn't asking for much, just a little reassurance, but

Luca still hadn't replied by the time I'd showered and dressed. The apartment smelled of synthetic lemon when I emerged from the bedroom, and I found Colt on his knees, scrubbing bloodstains from the couch.

"You don't have to do that."

"Thought you might need a hand."

"I'm so sorry about last night."

"Nothing to apologise for. You and Luca, eh?"

"Yeah." I felt myself blush. "Is that crazy?"

"Maybe. I always figured he had a thing for you. Didn't say anything to Aaron, obviously." Colt shrugged. "The heart wants what the heart wants. I made you a coffee, over there on the counter."

"Thanks." My heart might have known what it wanted, but my head had to be realistic. Luca had agreed to two weeks, and it had ended in a disaster. "Don't you need to take Kiki to school?"

"Meli Snyder offered. She has to take Sophie anyway." Colt glanced toward the back door. "Didn't know what state your brother would be in."

"He's still asleep?"

"I'd assume so."

"That's probably for the best."

"I'll give you a ride to work when you're ready."

"It's okay; I can take my car. Otherwise I won't be able to get home."

"After last night's conversation, Aaron'll want to pick you up."

"Well, I'm not sure I want Aaron to pick me up."

Colt sighed. "Look, I promised Luca I'd drive you, okay? He cares."

"Then why did he—"

"We both understand he had to. In high school, everyone said Luca was the volatile one, but…"

"He's gotten calmer and Aaron's gone the other way?"

"Aaron's like ice in court, but maybe bottling all that emotion up isn't so good for him? And Clarissa… Can't say I was her biggest fan, but there are ways to end it, and then there are *ways*. Any idea who the other guy was?"

"Not a clue. I didn't much care for her either, so we didn't hang out."

"Your brother's gonna need your support."

"Yes, I know, but is it wrong that I'm more worried about Luca right now? The last thing I wanted was to ruin their friendship."

"Luca knew what he was getting into. Give Aaron a week, and he'll most likely cool off."

"A week? I told you what he walked in on."

"Okay, maybe a month. Once he's had time to think things through, he'll realise he doesn't want to lose you or Luca either."

I hoped beyond hope that Colt was right. And in the meantime, I'd just have to be damn careful. Until Aaron came to his senses over Luca, I'd go nowhere alone until my stalker was caught. Aaron would look out for me, of that I was certain, and he'd also put pressure on the sheriff's department in Coos Bay to do more, but when it came to having a bodyguard, I preferred Luca's brand of close protection.

29

BROOKE

Darla took one look at me when I walked into work and opened her arms for a hug. Today's muumuu was green with pink flowers, but the bright colours did little to cheer me up.

"What happened, hun? You look as if your dog just died."

"Vega's fine." Deck was probably feeding him potato chips and sliced ham by now. "But everything with Luca went wrong. It was h-h-horrible. Aaron came back early from his trip and walked in on us, and there was a fight, and b-b-blood, and now Luca's gone."

"Oh, shoot." Darla's eyes saucered. "That's a lot to unravel. Who won the fight?"

"Aaron, but only because Luca didn't hit back. And I want to be mad at Aaron, but I can't even do that because we were in his apartment and I was in quite a, uh, compromising position, so he had every right to be upset, and also he just broke up with his girlfriend, and he'd been drinking and...and..."

Darla's arms tightened, and I cried onto her freaking

shoulder. For the briefest of moments, I was actually grateful to my stalker because if it weren't for him, I'd still have been working as an executive assistant, and my old boss would probably have had HR write me up for acting unprofessional.

"Are you looking for advice, or do you just want to unload?" Darla asked.

"I don't know. I don't know anything anymore. I guess advice? Honestly, I've never been in this situation."

"Have you spoken to Luca today?"

"I sent him a message, but he hasn't replied."

"Why don't you try calling him?"

"I... I... I suppose I'm scared."

"Why are you scared? Because the stalker guy's still around? Was it him who left the note on your car? You seemed pretty freaked out when Colt and Luca were here."

A laugh burst out of me. "Honestly? I've barely given him a thought since yesterday afternoon. But yes, he sent me a plant and another note. Left it outside Deals on Wheels. So I guess I should be worried, but what terrifies me is that I'll never see Luca again."

"So call him. Right now, you're scared of something that might never happen."

"But what if it does?"

"Once you have actual facts, you can react accordingly. Bury your head in the sand for long enough, and you'll suffocate."

What Darla said made so much sense, but there was a part of me that wanted to put off speaking with Luca. Because if he was going to devastate me, I didn't want to find out. Suffocation might even be preferable.

But Darla was still staring at me.

And deep down, I knew she was right.

Time to put my big-girl panties on.

The phone rang once, twice, and then Luca picked up. At least it hadn't gone to voicemail. I moved to the corner of the store to get some privacy and prayed.

"Hey."

Just the sound of his voice made my knees go weak. "Are you okay?"

"Shouldn't that be my question?"

"You were the one bleeding."

"Yeah."

One word. That was it. The silence stretched so long that I couldn't take it anymore.

"Are we over?" I blurted.

"Fuck, no." Then a note of caution entered Luca's voice. "Unless you want us to be?"

"Oh, thank goodness. I got so worried, and you didn't answer my message, and..."

"Because I wanted to speak to you in person. I don't do well with trying to put this shit into writing."

"Where are you?"

"In the forest behind the picnic ground."

That was practically next door. Well, three buildings away. The Craft Cabin was next to Annie's Hair and Beauty, which was next to Mary's Coffee House, and on the other side of the coffee house was an empty lot that had once been a bait and tackle store, but it had burned down when I was in elementary school and nobody ever rebuilt. Grass and bushes had taken over now, and Mart and Mary who owned the coffee house had set out picnic tables so their patrons could sit outside when the weather was good.

But why was Luca there?

Then it hit me, and my chest seized.

"Oh my goodness, you slept outside last night? Aren't

you freezing?"

The weather had turned unseasonably cold, and rain had been falling since I woke up. The thought of Luca hunkering under a bush made me angry at Aaron all over again.

Luca's laughter was unexpected. "Outside? Nah, I got a bed at the Peninsula."

"The Peninsula?"

"Figured I deserved room service after the shit Aaron pulled. The receptionist got snooty about the blood, but then that Belinsky guy showed up and bought me a drink."

"Then why are you in the forest?"

"I'm waiting for Asa Phillips to finish his cigarette and get off the phone so I can come see you. He's standing under the awning outside the coffee house."

Since Asa would be going from the coffee house to work with Aaron, that was a smart idea. "I'll sneak out to the parking lot for a few minutes. Darla won't mind."

"Don't leave the building until I get there."

"Okay, I won't. I promise."

"Five minutes, sweetheart." A pause. "I missed you last night."

"Missed you too."

I must have been smiling when I put the phone down because Darla had an "I told you so" look on her face.

"Good news?" she asked.

"He's here. Well, not *here*, here, but outside. Can I take a short break? I know I just arrived, but I'll make up the time over lunch."

"No problem, hun. Use the back room if you want. I'll hold the fort out here." She tilted her chin toward her laptop screen. "We had nearly fifty orders overnight, but most of them are straightforward."

On impulse, I flung my arms around Darla again. She'd proven to be a good friend through all of this. And thank goodness I was working with Darla and not Paulo today. Paulo would be either digging for details on the *exact* circumstances of the argument because gossip could never be juicy enough for him, or on his way to Deals on Wheels to berate Aaron for ruining Luca's good looks.

Five minutes passed before Luca knocked softly on the back door. I let him in and then locked it behind him again. Safety first. He'd drilled me well.

"It's so good—" I started, then gasped as he flipped his hood back. His nose was swollen, both eyes bruised. One of them was bloodshot, and although I wanted to kiss him, I didn't dare because the left side of his lip was scabbed over where Aaron had split it. "My gosh. You look... You look... Do you need to go to the hospital?"

"Nah. I've been better, but I've also been worse. I put some ice on my nose once I got to the hotel last night. The swelling's gone down now." He spread his arms, and I walked into the hug. Almost cried again, but this time with relief. "Go easy. I don't think my ribs are broken, but they sure are bruised."

"Why did you let Aaron do this? Why?"

"He needed to get it out of his system."

"But—"

"Shh. It's done. If I'd seen Romi in the position you were in last night, I'd have lost it too."

I laid my head against his shoulder, careful not to press too hard. While I might not have agreed with their methods, I guess I could understand why they'd gone at it. When they were teenagers, they'd let their fists do the talking, Luca more than anyone.

"We lost our last two days," I said, breathing him in.

He'd showered this morning. Whatever shampoo they gave out at the Peninsula, it smelled nice. Lime and mandarin and something sweet. Honey, perhaps.

"We'll have plenty more days."

"How? You're leaving."

"I'm not leaving."

I raised my eyes to his. "You're not?"

Luca pressed his lips against my forehead. "I can't. Not when you're here."

"But Aaron—"

"Will get used to the idea."

"What if he doesn't?"

Luca sucked in a breath, then winced. I winced with him.

"We'll have to cross that bridge when we come to it. I only know we have to try."

"What Aaron said about other women..."

"Maybe I did get crazy in New York. Back then, I was spending most of the year in the damn desert, and the only attention my dick got was from my hand. So when we went out to bars and women started throwing themselves at me, yeah, I let them. But none of them were you. That's why I was never interested in more than one night. Brooke, I love you. And I can't just go back to Africa and act as if the last month didn't happen."

"You...you love me?"

"Always have, always will. Fuck, why are you crying? I thought women liked that stuff?"

"We do. We definitely do." I didn't know which parts of him were safe to touch, so I had to settle for kissing him on the cheek. "I've been in love with you forever."

"Then we've got most of what we need. The rest is just logistics."

He was right. Love was the foundation. We could build on it over time, and it would only get stronger.

"Where do we go from here?"

"Figure the next couple of months are gonna be tough, but we'll get through them. Let Aaron do the brother thing. Don't push him away. Once he realises I'm not competition, that there's room in your life for both of us, he'll come around. And while we're waiting for him to do that, we'll catch that motherfucker who hurt you."

"How?"

"I already called Colt. We plan to start by keeping an eye on Steve. He's the best candidate right now, and either we'll catch him or we'll rule him out."

"Be careful."

"I'm—" Luca gave a wry laugh. "I was about to say I'm always careful, but after last night... Maybe in twenty years, we'll be able to see the funny side."

"I hope so."

"In the meantime, you need to watch your back. Stay at Deals on Wheels and make sure Aaron sleeps outside your door. Get him to drive you to work, and if you need to go anywhere else, make sure Aaron or Colt goes with you. This fucker's out there, watching. Waiting. And if he puts his hands on you again, I'm gonna do jail time."

"I promise I won't go anywhere alone."

Luca's expression softened. "Good. I'll call you later, okay? How do you feel about phone sex?"

"Addy always says I should try new things."

"Remind me to thank her." Luca cupped my cheeks in his hands and pressed his lips to mine. "Stay safe, Brooke. I love you."

This time when I walked into the store, I was grinning like an idiot.

30

BROOKE

It would take time, Luca had said.

So far, Aaron hadn't mentioned last night once, but he was trying hard to be nice to me. After he picked me up from work, he'd driven us to North Bend to collect dinner from La Cantina because he knew it was my favourite, but all that did was remind me of Mexican night with Luca.

"Did you go to the office today?" I asked as we spread the food out over the workbench. Yes, I still wanted to kick Aaron in the shins, but I forced myself to see the bigger picture and stick to Luca's game plan. Aaron actually looked as bad as Luca, although not quite so bruised. The dark circles around Aaron's eyes came from exhaustion rather than fists, and his hangover hadn't been kind either.

"For a couple of hours. Asa told me to go home and get some sleep."

"And did you?"

"Not really."

I sank onto the couch, trying to block out the bad

memories. Colt had done a good job on the bloodstains, so at least I didn't have those staring me in the face.

"Maybe if you took a pill? Or drank some of that herbal tea?"

"Can't. Colt said I needed to stay alert. Damn, Brooke, why didn't you tell me?"

"We already went through that."

"Yeah, I know." Aaron gave a heavy sigh. "I know. I hate that you've been dealing with this alone for so long."

"If I'd thought it would turn out like this, I'd have said something. But I wrote off that night as a moment of gross stupidity, swore I'd never put myself in that position again, and tried to push it to the back of my mind. Reporting it to the police would have meant rehashing it over and over, and I just wanted to forget. And it's not as if they'd have caught the person. They *still* can't catch him, and he's been following me all over town."

"Then they'll have to try harder. I called the sheriff earlier, and he's promised to assign more manpower to the case. They're going to start checking out people on the local sex offenders' register and look into similar crimes. Colt said he'd be surprised if it was the first time the guy's done this."

I shuddered at the thought. Had other girls suffered the way I was suffering? Did they feel that prickle of fear every time they stepped into a social situation? Had they changed their habits to ensure they didn't have to travel home alone at night? Did they have the nightmares? The low-level anxiety that never quite dissipated?

I wanted to tell Aaron that Luca had been helping too. That he'd kept me safe and made my living arrangements more secure. But now wasn't the time, so I kept my mouth shut.

"Thanks. How are you holding up? After Clarissa, I mean."

A shrug. "She says she's sorry, that it didn't mean anything."

"You spoke to her?"

"She called me."

"Do you know who the guy was?"

"Someone she works with. Now I realise why she spent so many late nights at the office."

"Wow, that really sucks. Want me to make you a voodoo Clarissa doll? I have plenty of pins."

"Tempting." Aaron managed a half-smile. "What stings is that I honestly thought we were good together. We both had our careers, and she didn't mind when I got caught up in a case. She was smart. We liked the same food, the same music, the same shows. She was great in— Never mind. You don't need to know that."

No, I definitely didn't.

"You might have had the same taste in TV, but you had different values. She cheated, and you stayed faithful."

Aaron's phone screen lit up, and he groaned.

"Is that her?"

"The third text this evening."

"Why don't you block her?"

"Because... I don't know. I just don't think I'm ready to do that yet."

"Why?" Surely he couldn't mean...? "You're not thinking of taking her back, are you?"

Silence.

"Aaron, no."

"She said it only happened twice."

"Twice. So she couldn't even claim it was a drunken one-off. And she was messaging with him while you were on vacation." He moved to pick up the phone, but I snatched it away. "Forget it. Forget her."

"I'm not sure I can."

"You want to hear the truth? I don't like Clarissa. I never liked Clarissa." Since he'd been brutally honest about Luca last night, I figured I'd return the favour. "She's smug and annoying and she thinks she's better than everyone else."

Aaron's eyes widened. "What? But I always thought you got along okay?"

"Well, now you know that we didn't." I tucked the phone down the side of the couch cushion, out of reach. Away from temptation. Not just Aaron's but mine too. Good thing I wasn't drinking tonight, or I might have been tempted to tell the witch what I really thought of her. "You want more guacamole?"

I hoped Aaron's weighty sigh might signify the release of Clarissa's hold over him. She didn't deserve to stand on the pedestal he'd put her on.

"A man can never have too much guac."

"AARON FOUND OUT ABOUT LUCA? Holy shit! I didn't say anything, I swear."

"Yes, I know that." I tried to keep things vague for Addy, but she filled in the gaps all by herself and dissolved into laughter. "It's not funny."

"You're telling me you had Luca's disco stick in your freaking mouth, and your brother walked in? That's, like, one of those stories you read on the internet and think 'no way, never happened.' Was it big? It was enormous, right?"

"Addy!"

"Sorry. I mean, no wonder Aaron went bananas. He

must've had a *really* bad day. Clarissa's such a bitch. Like, she probably barks at fleas in her sleep."

"A total bitch. But I'm worried that Aaron's not quite as over her as we'd like him to be. She told him she made a mistake—twice—but it'll never happen again."

"Yeah, right. A dog doesn't change its spots."

"I think that's actually a leopard."

"Whatever. Dogs have spots too. Brooke, we have to fix this. Aaron deserves better."

"Agreed."

"So you have to stop him from giving in to her tail-wagging while I do some investigation."

"Uh, what?"

"I know where she works. I have friends. Ergo, I can find out whether it really was a two-off. I bet you a pitcher of margaritas that it was more like a ten-off."

"I'm not allowed a pitcher of margaritas at the moment."

"Fine, you can have a glass. I hear Applejack's has started serving the *best* margaritas. Let's catch up for a progress meeting next week."

"I'm not allowed to go to Applejack's either."

"No, you're not allowed to go to Applejack's alone, and you won't be. I'll be there. Hell, bring Aaron too. We can tell him all Clarissa's dirty little secrets and hook him up with a new girl at the same time. What's the name of that girl who bought the bar?"

"Taya?"

"She's pretty. And he likes the strong, independent type."

"I don't even know if she's single."

"C'mon, it'll be fun."

"I'm not sure..."

"You don't need to be sure. *I'm* sure. Next Wednesday—save the date."

Dinner promised to be a disaster, but Addy was a force of nature. Arguing with a tornado would be easier. And I had to admit that asking around about Clarissa wasn't a terrible idea. Like Addy, I didn't believe it was the fleeting affair she claimed either, and I definitely didn't want her as a sister-in-law. If Aaron was hesitant to cut her out of his life, then it was my sisterly duty to help by handing him the knife.

"Fine, Wednesday. But I'm not getting drunk."

"Let's settle for tipsy."

"Addy..."

"Enjoy your dirty phone sex with Luca."

"Wait, how did you know...?"

"Just a lucky guess. Toodles!"

31

LUCA

"You're still here?" Nico Belinsky slid onto the next bar stool, still wearing a tie at eight o'clock in the evening.

"I needed somewhere to stay for a few weeks, and this seemed like as good a place as any. Nice gym, by the way."

That was an understatement. In my experience, most hotel gyms consisted of a treadmill and an exercise bike slung into a dusty corner with one of those "jack of all trades, master of none" weight machines if you were lucky. The gym at the Peninsula was an athlete's paradise. I'd spent an hour lifting free weights this morning and then gone for a swim in a pool actually big enough to do laps in.

The rates weren't cheap, but I'd thought "fuck it" and booked a room for three weeks anyway. I wanted to stay close to Brooke, and my years living in CHUs and tents and shitty cabins had let me build up my bank balance. I'd have to find a job in the next few months, but I wasn't in any burning hurry.

"Thanks. I drew up the specifications myself. Drink?"

"Not gonna say no if you're buying."

Belinsky signalled the bartender. "Two vodkas, Jeanette. The Beluga."

I'd never drunk vodka without a mixer before, but Jeanette poured it out neat into gold-rimmed shot glasses. Good thing Kiki had a sleepover tonight. Colt had offered to take the evening surveillance shift since I'd been following Steve for the previous four days and we didn't want him to get too familiar with my face. Last night, he'd gone to a strip club. Phoebe Gilmore was right about his character—the asshole was a lousy tipper and a real sleaze—but so far, he hadn't shown any signs of interest in Brooke. Then again, she hadn't received any more notes since Colt had spoken to him, so maybe he'd just backed off until the heat died down? I only hoped this didn't drag on. Brooke deserved to get her life back, and I didn't want to spend another year looking over our shoulders.

"Cheers."

I'd been about to knock back the vodka, shot style, when I noticed Belinsky was sipping his. I followed suit. The drink was smooth, almost fruity. Nothing like the paint stripper we'd drunk on base.

"Not bad."

"It's distilled five times rather than the usual three. They put honey in it afterward."

"You're a vodka connoisseur?"

"I like what I like." A non-answer. "And apart from the gym, how are you finding your stay?"

"Can't complain. My girlfriend would say you need more pillows."

Belinsky threw his head back and laughed. "More pillows. I'll bear that in mind. Your girlfriend isn't staying here with you?"

"No, she isn't."

"And yet she lives in town?"

Had he been checking up on us? On Brooke? A chill prickled at the back of my neck.

"Not sure our living arrangements are any business of yours."

Another laugh. "On the contrary—I made it my business when you showed up in my hotel covered in blood. The staff were concerned you were here to make trouble, but I believe you're a man who knows how to show restraint, no? When we first met, you looked as if you wanted to knock Easton Baldwin's head off his shoulders, and not many men would have blamed you if you did. And yet you didn't. Then you had a difference of opinion with your girlfriend's brother, if rumour is correct? Again, you held back. I can't imagine you losing a fight if you put the slightest effort into it."

Should've known the Baldwin's Shore gossip network was working overtime.

"He'd had a bad day."

"And you didn't want to make it worse? Admirable." Belinsky set his glass down on the bar and studied me. "Restraint. I believe that's one trait we share. When necessary." He pushed his stool back and stood. "Invite your girlfriend over. Make the most of the facilities. I'll ensure those extra pillows get delivered."

Belinsky left without another word, a pair of shadows following behind like trained guard dogs. I'd met a lot of interesting characters in my time, but I didn't quite know what to make of him. After some deliberation and another glass of vodka—the regular stuff rather than top-shelf this time—I came to the conclusion that I wouldn't mind him as a friend, but I wouldn't want him as an enemy.

"How did the painting class go?" I asked Brooke over FaceTime. I had a light buzz from the vodka, but what really put the warmth in my chest was her.

"Great. Can I open my gift yet?"

In truth, I was surprised she hadn't already. Yes, I'd told her to wait, but I hadn't expected her to heed the instruction. When we were kids, she'd once found all her Christmas gifts in mid-December, opened them, panicked, and tried to rewrap them. But since she was only seven, she'd managed to wrap herself up in sticky tape instead, including her hair. The day after, she'd shown up at school in tears with a pixie cut. Cute. Damn cute. Eventually the hair had grown back, and she'd worn it long ever since.

"Patience, pixie."

"Don't call me that."

"Have you ever tried selling your paintings? People would pay good money for them, especially tourists."

"A couple of people have bought my demo paintings from the Craft Cabin."

"You should set your sights higher. Is the gift store in Coos Bay still open? The one on South Broadway? I bet they'd be interested."

"Do you really think they're good enough?"

"You know me, sweetheart. If they were shit, I'd tell you."

"I'll think about it."

This whole talking-before-sex thing was a novelty, but I'd begun to enjoy our nightly calls. It was all about the connection. We discussed everything and nothing, the past and the present. Not the future. We'd settled on an unspoken rule that said we needed to tidy up our loose ends before we moved on. I wanted Brooke in my bed again, but for now, the calls would have to be enough. At least I could visit her at the store. Darla was good about letting her take a break when I showed up.

"How's it going with Aaron? Any sign of a thaw?"

"Maybe." A pause. "He knows I'm speaking to you right now."

"He's okay with that?"

"Not exactly *okay*, but he called Clarissa earlier, and she freaking cheated on him, so I figure he doesn't have much authority when it comes to telling me who I can and can't phone."

"What did he say?"

"To Clarissa? I couldn't hear—he disappeared up the ramp. Goodness, if he knew what we did on that landing..."

Some things were better kept secret. "I meant, what did he say when he found out you were calling me?"

"Nothing. He just shrugged and changed the channel." That was a definite step in the right direction. Yeah, Aaron would come around after he'd gotten over his snit. "He'd better not get back together with Clarissa. I mean, Addy's got a plan for that, but..."

"*Addy's* got a plan? This should be fun."

"It's nothing drastic. She's just digging for dirt, although that got a bit delayed because she went on a date last night, and the guy was... Uh, I probably shouldn't tell you those details. And she also thinks Aaron should get out more. Did I tell you we're going to Applejack's for dinner tomorrow?"

"No, you didn't. And I'm not sure going out is a good idea at the moment."

"I won't be alone. Aaron and Addy are both coming. And Deck, and Colt, and Brady—he's almost finished at Deals on Wheels now, so it's a thank-you-slash-goodbye drink as well as phase one of Operation Find Aaron a Better Girlfriend. I can't let them down."

I didn't like it, but I understood. As much as we all wanted this to be over in a month, that might not happen, and if Brooke became a prisoner in her own home, Cupid would win. His games had a sexual flavour, but when you dug deeper, what he really got off on was control. He wanted Brooke scared. Cowering.

And my girl did not cower.

I was proud of her for that.

Plus Brady deserved thanks for fitting those cameras. He'd worked long hours, and they covered the front, back, and sides of the building, four units, all motion activated. If they sensed movement, I'd get an alert on my phone and they'd start recording.

"Just be damn careful."

"I will be, I promise. *Now* can I open my gift?"

"Yeah, you can open your gift, sweetheart. You're not anywhere near Aaron, are you?"

"Uh, no? I'm in the bedroom. Why? Is it *that* kind of gift?"

A grin crept onto my face. "It's that kind of gift."

She tore through the paper the concierge at the Peninsula had found for me and studied the box.

"A remote-controlled love egg? What does that even…?" Her cheeks turned nicely pink. "Oh!"

Oh, yeah. And guess who had the remote?

32

BROOKE

It was good to be out, and even better because I was with friends. Of course, there was one person missing, and a part of me wanted to be at home so I could spend more time playing with him and my new toy—Luca had studied the operating manual like a pro—but he was in Roseburg following Steve. Combining what I'd learned about Steve while we were dating and the new facts that had come to light since, that meant Luca was either skulking around in the bushes while Steve played *World of Warcraft*, or he was in a strip club.

I didn't particularly want to think about that second option. I trusted Luca, but those women all had better boobs than me, and— *Stop it, Brooke.*

Luca loved me.

He *loved* me.

"Brooke, what are you drinking?" Aaron asked.

"Diet Coke."

"No, she's drinking a pineapple mint mojito," Addy told him, and before I could argue, she put a hand over my mouth. "You can have one drink."

"Okay, okay. *One* drink."

I'd promised Luca I'd be careful, and I *was* being careful. I'd been eating as well as drinking. I was surrounded by people who cared. Cupid wouldn't try to snatch me from a crowded bar, and Addy had promised to come to the bathroom whenever I needed to go. Plus I'd mentioned dinner to Paulo when he dropped by with cookies at lunchtime—apparently, he'd hooked up with a pastry chef last night, which meant we had to hear all the excruciating details, but at least we got to share the spoils—and he'd shown up tonight and dragged Darla along with him.

Addy put the mojito in my hand and gave me a gentle shove toward the table she'd reserved. Applejack's was packed, and I spotted Isaac the veterinarian in the far corner with a pretty blonde I didn't recognise and waved. He waved back, and the blonde narrowed her eyes at me. Some women were so petty.

"That didn't last long, did it?"

The voice came from over my left shoulder, slightly nasal with a hint of a sneer, and I stiffened as soon as I heard it.

"The Neanderthal ditched you already?"

Addy got in first. "Shut up, Easton."

"You got a new guard dog?"

I saw her eye up her own drink, and I knew exactly what was going through her mind. Should she waste her cocktail by throwing it over the jerk in front of us?

But Parker materialised behind his brother and put a hand on his arm.

"Leave it."

"This bitch got me banned from the bar at the Peninsula."

Oh, that was too much. "You didn't need any help with that. Acting like a dumbass comes naturally to you."

A cross between a growl and a gurgle sputtered out of Easton's throat. Perhaps it was meant to be a snarl? He took a step forward, and I felt rather than saw Aaron appear at my shoulder.

"You should heed your brother's advice," he said to Easton. "If you've got a problem with door policy at the Peninsula, take it up with the management."

"Management." Easton snorted as he turned away. "Bet she's fucking Nico Belinsky too."

Thankfully, Aaron was back to his usual controlled self today, so I didn't have to hunt for another bucket of water.

"Such a creative insult. I'd expect nothing less from a man who had to climb over the fence to get into college."

"Probably paid someone to lift him," Addy muttered. "Go play with your dick, Easton. Nobody else is gonna do it for you."

"Is there a problem here?" Taya Swann asked. Great, we'd attracted an audience. Taya might only have been an inch taller than me, but she still kept Skip's baseball bat behind the bar and rumour said she knew how to use it.

Parker's grip on Easton's arm tightened. "No, there's no problem."

The pair of them walked away, and I felt both relieved and disappointed. If Easton had gotten banned from two bars in one week, I'd have been the first to laugh.

"Thanks," I said to Aaron and Addy, and Addy slung her free arm around my shoulders.

"What are friends for? Now, forget those two and enjoy yourself. Want to split a plate of nachos with me? I'm famished."

"Extra cheese?"

"Extra cheese."

I tried to follow Addy's instruction to have fun, and for the most part, I managed it, despite Easton's best efforts to cast a cloud over the evening. Applejack's was much more of a "me" place than Beer Me Up. I'd always found Skip a bit weird, even before he got arrested, and Taya seemed far more personable. Tough, but personable. When she took over, she'd completely remodelled, and now there was a small dance floor nestled among the blue-and-pink neon lights that illuminated every wall. I bent my "one drink" rule when Addy bought a round of the bar's signature cocktails —applejack, blue curaçao, and lemon juice, garnished with apple slices and a sugared rim—and then joined the others on the dance floor, at least until Colt left to pick Kiki up from the sitter and Paulo abandoned me for a guy who had better hair than I did.

By then, my feet hurt, so I sat my sweaty ass down next to Aaron at the table. What had Luca told me? Right, that I needed to make Aaron realise I wouldn't abandon him just because Luca and I were dating. A psychological thing, he said.

"Not dancing tonight?"

"Huh? Uh, no."

Why was he distracted?

"Work so busy you can't take a break?" I asked, hoping it was lawyer stuff but getting a sinking feeling it wasn't.

"Wish that were the case." He waved the phone at me. "It's Clarissa."

My heart plummeted to my feet. *So much for Addy setting him up with Taya.* "You're not still thinking of getting back together with her?"

"Now that I've had the chance to step back, I realise I had a lucky escape." Oh, thank goodness. No more Clarissa. And it meant Addy's grand master plan wouldn't be needed anymore, so I wouldn't have to fork out for a pitcher of margaritas. "She wants to talk in person, but I don't think that's a good idea."

"So tell her that."

"I did. She disagrees."

"There's a surprise. Why don't you just block her number?"

"I—" The phone buzzed in his hand, and he glanced at the screen. "Ah, hell."

"What happened?"

Was it the weird lighting, or had he gone a shade paler?

"I'm worried Clarissa might do something stupid."

"Something more stupid than cheating?" Then I realised what he meant. "Holy crap—she's suicidal?"

"Yes. No. Maybe?" He scrubbed a hand through his hair. "I don't fucking know. If there's one thing she's proven to be a master at, it's screwing with my mind." A sigh. "I should go over there."

"That's the last thing you should do. Call the police and let them deal with it. If she is thinking of harming herself, they'll get her the help she needs."

"And if she's just messing me around? I don't want to waste their time."

"Hey, guys!" Addy bounded up and grabbed both of our hands. "Come dance."

I shook my head, tried to send "not now" vibes. "Maybe in a while, okay?"

"What's up? Smile, babe."

"Clarissa's threatening to kill herself."

Addy glanced from me to Aaron, searching for signs of a joke. When neither of us laughed, her forehead creased in confusion.

"Is that 'yay' or 'oh no'?"

"I need to go check she's okay," Aaron said. "I'll drop you guys off at home on the way."

"Home isn't on the way, it's in the opposite direction. And we're having *fun* here."

"I can't leave Brooke here on her own."

"She's not on her own, dummy. There's a whole group of people with her. You can pick us up on your way back."

I wanted to say I could call Luca, but that wasn't a good idea. Aaron was gradually coming around to the idea that we were a couple, but I didn't want to push things and damage the fragile peace that seemed to be holding.

Finally, Aaron made up his mind.

"I'll call you when I leave Clarissa's place. Don't let Brooke go anywhere alone."

"No, sir." Addy saluted, and when Aaron was on his way to the door, she rolled her eyes. "Clarissa isn't suicidal. She's just manipulative."

"I'm inclined to agree with you, but what if...?"

"Like brother, like sister. Come back to the dance floor. Paulo's lined up the jukebox to play the Macarena."

I choked out a laugh because that song would always remind me of my first time with Luca.

"One dance. *One*. My feet ache."

"So take your shoes off." Addy stood on tiptoes and waved over my shoulder. "Bye, Deck! Enjoy your date. Come *on*, Brooke. Do you need painkillers? I have some in my purse."

A dose of Advil and who-knew-how-long later, I collapsed onto a chair. Paulo had taught everyone in the damn bar the Macarena—everyone drunk, anyway—and I must've lost at least three pounds in sweat. I poured half of my Coke down my throat, then fumbled in my pocket as my phone vibrated against my thigh.

Did Aaron have an update?

Luca: On my way back. Hope you're having a good time.

Well, no news was good news, right?

Me: The best! Blue is my new favourite colour xxx

I snapped a picture of Addy's garish three-quarters-full cocktail and pressed send.

Me: I recharged the thingy. Can't wait for you to push my buttons ;)

Luca: The speeding ticket will be worth it.

Damn, I loved that man.

Brady crouched beside me, one hand on the back of my chair. "Thanks for the send-off tonight, Baby."

"Baby?"

"Nobody puts Baby in a corner? The song you were just dancing to?" Now he looked confused. "Or did I get that wrong?"

"No, no, you're right." I was a bit slow this evening. I also hadn't done the lift because there was a ninety-nine percent chance Paulo would have dropped me. "You're leaving already?"

"Got a new job starting tomorrow morning, and Addy wouldn't let me finish packing up my tools earlier."

"She can be quite persh...press..." I gave up trying to think of the right word. "...quite pushy, can't she?"

"She sure can. Tell your brother to call me if there are any electrical problems, okay?"

"Electrical problems? Yes, I'll tell him."

I wasn't sure if it was the cocktails or the dancing or the dehydration, but I suddenly felt really tired.

"Take care of yourself, Brooke."

"You too."

I drained the rest of my Coke and yawned. What time was it? Only ten o'clock, but I wasn't used to dancing all night. And I'd neglected my fitness for the last month. The only exercise I'd gotten was sex, and I wasn't sure that took as much effort as my daily hikes. Probably I should look that up. Someone on the internet would know.

"Penny for them?"

"Huh?"

Darla stood watching me. "Your thoughts, hun. You look puzzled."

"Oh, it doesn't matter." Was I blushing? "Nothing important. Are you leaving too?"

She leaned down to give me a hug. "I've always been an early bird rather than a night owl. If Paulo's totally hungover in the morning, call me. I can come in for a few hours."

I glanced over at him. He'd organised a limbo contest for the few people who could still stand, a mop balanced across two chairs, and I could see that ending in tears or possibly a concussion.

"You're the best. I'm gonna go home myself soon."

At least, I hoped so. How much longer would Aaron be? I began to worry that we'd been wrong about Clarissa, that she genuinely had hurt herself. Aaron should have...should have...called...the police. Maybe I should message Luca? He was already on his way to Baldwin's Shore, and he might be back faster. But Aaron and his stupid macho-ness... Was that a word? If it wasn't, then it should be. *Macho-ness.*

"You okay, sweetie?" Addy slid onto the chair beside me. "You look kinda glazed."

"Just tired. I think I'm just tired. Although I feel a little sick."

"Probably dehydration. Have you drunk enough?"

"I had a Coke two minutes ago. And a cocktail before that."

"Hmm..." Addy studied me, head tilted to one side. "Maybe you should go to the bathroom, just in case. Here, let me help you."

I clung to Addy as I wobbled my way toward the door. Next time, I'd remember to drink more water. At this rate, Darla would be covering for me and not Paulo tomorrow.

"My head feels all jumbled."

"I know, sweetie. Mine too, but those cocktails were soooo good. Is Aaron done with the drama queen yet?"

"He said he'd call when he...when he was on his way... back. And he...he hasn't."

"You look kind of weird. Was that last drink a double or a single?"

"I don't know?"

I was almost certain I hadn't ordered the pretty green cocktail myself. But I wasn't sure who had. It just sort of... appeared in my hand. Taya? Was it Taya who'd given it to me?

The bathrooms were in a vestibule by the entrance, and I sucked in fresh air when the breeze hit me through the open front door. Perhaps I had heatstroke too? Could you get heatstroke from dancing? I tripped sideways, and my shoulder hit the wall.

"Ow."

"I've got ya, sweetie."

"Addy?"

"Yeah?"

"I just want to go home."

"But Aaron said..." Addy turned, and both of her studied me. "You know what I'm gonna do? I'm gonna call Selwyn."

Selwyn… Selwyn… Oh, *Selwyn*. He'd been driving his cab in Baldwin's Shore for as long as I'd been alive. "We know he's not your stalker because he's, like, a hundred years old and Black. He can drive us to your brother's place, and we can wait for Aaron there."

"Okay. That…that shounds good."

There was a little wall right outside the door, and I collapsed onto it, but what I really wanted was to lie down. And sleep. I needed sleep. Was the ground wet? Yeuch, it was.

"Shit, I can't find my phone. It must've fallen out when I put my purse under the table. I…uh…"

"Go…just go get it."

"But I'm not allowed to—" Addy glanced around the parking lot. "I'll be two seconds. Don't go anywhere."

I couldn't have gone anywhere if I'd tried. My legs had turned to mush, like half-set jello. And the parking lot was fuzzy too. Lights blinded me for a second, and then a shiny red car splashed past. Another car followed, black, black, black, even the windows. *Was* it a car? It sort of…purred along. Maybe Skip had been right and UFOs really did exist?

"Brooke, are you okay?"

What? Who? A head came into view, floating, and I smiled. I think I smiled. I knew that face. But now he had a twin. That was…special?

"I'm…fine."

I leaned against the back of the chair and fell straight off. So…not a chair? At least I was wearing pants. Not skirts or dresses, not anymore. A girl needed to stay safe.

"You shouldn't be out here like this."

"Addy… Addy…"

"Shouldn't have left you alone. I'll take you home."

"But... But... Aaron..."

"I'll call Aaron."

Then I wasn't on the ground anymore, and this seat *did* have a back. And an engine. And nice music. Maybe if I just closed my eyes for a few minutes...

33

LUCA

"Do you have Brooke?"

What the fuck?

"No, I don't have Brooke. Buddy, you literally broke my nose for having Brooke." Then the implications of Aaron's words hit, and I gripped the steering wheel of my rental car hard enough to bend the damn thing. "I thought Brooke was with you? She's meant to be with you."

Aaron's voice was tight. "There was a Clarissa-related incident. I had to go see her."

"You left Brooke *alone*?"

My foot hit the gas without me even thinking about it.

"Not alone. She was with Addy, and the bar was still half-full."

"Where's Addy now?"

"At her parents' place. Colt's on his way to get her. I'm ten minutes out." A horn blared. "Five minutes out."

"Start at the beginning. What happened?"

If any harm had come to my girl, blood was gonna be spilled. Cupid's, and maybe Aaron's too because he had *one* damn job and he'd fucked it up royally.

"Clarissa texted me a photo of a knife and said she couldn't bear to live without me. I could hardly just ignore it."

"She still alive?"

"Yeah." Aaron's tone said he might have regrets about that. "Brooke and Addy were supposed to stay inside the bar until I got back, but Addy said Brooke got wobbly, so she decided to call Selwyn and take her home."

Selwyn was still driving his cab? Damn, I thought he'd have retired long ago.

"And they never got there?"

"Addy lost her phone, and she left Brooke outside the bathrooms while she went to look for it. When she got back, Brooke had disappeared."

"Addy checked the bathrooms? The parking lot?"

"Yes, and yes. Then she borrowed the bar's phone to call Selwyn, and he drove her to Deals on Wheels in case Brooke tried to walk."

"Brooke wouldn't have tried to walk." I'd told her a hundred times not to go anywhere on her own. Even if she'd been drinking, she wouldn't have taken that risk.

"Addy didn't think so either. She wasn't even sure she *could* have walked. Buddy, I swear she wasn't that drunk when I left."

What's done was done. We could argue about whose fault it was later.

"We just need to find her."

"Fuck, I know. Anyhow, she didn't go to Deals. Brady's still there packing up, and he said he hasn't seen anything suspicious. Not Brooke, not a car slowing outside, nothing. He's gonna hang around for a while in case she shows."

"You said Addy checked the Crowe place too?"

"Yeah, and then she freaked out totally and called me."

"Does the bar have security cameras?"

"Colt's gonna check."

Fuck. I'd dealt with critical situations a hundred times, seen more tragedy than any man should, held good friends as they died, but the pain I'd felt in those situations paled into insignificance beside my fear for Brooke. A woman couldn't vanish into thin air. *He* had her. Cupid. He'd been watching, waiting in the shadows, and the second he saw an opening, he'd pounced.

And Cupid wasn't Steve. Steve was at home, nursing his wounded pride after getting slapped by a brunette whose ass he'd groped.

So that left the million-dollar question. Who the fuck *was* Cupid?

ADDY WAS CRYING when I arrived at the Crowe place. Judging by the state of her face, she'd been crying for a while. She was in an armchair, legs curled up against her chest, her parents hovering in the background. When I walked in with Aaron, she scrambled to get up, swayed alarmingly, and grabbed the mantlepiece to keep her balance.

"I'm so s-s-sorry. I don't know what h-h-happened."

"Cupid took her. That's what happened. Why did you leave her?"

"C-C-Cupid?"

"Her stalker. That's what she calls him. Who did you see in the parking lot when you headed outside with Brooke?"

"Nobody! We barely even *got* outside. She was right next to the door. And I was only gone for a minute, literally a minute, and definitely no more than two. I'm sorry, I'm s-s-so sorry."

Crying wouldn't help us to find Brooke, and neither would playing the blame game. "Okay, so who was inside?"

"Hardly anyone. There was, like, this mass exodus in the half hour before we went to leave. I g-g-guess that's because it's a Wednesday and people have to work tomorrow."

"Think, Addy. Was Deck still there?"

Brooke had said he'd be going tonight, hadn't she? Dammit, I should have been there.

"N-n-no, he left hours ago. Not long after Colt."

"Who in your group stayed to the end? Who else might have seen Brooke?"

"Uh, Paulo?"

Aaron let out a growl of frustration. "Paulo was in no state to remember his own damn name, even before I went to Clarissa's place. What about the others? When did Brady leave?"

She screwed her eyes shut, trying to remember. "Uh, before us, but maybe not too long before? And Darla left around that time too."

The door crashed open, and Colt ran in. "Any news?"

"Nothing from Brooke," I said, willing the quake out of my voice. Losing my head wouldn't help us tonight. "Her phone's turned off now. Going straight to voicemail."

I'd tried calling it ten times on the drive over, hoping she'd just moved out of signal range temporarily, but knowing deep down that wasn't the case. Cupid had probably ditched the device. Where had that son of a bitch taken her? Hell, forty minutes had passed since Addy last saw Brooke. She could be on her way to California right now. Or Canada.

"I stopped at Applejack's on my way here. The bar has a camera outside the door, but somebody tampered with it. Hit it with a stick or something. It's meant to watch over the parking lot, but now it's pointing at the sky. Taya's gonna check through the footage to see if she can work out when and who."

Cupid had planned this. He'd fucking planned it. Carved Brooke away from the herd, then lay in wait for the strike.

"Did Taya see Brooke with anyone?"

"'Bout that time, some girl puked on the dance floor, and Taya was cleaning up the mess."

"What about Paulo? Did you talk to Paulo?"

"Paulo was sleeping in the corner. Everyone I spoke with said the same thing—one minute Brooke was there, and the next she wasn't."

"Can we do anything to help?" Mr. Crowe asked. "Go out and search?"

Addy scrambled to her feet. "I want to go too. This is all my fault."

"It's not," Aaron said, cutting his eyes sideways toward me. "If it's anyone's fault, it's mine. I was the asshole who kicked Luca out."

Okay, so that was progress, but under the worst possible circumstances. I'd rather have been excommunicated for good if it meant Brooke was tucked up safely in bed tonight.

"I'll call Brady and see if he saw anyone hanging around. Can somebody call Darla?"

"I'll do it," Colt offered. "Do you have her number?"

Aaron fumbled for his phone. "I have it."

Brady picked up on the second ring. "Hey, did you find Brooke?"

"Not yet. That's why I'm calling. Addy reckons you left the bar not too long before they did."

"I called it a night around ten. Should've left earlier, but... Never mind. I don't know how much longer they stayed, but I guess not long because Brooke was looking tired when I said goodbye. Sounded kinda slurry."

Tired.

Kind of slurry.

That *motherfucker*.

Cupid had slipped something into her drink again. I believed Aaron when he said Brooke had been in reasonable shape when he took off, and I also believed Addy when she said Brooke was having trouble walking later. There was one obvious explanation for that. Cupid had been in the bar.

He'd been up close, brazen enough to attack in front of her friends.

"Did you notice anyone paying attention to Brooke around that time? A little *too much* attention?"

"Not really. I mean, she was sitting in a chair, watching people on the dance floor. It was just a regular evening out. Apart from the altercation with Easton Baldwin at the start, anyway."

Hair prickled on the back of my neck. I'd felt that niggle a thousand times before, usually before somebody shot at me.

"What altercation?"

"I'm not sure how it started, but there were words. Aaron and Addy backed her up, and Parker talked Easton down. The Baldwins ate dinner on the other side of the bar. I saw them looking over at her a couple times after that, but..."

Easton Baldwin again. Why did he keep turning up like a bad penny? We already knew he wasn't Cupid. Unless Lydia had been wrong about the man she saw with Brooke on the night of Addy's party. Or...

"Do you know if Easton Baldwin ever dyed his hair?"

"Huh?"

"I've got to go."

"You need a hand with the search?"

If I was going to mount Easton's head on a plaque, the fewer witnesses, the better.

"Can you stay at Aaron's place in case a miracle happens and Brooke shows up?"

"Sure I can, but—"

I hung up and turned back to Addy and Aaron. "What happened with Easton Baldwin?"

Aaron's forehead creased. "Easton? He started out as his usual belligerent self, but Parker convinced him to simmer down."

"Taya helped too," Addy said. "She has a bat."

"Does it matter? Brooke said you ruled him out."

"Yeah, I thought we had, but I'm not a great believer in coincidences. Did he change his hair last year? Dye it brown?"

"Not that I recall."

Addy hiccuped, still on the wrong side of sober. "Parker's the one with the brown hair."

The gears were turning faster now.

Parker Baldwin. Parker motherfucking Baldwin. Addy was right—he *did* have brown hair. And he was taller than Brooke, shorter than me. Not skinny, not bulky either. He'd been in Coos Bay that night. He was in Applejack's tonight. *Two brothers...* If Parker had decided to take Brooke, would Easton have gone along with it? Probably. He had the ethics of a swamp rat. Colt mouthed, "Voicemail," at me, but I didn't much care what Darla had to say now, not when I had a good idea who was behind Brooke's abduction.

"Addy, think hard—when you headed out with Brooke, were the Baldwin brothers still inside?"

"Uh...uh... I'm almost sure they weren't. They were

sitting over by the jukebox earlier, and that table was empty when we walked past."

I palmed my keys and headed for the door.

"Wait!" Colt called. "Where are you going?"

"You know where I'm going."

"You're not going alone."

I glanced at Addy's parents, still loitering in the background, and forced what I hoped was a smile. "Chill, I'm just gonna have a little chat."

Mr. Crowe nodded once. "Well, when you do, give those boys a kick up the rear from me."

34

LUCA

The imposing metal gates of the Baldwin mansion were closed when we drew up outside, but I didn't bother with the intercom. Instead, I nosed the rental car alongside the six-foot-high wall, hopped up on the hood, then the roof, and vaulted over into the grounds. Behind me, Colt was trying to convince Aaron to stay in the car, but good luck with that plan.

"Shhh!" I hissed as they both followed me up the driveway. Parker was home. His shiny red BMW glinted in the moonlight to the right of the tacky Doric columns that framed the front door.

"Are we gonna break in?" Aaron whispered.

That would waste time we didn't have. "I'll try knocking first."

If Parker came to the door, it would save us from hunting him down in this monument to bad taste. The place was huge—two wings flanked the main building, and if memory served me correctly, there was a detached garage and a guest house out back too.

I hammered on the brass knocker, custom made with

the family crest, a shield and a swirl of filigree they'd probably stolen from some English nobleman. Or maybe a French family? The engraved banner at the top read "*Je n'oublierai pas*."

"I will not forget," Aaron murmured.

"What?"

He traced the words with a fingertip. "Their family motto. 'I will not forget.' Perhaps that's why Easton bears so many grudges?"

Well, I wouldn't forget either. I wouldn't forget the way he'd accused me of stealing his billfold, or how Parker had reported me to the school principal for vandalising a classroom, neither of which I was guilty of. I was about to bang on the door again when the lock clicked and it swung open. Sara Baldwin stood there, eyes widening as she took in the three of us.

"Luca? Luca Mendez? What are you doing here?"

"Where's Parker?"

"Uh, in the living room? What's all this about?"

I brushed past her, then realised I didn't know where the fuck the living room was. And if Parker was in the living room, where the hell was Brooke? I could see Easton being complicit in her abduction, but Sara wouldn't go along with that shit. Had Parker stashed her somewhere?

"Could you please show us the way?" Colt asked, good cop to my Frank Castle.

"Sure, but I don't understand why you're here."

"We have a few questions about an incident that happened at Applejack's earlier."

Sara groaned as she started along a hallway to the left. "Did Easton pick another fight?"

"He told you about that?"

"No, but he's in a foul mood this evening, the same way

he always is when he loses whatever argument he gets into." She waved at a door ahead. "In there."

I stormed ahead, ready for a fight of my own, but some of the steam evaporated when I spotted Parker in a pair of plaid pyjamas, feet propped up on a burgundy padded footstool that matched the velvet couch. When he saw the three of us, he appeared more puzzled than anything else.

"What the...?" He looked past us to Sara, who shrugged. "It's almost midnight."

"Where's Brooke?" I demanded.

"How should I know?"

"What do you mean?" Sara asked. "Brooke's missing?"

Aaron had brought his cool head this evening. His lawyer head. "We believe she was drugged and abducted from outside the bar tonight."

Sara gasped. "My gosh!"

"Your brothers left around the same time she disappeared."

Parker got to his feet. "And you think we were involved? I know Easton was a tad rude earlier, but you're clutching at straws."

"Last year, he was also at a party where Brooke got drugged and sexually assaulted." Aaron winced as he said the words. "You fit the description of the last man seen with her."

Now Parker paled a shade. "What party?"

"Adeline Crowe's birthday celebration."

"Well, I'm sorry to hear that happened, but I assure you I had nothing to do with the matter."

"He really didn't," Sara put in. "March last year, right? I was in the car with Parker when he picked Easton up from Addy's place. Another fricking fight." She rolled her eyes. "Parker only went inside for two minutes, if that."

I didn't trust Parker, but I was inclined to believe Sara. She might have had the Baldwin name, but she'd never lorded it over the serfs the way the rest of the clan did. And she'd once covered for me when I put a live rat in Tucker Jones's locker. When I thanked her afterward, she'd just smiled and said he deserved it.

"Fuck," Aaron muttered under his breath.

"Did you see Brooke or anyone else in the parking lot when you left Applejack's?"

"Can't say I did."

And we were back to square one. For the ten-minute trip to the Baldwin place, I'd been so certain it was Parker, but all we'd done was waste time. Brooke was at the mercy of a madman, and… I couldn't think about it. If I went down that rabbit hole, I'd lose my damn mind.

"We need to go back to the bar," Colt said. "See if Taya's found anything on the cameras."

Except Easton Baldwin blocked the way.

"What the hell are you doing in my house?" His gaze homed in on Sara. "Why are they here? Did *you* let them in?"

She took a couple of steps back, and I got the impression the move was as natural to her as breathing.

"They knocked," she said, so softly I barely heard her.

"Luca and his friends were just leaving," Parker told him. "Brooke Bartlett went missing from the parking lot at Applejack's, and they thought we might have been involved."

"So there's a problem, and right away, you thought, 'Oh, it must have been Easton.' That's discrimination."

Discrimination? Not if it was usually true. "Save it."

"And get out of our way," Aaron added.

"No, I think you should apologise for disturbing our

evening first."

From zero to full-asshole in five seconds. Some things never changed. "Fine, we're all very sorry. Now move before I make you."

Behind me, Parker sighed. "Just let them leave."

"Why should I? You're not upset that Luca has a vendetta against us? His girlfriend goes missing, and his first instinct is to come over here and make accusations when he should be looking closer to home."

"I don't have a damned vendetta."

Sara twisted her hands. "Please, Easton. Don't do this."

But it was Aaron who grabbed the thread Easton had given us and tugged it. "What do you mean, closer to home?"

"*I* wasn't the one skulking in the parking lot this evening."

"You saw someone?"

Easton folded his arms, smug now, and I wanted to knock his teeth out. "I might have done."

"Who?"

Parker huffed out a breath. "For goodness' sakes, just tell them. A woman's *missing*."

"Oh, fine. It was that friend of yours." He jerked his head at Aaron. "The one working on the derelict building you call a home."

"You're sure? Which friend? Deck? Brady?"

But I already knew the answer. *Brady*. He fit Lydia's description too. He was friends with Addy. He'd handed Brooke the damn plant. He'd been the one to point us toward the Baldwins. The fox had been in the fucking henhouse the whole time.

And he'd been alone with Brooke at Deals on Wheels for almost two hours.

35

LUCA

"I'll kill him." Aaron was riding shotgun, although I suspected he'd rather be driving. "If Brady's hurt Brooke, I'll choke the damn life out of him."

He'd have to get in line.

"No, you won't," Colt said from the back seat, the voice of reason. "If one of us kills Brady, we're gonna need a good defence attorney, and that's *your* job."

"You've got a kid," I reminded him. "You can't go to jail."

That was *my* fate. I was no stranger to death, but inflicting it had never given me pleasure. Tonight, I'd make an exception.

Then my phone buzzed. I juggled it out of my pocket and read the message that had flashed up on the screen.

Brooke: Could you come to Deals on Wheels? I'm fine, just need a hand with something xx

"What the fuck?"

"What is it?" Aaron asked.

I tossed the phone across. "A message from Brooke's phone."

He took a second to read it, and I heard his misplaced sigh of relief. "She's okay. Brooke's okay. So what the hell happened earlier?"

"She's not okay. That message didn't come from Brooke."

"How do you know?"

"Because she always puts three x's at the end, not two."

"Are you—"

"Of course I'm sure," I snapped, then felt guilty for biting his head off. "Try calling her."

Aaron dialled, pressed the phone to his ear. "She's not answering."

"Told you."

It was an ambush. Brady had Brooke's phone, and he was trying to lure us in.

But he'd made a mistake.

The drive across town usually took ten minutes, but I did it in seven. Deals on Wheels was in darkness apart from a faint glimmer around the drapes near the sitting area. Somebody had put a lamp on. The worst part of this whole nightmare was that it wasn't just Brooke's body Brady had violated; it was her home too. He'd come into her safe space and turned it into a house of horrors.

"He's still here," Aaron muttered.

Brady's truck was parked out front, doors closed. Had he dumped Brooke in the back like cargo? Or risked driving with her slumped in the passenger seat? I checked the gun at the small of my back and tamped down my emotions. Brady was gonna suffer, but my priority was ensuring Brooke's safety. Once Aaron had gotten her out of there, all bets were off.

I motioned Colt and Aaron toward the front door.

"I go in first. When it's safe, I'll call you forward."

"But—" Aaron started.

"I'm trained for this. You're not."

In truth, I didn't know how dangerous Brady was. A day ago, I'd have put him at the lower end of the scale, but now I realised I didn't know him at all. He had to know we'd be back. That we'd work out his secret. Had he prepared? Was he lying in wait? Hell, he'd installed the damn camera over my head. I glanced up, but the red light wasn't on. Had he turned off the system? I checked my phone—I'd only had one alert from the motion sensors, hours ago when he arrived to "pick up his tools."

PERIMETER DEACTIVATED.

That motherfucker.

I turned my key in the lock. Waited.

Nothing.

Slowly, slowly, I inched through the door. Checked the ramp to my right. No movement. But I did hear the faint strains of music drifting through the air, and...fuck...

I knew that smell.

Unwanted images flashed through my head. The blast of an IED. Flames. Red-hot razor blades flying through the air. Brothers writhing on the floor, screaming. Our driver's legs, cut off at the knees. He'd have bled out if the shrapnel hadn't cauterised the wounds.

"What's that stink?" Aaron whispered, because of course he hadn't stayed where I told him to. Would I have listened if my sister had been in trouble? Probably not.

"Burning flesh."

I swallowed down the bile in my throat. Forced the images out of my head and carried on.

The music got louder. A woman's voice, sweet, slow, and sad. Where was Brady? Where was that traitorous snake hiding? Although the place was only half-finished, there were plenty of nooks and crannies a man could duck into, and in a moment of clarity, I recalled him mentioning he had a gun.

I'd die for Brooke in a heartbeat, and I'd give up my future to avenge her past, but I wanted to take him with me.

Vega whined from his little pen, standing by the gate, begging to be let out. Brooke had got the mutt to act as a guard dog, but to him, Brady was practically family. This was so messed up.

Then I saw her.

And my face must have mirrored Parker's from earlier.

What the...?

Was Brady using her as bait?

Brooke was sleeping on the couch, snuggled under a blanket, the lamp illuminating the faintest smile on her face. Gleaming hair tumbled over one bare shoulder, and as my chest suddenly hitched *because what if she was dead*, she stirred and turned onto her back.

She was safe.

My girl was safe.

But was I?

The stench was stronger here, a cloying odour that slithered down my throat and turned my stomach. I ran forward, instinct taking over, and I was halfway to Brooke when I heard a muffled groan.

Company.

I could see five doors from where I was standing, leading to the gym, Aaron's home office, the guest bathroom, and two bedroom suites. The rooms lay empty for the most part, a house waiting to become a home.

Only one door was closed.

The door to the bedroom Brooke had been using.

And I knew, I fucking *knew*, that I'd find Brady in there. He'd raped Brooke in her own bed a year ago, and tonight, he'd followed the same playbook.

But why was Brooke on the couch?

I motioned Aaron forward. "Get her out of here."

"What about Brady?"

"I'll deal with Brady."

Colt stacked up one side of the bedroom door, and I took the other. There was no lock, just a handle. I pushed down, the world slowing around me, my pulse loud in my ears. Eased the door open with one foot.

Held my breath.

When I was eight, me, Aaron, and Colt had "borrowed" *The Silence of the Lambs* from Colt's dad's movie library and watched it in Aaron's room. We'd stuffed our faces with popcorn and candy and potato chips, and when it came to the scene with the cage, the one where Hannibal Lector strung up the cop like Christ on the cross with his guts hanging out, I'd almost puked all that shit up again.

Tonight, I got that same feeling again when I saw Brady.

"Holy fuck," Colt breathed in my ear.

Brady jerked his head when he saw us, eyes wide, and I took in the details. He'd been tied to the bed with what looked like electrical cord, naked and spread-eagled. The soldering iron on top of his toolbox told me where the smell had come from. Whoever got there before us had used Brady's body as a canvas, a vessel for their macabre artwork. Words were seared into his skin from his forehead to his feet, embellished with swirls and flourishes.

Rapist.

Pervert.

Traitor.

Snake.

Stalker.

They'd taken wire and threaded it into his skin, carved into him with his own Stanley knife. I winced myself when I saw the G-clamps crushing his testicles. There was a message written on his chest in black marker, neat block letters not so dissimilar from those he'd written to Brooke. The letters were upside down, the words meant for him and not me. I took a moment to read them before I removed the duct tape from his mouth.

CONFESS, OR I'LL COME BACK AND FINISH THE JOB

As Colt had said, *holy fuck.*

Free to speak, Brady said nothing, just glared at me mutinously.

"Why'd you do it?" I asked. "Why'd you betray your friends and put Brooke through hell?"

There was some kind of white powder on his stomach, and when I looked up, I saw a hole in the ceiling. The visitor had taken a claw hammer to the Sheetrock, and wires were hanging out beside the light fixture. Black wires and a tiny gleaming lens.

My semiautomatic was in my hand before I had time to think. That cunt had wired Brooke's room with a camera. He'd been watching her. Watching *us.*

"Do it," he croaked. "Shoot me."

Oh, it was tempting. One tiny squeeze and he'd be out of Brooke's life. But so would I, and realisation dawned that in death, he'd still win. I put the gun away. Brady would be the asshole going to jail, not me. I was going to a tropical island somewhere. With Brooke.

I headed for the door.

"Good luck with the jury, *pal*."

36

BROOKE

The most dramatic evening of my life, and I'd slept through the whole thing.

Although on balance, I had to be grateful for that. When I awoke, I was in Luca's room at the Peninsula, nestled among a million pillows with his heavenly arms wrapped around me. And utterly mystified as to how I'd gotten there.

"Luca?"

He kissed me on the forehead, on the nose, on the lips. "Hey, sweetheart."

"I don't think I'm meant to be here. Aaron—"

"Is fine with it. We had a talk last night, and we agreed that I'm the best person to guard your body." Another sweet kiss. "That's a role I intend to take *very* seriously. How are you feeling?"

Honestly? "Like I got run over by a truck. I think I drank a little too much last night. I'm so sorry—I know I promised to be sensible."

"You *were* sensible. Cupid played everyone for fools."

I went rigid. "Cupid was there?"

"He spiked your drink again. Snatched you from right under our noses."

"Then how...how am I here? Did he...?" I felt sick now. Sicker. Did I have that ache between my thighs, the one I'd woken up with last time? I moved my legs, testing. No, I didn't hurt, not that way. "I don't understand."

"It's a long story."

And when Luca told it, I went through the full spectrum of emotions. Shock, horror, disgust, confusion, and disbelief.

"Brady? *Brady* was Cupid?" Aaaaaaand we were back to the horror. "But he was my friend. I thought he was my friend."

"Everyone thought he was their friend. Addy's devastated."

Because she was the one who'd introduced us. "It wasn't her fault."

"In time, she'll learn to accept that, but right now, she's taking it hard."

"I should call her."

"Later. You can call her later. Her mom gave her a sleeping pill at three a.m., so she'll still be dead to the world. We can have breakfast first, and then I'll take you to see her. Colt's gonna have questions too."

"I'm not sure I'll have any answers. The last thing I remember is falling off the wall outside Applejack's, and then it's all a blank. Do you have any idea who this...this... I can't call them a Good Samaritan because what they did was very, very bad, but..."

"The Bad Samaritan. That works."

"You don't know who they were?"

"They covered their tracks well. Colt's gonna question

Brady when the doctors let him, see if he remembers anything."

Brady. I shuddered at the mention of his name. Probably I always would. The wolf in sheep's clothing who'd infiltrated my life and upended it, only to get taken out by a bigger predator. The biggest. A shark? A bear? A Siberian tiger? That's when I felt the relief flood through me. It was done. Finished. Cupid's grip on me was gone. It was *finally* over. And do you know what? Even if my memories were crystal clear, if I remembered the Bad Samaritan's face in perfect detail, I wouldn't tell a soul.

I'd send a thank-you note.

And also some cookies.

"I hope Brady doesn't remember."

"Me too, sweetheart. Me too. Do you want me to order breakfast? Aaron's gonna feed Vega and bring more clothes over for you if he hasn't already."

"He's truly okay with us?"

"Yeah, he is. Clarissa did a real number on his head, and we caught the tail end of that. But we're good now. Told you he'd come around."

"I hated the thought of losing either of you."

"Well, you're stuck with me now, for better or for fucking worse."

"For better or for worse?" My breath hitched, but maybe I was just reading too much into a throwaway comment. "You don't mean...?"

He gifted me one of those sweet Luca-smiles, the ones he saved for me and no one else. "Give me a few weeks to find a job and somewhere to live, and then...yes. I do mean."

"We're not going to live together? I have an apartment."

"Guess that timescale just shortened."

"Did I mention that I love you?"

"I'll never get tired of hearing it. Love you too, Brooke soon-to-be Mendez. About that breakfast..."

A giggle burst out of me. "If you're hungry, you only have to say so."

"I'm hungry."

"Can we get room service?"

"We can get anything you want, sweetheart."

And just like that, everything was right with my world.

Really.

Thanks to a stranger, the last barrier to happiness had been removed.

Cupid might have missed with his arrow, but as the fuzziness in my head faded, clarity hit me like a warm ray of sunshine. For so long, I'd clung to my outdated view of what happiness meant, but now I realised that not everybody was destined to follow the same path. I didn't need a million bucks or a college degree or a fancy job title in order to smile in the mornings. I'd needed to change my mindset, not my lifestyle.

Luca made me happy.

Being part of the community made me happy.

My job made me happy.

That was one life goal checked off the list, and a second too. I'd fallen in love. Not only with Luca, but with myself as well. We all had flaws, and in time, I could learn to embrace mine.

As for the third goal, I still had lessons to learn. I'd *always* have lessons to learn. And that was okay.

37

LUCA

"The good news is that Brady's gonna have a fuck-ton of scars," Colt told us. Kiki was at the Craft Cabin with Brooke for the Saturday morning kids' session, so we'd gathered in his kitchen. "The doctor said there's no way 'rapist' is coming off without removing his entire forehead. Oh, and..." His lips twitched at the corners. "Brady's testicles were too badly damaged to save. They had to remove them both."

I clinked my glass against Aaron's, then Colt's. OJ, since it was eleven o'clock. We'd switch to beer later, or hell, maybe I'd even buy champagne. There was a lot to celebrate.

"You're right; that's the best news I've had all day. Is Brady talking?"

"Singing like a choirboy. Falsetto." Colt couldn't keep the smile off his face. "Seems as if he's taking the mysterious visitor's words to heart."

"Brooke's calling him the Bad Samaritan."

"The Bad Samaritan—yeah, that fits."

"Does Brady know who he is?"

"He says not. I'm inclined to believe him after what we saw on that video."

The message on Brady's chest wasn't the only one the Bad Samaritan had left. We'd found the second note on the counter outside, next to Brady's phone. Short but sweet.

CHECK THE CAM APP

Turned out Brady had been running a second, parallel camera system alongside the one I'd paid him to install, and it was a good thing he had police guards in the hospital because when I found out, I'd wanted to kill him all over again.

His system was more sophisticated, a live feed hooked into Aaron's Wi-Fi. There were spying eyes everywhere—in each bedroom, the bathrooms, the living room, and Brooke's new home upstairs. And that was just at Deals on Wheels. He'd also wired Brooke's rental place above the Crowes' garage, plus apartments belonging to six other girls. The police in Coos Bay were involved now, trying to locate those women based on what they could spot in the recordings.

And speaking of recordings, we'd found several from last night. The Bad Samaritan had erased most of his parts, but he'd thoughtfully left enough for us to understand how the evening went down. My blood pressure had risen as we watched Brady drag Brooke through the house by her armpits, lay her on the bed, and undress her slowly, stroking her skin as he went. Gently, almost reverently. The sick fuck. He'd arranged her the way he wanted, dimmed the lights, and then shucked his own clothes. Jacked off a while. She was lying in a pose reminiscent of his, arms and legs splayed but mercifully oblivious, when a blurry black-clad figure darted into shot and jabbed what appeared to be a syringe into Brady's neck. Brady had stayed standing for a second, then swayed and crumpled forward onto the bed.

The camera feed ended there.

Some words were better left unsaid, some home movies better left unwatched.

There were no good clues to the Bad Samaritan's identity. He was fast, clearly strong, and sneaky as a ninja on tiptoe. Proficient with a set of lock picks since there was no damage to any of the doors or windows. Smart, because he'd found Brady's hidden network of cameras. Confident. Perhaps even arrogant. And nobody we knew fit that profile.

Everybody in Baldwin's Shore had a secret, but some secrets were dirtier than others.

A secret...

Before he left, the Bad Samaritan had set Brooke's phone to play Sarah McLachlan's "Dirty Little Secret" on repeat, and I thought that might have been another message, but I didn't quite understand what he was trying to say.

Maybe I never would.

Maybe I didn't care.

If he wanted to fade away, to keep his secrets and stay in the background, I was good with that.

Because I had Brooke.

I had Brooke, and the Bad Samaritan had saved us both a world of heartache.

"I don't care who the guy is. I'd buy him a beer if I could."

Colt snorted. "A beer? I'd buy him a six-pack."

Aaron drained his own can. "I'd buy him a damn brewery. Although that might have to wait a few months. I'll have to get all the electrical work redone at Deals on Wheels first, and that's gonna put a dent in my finances."

"You know Brooke wants me to move in with her, right?"

"Yeah. Can't say I hate the idea. Not anymore."

"So I can chip in toward the electrical costs."

"You don't have to—"

"Yeah, I do. I'm gonna marry your sister one day, and I'm gonna take care of her."

Aaron choked on his OJ. "You're gonna marry Brooke?"

"Just laying my cards on the table, so if you want to punch me, go ahead and do it now. She hates it when you hurt me in front of her."

He scowled for a second, only a second, then broke into a smile. I'd been bracing for impact, but now the tension in my abs released.

"You as a brother-in-law? Can't say I hate that idea either."

EPILOGUE - BROOKE

"C'mon, boy. You already sniffed that clump of grass on the way out. And peed on it too."

How things had changed in three months... Vega's leg had healed well, and I could walk him alone again. Between the early morning hikes, all the sex, and the gym membership at the Peninsula that Luca had signed us up for, I was the fittest I'd ever been. Not necessarily the thinnest, because Luca bought me an extraordinary amount of chocolates, but the fittest.

We were still living in the garage apartment behind the Crowes' house, but I didn't much mind. Home was where the heart was. And also the hot guy. Besides, our address would soon change. Deals on Wheels was being completely rewired, every trace of Brady erased. Deck was working overtime to help, and when the new electrician heard what had happened, he'd offered us a discounted rate, and over the weeks, he'd found nineteen cameras hidden around the place. Microphones too. And while I hated the fact that Brady had abducted me from the bar, in a strange way I was thankful, because if he hadn't seen an opportunity that night, we'd all have been walking around our new home oblivious.

And Brady had gotten his just deserts.

The Bad Samaritan's identity remained a mystery, but reading between the lines, nobody had looked for him too hard. He'd become another Baldwin's Shore legend, along with Skip's hidden treasure and the siren on Turtle Rock.

Vega finally gave up on the grass and trotted along at my side again. He passed all his check-ups with flying colours, and although he wasn't allowed off-leash yet, just in case he overdid things, he seemed pretty cheerful these days. His tail rarely stopped wagging, and Luca was his new best friend, mainly because he bought him hotdog wieners and ham slices and steak. Freaking *steak.*

"You want to ride in the truck this afternoon? Do you?"

I took the cold, wet nose nudging my hand to mean "yes." Since I had a day off today, I'd promised to go to Alma's Furniture Emporium with Colt, and we were going to drop a couple of my paintings off at the gift store on the way. I'd finally plucked up the courage to ask if they'd stock them, and they'd sold three in the last month. Plus the boutique at the Peninsula had sold four, and those folks paid top dollar. The extra income meant that I could afford to buy brand-new furniture if I wanted to, but there was something satisfying about browsing through pre-loved treasures. Every piece had a story.

Kiki wanted a dressing table, Colt wanted to take her mind off the fact that their cat had gone missing, and I wanted to look for another bed since Luca and I would be moving to the new apartment soon. The old iron bed frame I'd once loved so much had gone into the dumpster for obvious reasons. I was grateful I hadn't seen Brady tied to it, but that didn't stop my imagination from running wild at times.

At least Brady was in jail now. He'd opted to plead guilty to everything, which Aaron said was a smart move given the circumstances. Any juror would have struggled to remain impartial when the defendant had the word "rapist" burned into his forehead and "pervert" scarred across both cheeks, and Brady was also terrified the Bad Samaritan would make good on his promise to come back. He'd said as much in his interviews, and his signed confession ran to nine pages. I wasn't the only woman he'd assaulted. Thankfully, he was serving twenty years in the Oregon State Penitentiary now, hopefully with a three-hundred-pound cellmate who had a taste for pasty white ass.

My phone rang as we got back into town, and I smiled at the sound. Savage Garden's "To the Moon & Back," the song I'd set for Luca.

"Hi."

"Hey, sweetheart."

My heart rate still spiked every time I heard his voice. It probably always would. "How's the first-aid course?"

"Not as comprehensive as the training I had in the army, but it's always good to have a refresher. Rumour says we might get let out of school early today. Want to go out for dinner?"

Yes, Luca was back at school. Well, the Sheriff's Academy. The job had been Colt's idea. Apparently, Luca got preference points for being a veteran, so the interview process had been relatively straightforward, and now he had a week left at the academy before he switched to field training. Field training meant Colt got to tell him what to do for six months, something Colt was looking forward to but Luca was not. But I'd come to realise that what drove Luca was a need to help people, and being a deputy would fulfill that need. Plus he'd be coming home to me every night. And he got a uniform. Overall, the new job was a win for everyone.

"I thought you were watching football with Colt and Aaron this evening?"

And I'd promised to teach Kiki how to knit a scarf, even though it was the end of July. She wanted to be prepared for winter. Seven years old, and her organisational abilities put mine to shame. And Luca's.

"I thought the football was next week?" he said.

"No, it's definitely this week. Want me to pick up takeout after I've been to the furniture store?"

I could almost feel Luca's shudder through the phone. He'd turned out to be surprisingly domesticated, but he still didn't do well with shopping. When I'd suggested I tag along to the Emporium with Colt rather than waiting until the weekend and going together, he'd actually sighed with relief.

But he had managed to buy one thing in the last month. I held my hand up to the light, loving the way the diamond on my finger sparkled in the sun. It wasn't a huge rock—I hadn't wanted that—but he'd had the white gold band engraved on the inside. *My everything*. I'd cried when he got down on one knee, late one evening on the beach at the Peninsula. Kissed him silly after I'd choked out a "yes." And when we got back to the bar, there'd been a bottle of champagne waiting, courtesy of Nico Belinsky.

"Takeout sounds good. Anything you want."

"Which means Mexican. *Te quiero*."

"Love you too, sweetheart. And before I forget, I told the guys at the academy about Thrive, and they want me to bring in some flyers."

My heart swelled.

Since I'd come up with the idea of starting a support group for survivors—of sexual assault, of domestic violence, of any kind of abuse that left them feeling the pain and shame I once had—Luca had been nothing but supportive. I'd grown to realise how much talking had helped me, and art too, so I'd created an environment that encompassed both.

Thrive met twice a month on Wednesday evenings at the Craft Cabin, and any woman was welcome to drop by to talk, paint, or just listen. They shared their experiences, their coping techniques, and other advice, and I'd convinced a therapist to facilitate the sessions in exchange for painting lessons.

The first time, three people had shown up, all wary, all nervous. The next time, four more joined us. At the last session, there'd been eighteen women, each at a different stage of processing their trauma, and I was beginning to realise what a vast, hidden problem existed. I hadn't been the only one suffering. I was but one tiny snowflake in what needed to become an avalanche if society was going to change.

Initially, I'd thought that if I could help just one person, the effort would have been worth it, but now I had bigger plans. I wanted *every* woman to find happiness, not only me.

"I have plenty of flyers."

"Then I'll make sure they get where they need to go."

"Wow! His tongue flaps *and* his ears flap."

Oh, to be a child again. A dog sticking its head out of the

truck window could provide endless hours of entertainment.

Kiki's tiny pink dressing table was in the back, along with a pink stool and a pink-framed mirror bundled in fifty layers of bubble wrap. Can you guess what Kiki's favourite colour was? We'd even stopped at the bakery and bought pink cupcakes on the way home. Colt was such a pushover when it came to his daughter, but after Hannah died, he'd said he needed to give Kiki enough love for two, and over the years, he'd stuck to his word. The early days had been hard. I still remembered his frustrations as I'd taught him to braid Kiki's hair, but now he was a pro, and he'd worn stubby pigtails and a full face of make-up himself more times than I could count thanks to her efforts.

"Do you think *my* ears would flap if I stuck my head out the window?" Kiki asked.

Colt groaned quietly. "Absolutely not."

"How about my tongue?"

I still had all this to look forward to. Not yet, but one day. I twisted in my seat to face Kiki. She'd dressed as Tinker Bell today, complete with a wand Paulo had made for her.

"You might swallow a fly, and flies taste yucky."

"Yuck, yuck, yuck! Vega, get your head in!"

He turned and slurped his tongue up her face, then stuck his head out the window again.

"*Euch*. Now I'm all slimy."

"The wet wipes are in the centre console," Colt reminded me.

At least one of us had come prepared. I was rummaging for the package when Kiki shrieked in my ear.

"Look! A princess!"

"We don't have any princesses in Baldwin's Shore."

"No, she's right," Colt said, and the truck began to slow. "Looks like a lady's broken down."

Holy heck, Kiki hadn't been kidding. Up ahead, a stunning blonde was standing beside a dark green Audi. In what was unmistakably a wedding dress. The bodice twinkled in the sunlight, and her hair had been fastened into an elaborate updo with stray tendrils floating around her face. As we got closer, I could see she'd been crying.

Colt sucked in a breath. "Well, you can say one thing about life in this town—it's never dull."

We drew up beside the bride just as she kicked one tyre with a dainty satin shoe, and Colt clipped on his badge and climbed out.

"What seems to be the problem, ma'am?"

I quickly tapped out a text to Luca.

Brooke: We might be a few minutes late for the football xxx

A FEW WORDS FROM THE BAD SAMARITAN…

Curious about the Bad Samaritan? Well, so was I, so I took a little journey into the mind of Baldwin's Shore's favourite vigilante.

If you'd like to hear a few of their thoughts, the bonus chapter is FREE to members of my reader group. You can join here:

www.elise-noble.com/t1g3r

WHAT'S NEXT?

The next book in the Baldwin's Shore series is Colt and Gabrielle's story, *Secrets, Lies, and Family Ties*.

After leaving her fiancé at the altar, all Gabrielle wants is a day alone to reflect on the mistakes she's made. But when her car breaks down in Baldwin's Shore, a day turns into a week, and perhaps—if the goddesses of fate smile kindly—a little longer. But someone from her past has a different plan.

Sheriff's deputy Colt Haines isn't looking for love, and he definitely isn't looking for a flighty blonde to move into his spare room and complicate his life. But his young daughter has other ideas. So too does his heart, and when Gabrielle's secrets catch up with her, he's left with no choice but to fight for her future and for his.

For more details:
www.elise-noble.com/secrets-lies

The Baldwin's Shore series will tie in with the Blackwood Security series later on. If you haven't read any of the Blackwood books yet, why not start for FREE with *Pitch Black*?

After the owner of a security company is murdered, his sharp-edged wife goes on the run. Forced to abandon everything she holds dear—her home, her friends, her job in special ops—assassin Diamond builds a new life for herself in England. As Ashlyn Hale, she meets Luke, a handsome local who makes her realise just how lonely she is.

Yet, even in the sleepy village of Lower Foxford, the dark side of life dogs Diamond's trail when the unthinkable strikes. Forced out of hiding, she races against time to save those she cares about.

For more details:
www.elise-noble.com/pitch-black

If you enjoyed *Dirty Little Secrets*, please consider leaving a review.

For an author, every review is incredibly important. Not only do they make us feel warm and fuzzy inside, readers consider them when making their decision whether or not to buy a book. Even a line saying you enjoyed the book or what your favourite part was helps a lot.

WANT TO STALK ME?

For updates on my new releases, giveaways, and other random stuff, you can sign up for my newsletter on my website:
www.elise-noble.com

If you're on Facebook, you might also like to join Team Blackwood for exclusive giveaways, sneak previews, and book-related chat. Be the first to find out about new stories, and you might even see your name or one of your suggestions make it into print!

And if you'd like to read my books for FREE, you can also find details of how to join my advance review team.

Would you like to join Team Blackwood?

www.elise-noble.com/team-blackwood

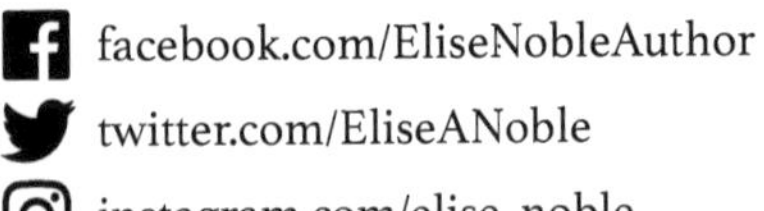

END-OF-BOOK STUFF

My other half works in London, and each day we're not in lockdown, he takes the train to work. Muggins here drives him to the station each morning and picks him up in the evening. Pre-COVID, he'd take the train to Paddington, then catch the Tube to travel across London, but if you've ever been on the Bakerloo line in rush hour, you'll know that it isn't a place you want to be in a pandemic. So we switched it up, and instead of taking the train and then the Tube, he began taking a different train from a different station, riding to Waterloo, and walking the rest of the way to work. That makes my drive twice as long, but I don't mind because it's safer.

It also gives me more thinking time.

And it means that every day, twice a day, I drive past a road called Baldwin's Shore.

Which is a pretty dumb name for a road, really. I mean, it's nowhere near a shore, and who the hell is Baldwin, anyway?

But as I tend to do, I started making up stories in my head. It's a bad, bad habit. And I decided that Baldwin's

Shore would be a good name for a small town on the Oregon coast. And because it's the kind of town that people end up in when they run away from their lives and can't go any further, it has a whole bunch of interesting people among its inhabitants.

Since I couldn't get these stories out of my head, and because of the way they jigsaw in with the Blackwood series, I put my other projects on hold to write a few of them. So the plan is to do three Baldwin's Shore books followed by Hallie's story in the Blackwood Security series (which I've changed the plot of yet again), and then a crossover book that ties both of those series together.

And after that, I'll finally be able to get back to the Blackstone House series that I started writing in 2018...

Elise

ALSO BY ELISE NOBLE

Blackwood Security

For the Love of Animals (Nate & Carmen - Prequel)

Black is My Heart (Diamond & Snow - Prequel)

Pitch Black

Into the Black

Forever Black

Gold Rush

Gray is My Heart

Neon (novella)

Out of the Blue

Ultraviolet

Glitter (novella)

Red Alert

White Hot

Sphere (novella)

The Scarlet Affair

Spirit (novella)

Quicksilver

The Girl with the Emerald Ring

Red After Dark

When the Shadows Fall

Pretties in Pink (2022)

Secret Weapon (Crossover with Baldwin's Shore) (2022)

Blackwood Elements

Oxygen

Lithium

Carbon

Rhodium

Platinum

Lead

Copper

Bronze

Nickel

Hydrogen (TBA)

Blackwood UK

Joker in the Pack

Cherry on Top

Roses are Dead

Shallow Graves

Indigo Rain

Pass the Parcel (TBA)

Blackwood Casefiles

Stolen Hearts

Burning Love (TBA)

Baldwin's Shore

Dirty Little Secrets

Secrets, Lies, and Family Ties

Buried Secrets

Secret Weapon (Crossover with Blackwood Security) (2022)

Blackstone House

Hard Lines (2022)

Hard Tide (TBA)

The Electi

Cursed

Spooked

Possessed

Demented

Judged

The Planes

A Vampire in Vegas

A Devil in the Dark (TBA)

The Trouble Series

Trouble in Paradise

Nothing but Trouble

24 Hours of Trouble

Standalone

Life

Coco du Ciel

A Very Happy Christmas (novella)

Twisted (short stories)

Books with clean versions available (no swearing and no on-the-page sex)

Pitch Black

Into the Black

Forever Black

Gold Rush

Gray is My Heart

Audiobooks

Black is My Heart (Diamond & Snow - Prequel)

Pitch Black

Into the Black

Forever Black

Gold Rush

Gray is My Heart

Neon (novella)

Printed in Great Britain
by Amazon

66052008R00184